# CHRISTOPHER BUSH
# THE CASE OF THE
# GREEN FELT HAT

CHRISTOPHER BUSH was born Charlie Christmas Bush in Norfolk in 1885. His father was a farm labourer and his mother a milliner. In the early years of his childhood he lived with his aunt and uncle in London before returning to Norfolk aged seven, later winning a scholarship to Thetford Grammar School.

As an adult, Bush worked as a schoolmaster for 27 years, pausing only to fight in World War One, until retiring aged 46 in 1931 to be a full-time novelist. His first novel featuring the eccentric Ludovic Travers was published in 1926, and was followed by 62 additional Travers mysteries. These are all to be republished by Dean Street Press.

Christopher Bush fought again in World War Two, and was elected a member of the prestigious Detection Club. He died in 1973.

# By Christopher Bush

# CHRISTOPHER BUSH

# THE CASE OF THE GREEN FELT HAT

With an introduction
by Curtis Evans

DEAN STREET PRESS

# INTRODUCTION

THAT ONCE vast and mighty legion of bright young (and youngish) British crime writers who began publishing their ingenious tales of mystery and imagination during what is known as the Golden Age of detective fiction (traditionally dated from 1920 to 1939) had greatly diminished by the iconoclastic decade of the Sixties, many of these writers having become casualties of time. Of the 38 authors who during the Golden Age had belonged to the Detection Club, a London-based group which included within its ranks many of the finest writers of detective fiction then plying the craft in the United Kingdom, just over a third remained among the living by the second half of the 1960s, while merely seven—Agatha Christie, Anthony Gilbert, Gladys Mitchell, Margery Allingham, John Dickson Carr, Nicholas Blake and Christopher Bush—were still penning crime fiction.

In 1966--a year that saw the sad demise, at the too young age of 62, of Margery Allingham--an executive with the English book publishing firm Macdonald reflected on the continued popularity of the author who today is the least well known among this tiny but accomplished crime writing cohort: Christopher Bush (1885-1973), whose first of his three score and three series detective novels, *The Plumley Inheritance*, had appeared fully four decades earlier, in 1926. "He has a considerable public, a 'steady Bush public,' a public that has endured through many years," the executive boasted of Bush. "He never presents any problem to his publisher, who knows exactly how many copies of a title may be safely printed for the loyal Bush fans; the number is a healthy one too." Yet in 1968, just a couple of years after the Macdonald editor's affirmation of Bush's notable popular duration as a crime writer, the author, now in his 83rd year, bade farewell to mystery fiction with a final detective novel, *The Case of the Prodigal Daughter*, in which, like in Agatha Christie's *Third Girl* (1966), copious references are made, none too favorably, to youthful sex, drugs and rock and roll. Afterwards, outside of the reprinting in the UK in the early 1970s of a scattering of classic Bush titles from the Golden Age, Bush's books, in contrast with those of Christie, Carr, Allingham and Blake, disappeared from mass circulation in both the UK and the US, becoming fervently sought (and ever more unobtainable) treasures by collectors and connoisseurs of classic crime fiction. Now, in one of the signal developments in vintage mystery publishing, Dean Street Press is reprinting all 63 of the Christopher Bush detective novels. These will be published over a period of months, beginning with the release of books 1 to 10 in the series.

Few Golden Age British mystery writers had backgrounds as humble yet simultaneously mysterious, dotted with omissions and evasions, as Christopher Bush, who was born Charlie Christmas Bush on the day of the Nativity in 1885 in the Norfolk village of Great Hockham, to Charles Walter Bush and his second wife, Eva Margaret Long. While the father of Christopher Bush's Detection Club colleague and near exact contemporary Henry Wade (the pseudonym of Henry Lancelot Aubrey-Fletcher) was a baronet who lived in an elegant Georgian mansion and claimed extensive ownership of fertile English fields, Christopher's father resided in a cramped cottage and toiled in fields as a farm laborer, a term that in the late Victorian and Edwardian era, his son lamented many years afterward, "had in it something of contempt....There was something almost of serfdom about it."

Charles Walter Bush was a canny though mercurial individual, his only learning, his son recalled, having been "acquired at the Sunday school." A man of parts, Charles was a tenant farmer of three acres, a thatcher, bricklayer and carpenter (fittingly for the father of a detective novelist, coffins were his specialty), a village radical and a most adept poacher. After a flight from Great Hockham, possibly on account of his poaching activities, Charles, a widower with a baby son whom he had left in the care of his mother, resided in London, where he worked for a firm of spice importers. At a dance in the city, Charles met Christopher's mother, Eva Long, a lovely and sweet-natured young milliner and bonnet maker, sweeping her off her feet with a combination of "good looks and a certain plausibility." After their marriage the couple left London to live in a tiny rented cottage in Great Hockham, where Eva over the next eighteen years gave birth to three sons and five daughters and perforce learned the challenging ways of rural domestic economy.

Decades later an octogenarian Christopher Bush, in his memoir *Winter Harvest: A Norfolk Boyhood* (1967), characterized Great Hockham as a rustic rural redoubt where many of the words that fell from the tongues of the native inhabitants "were those of Shakespeare, Milton and the Authorised Version....Still in general use were words that were standard in Chaucer's time, but had since lost a certain respectability." Christopher amusingly recalled as a young boy telling his mother that a respectable neighbor woman had used profanity, explaining that in his hearing she had told her husband, "George, wipe you that shit off that pig's arse, do you'll datty your trousers," to which his mother had responded that although that particular usage of a four-letter word had not really been *swearing*, he was not to give vent to such language himself.

Great Hockham, which in Christopher Bush's youth had a population of about four hundred souls, was composed of a score or so of cottages, three public houses, a post-office, five shops, a couple of forges and a pair of churches, All Saint's and the Primitive Methodist Chapel, where the Bush family rather vocally worshipped. "The village lived by farming, and most of its men were labourers," Christopher recollected. "Most of the children left school as soon as the law permitted: boys to be absorbed somehow into the land and the girls to go into domestic service." There were three large farms and four smaller ones, and, in something of an anomaly, not one but two squires--the original squire, dubbed "Finch" by Christopher, having let the shooting rights at Little Hockham Hall to one "Green," a wealthy international banker, making the latter man a squire by courtesy. Finch owned most of the local houses and farms, in traditional form receiving rents for them personally on Michaelmas; and when Christopher's father fell out with Green, "a red-faced, pompous, blustering man," over a political election, he lost all of the banker's business, much to his mother's distress. Yet against all odds and adversities, Christopher's life greatly diverged from settled norms in Great Hockham, incidentally producing one of the most distinguished detective novelists from the Golden Age of detective fiction.

Although Christopher Bush was born in Great Hockham, he spent his earliest years in London living with his mother's much older sister, Elizabeth, and her husband, a fur dealer by the name of James Streeter, the couple having no children of their own. Almost certainly of illegitimate birth, Eva had been raised by the Long family from her infancy. She once told her youngest daughter how she recalled the Longs being visited, when she was a child, by a "fine lady in a carriage," whom she believed was her birth mother. Or is it possible that the "fine lady in a carriage" was simply an imaginary figment, like the aristocratic fantasies of Philippa Palfrey in P.D. James's *Innocent Blood* (1980), and that Eva's "sister" Elizabeth was in fact her mother?

The Streeters were a comfortably circumstanced couple at the time they took custody of Christopher. Their household included two maids and a governess for the young boy, whose doting but dutiful "Aunt Lizzie" devoted much of her time to the performance of "good works among the East End poor." When Christopher was seven years old, however, drastically straightened financial circumstances compelled the Streeters to leave London for Norfolk, by the way returning the boy to his birth parents in Great Hockham.

Fortunately the cause of the education of Christopher, who was not only a capable village cricketer but a precocious reader and scholar, was taken up both by his determined and devoted mother and an idealistic local elementary school headmaster. In his teens Christopher secured a scholarship to Norfolk's Thetford Grammar School, one of England's oldest educational institutions, where Thomas Paine had studied a century-and-a-half earlier. He left Thetford in 1904 to take a position as a junior schoolmaster, missing a chance to go to Cambridge University on yet another scholarship. (Later he proclaimed himself thankful for this turn of events, sardonically speculating that had he received a Cambridge degree he "might have become an exceedingly minor don or something as staid and static and respectable as a publisher.") Christopher would teach in English schools for the next twenty-seven years, retiring at the age of 46 in 1931, after he had established a successful career as a detective novelist.

Christopher's romantic relationships proved far rockier than his career path, not to mention every bit as murky as his mother's familial antecedents. In 1911, when Christopher was teaching in Wood Green School, a co-educational institution in Oxfordshire, he wed county council schoolteacher Ella Maria Pinner, a daughter of a baker neighbor of the Bushes in Great Hockham. The two appear never actually to have lived together, however, and in 1914, when Christopher at the age of 29 headed to war in the 16th (Public Schools) Battalion of the Middlesex Regiment, he falsely claimed in his attestation papers, under penalty of two years' imprisonment with hard labor, to be unmarried.

After four years of service in the Great War, including a year-long stint in Egypt, Christopher returned in 1919 to his position at Wood Green School, where he became involved in another romantic relationship, from which he soon desired to extricate himself. (A photo of the future author, taken at this time in Egypt, shows a rather dashing, thin-mustached man in uniform and is signed "Chris," suggesting that he had dispensed with "Charlie" and taken in its place a diminutive drawn from his middle name.) The next year Winifred Chart, a mathematics teacher at Wood Green, gave birth to a son, whom she named Geoffrey Bush. Christopher was the father of Geoffrey, who later in life became a noted English composer, though for reasons best known to himself Christopher never acknowledged his son. (A letter Geoffrey once sent him was returned unopened.) Winifred claimed that she and Christopher had married but separated, but she refused to speak of her purported spouse forever after and she destroyed all of his letters and other mementos, with the exception of a book of poetry that he had written for her during what she termed their engagement.

Christopher's true mate in life, though with her he had no children, was Florence Marjorie Barclay, the daughter of a draper from Ballymena, Northern Ireland, and, like Ella Pinner and Winifred Chart, a schoolteacher. Christopher and Marjorie likely had become romantically involved by 1929, when Christopher dedicated to her his second detective novel, *The Perfect Murder Case*; and they lived together as man and wife from the 1930s until her death in 1968 (after which, probably not coincidentally, Christopher stopped publishing novels). Christopher returned with Marjorie to the vicinity of Great Hockham when his writing career took flight, purchasing two adjoining cottages and commissioning his father and a stepbrother to build an extension consisting of a kitchen, two bedrooms and a new staircase. (The now sprawling structure, which Christopher called "Home Cottage," is now a bed and breakfast grandiloquently dubbed "Home Hall.") After a falling-out with his father, presumably over the conduct of Christopher's personal life, he and Marjorie in 1932 moved to Beckley, Sussex, where they purchased Horsepen, a lovely Tudor plaster and timber-framed house. In 1953 the couple settled at their final home, The Great House, a centuries-old structure (now a boutique hotel) in Lavenham, Suffolk.

From these three houses Christopher maintained a lucrative and critically esteemed career as a novelist, publishing both detective novels as Christopher Bush and, commencing in 1933 with the acclaimed book *Return* (in the UK, *God and the Rabbit*, 1934), regional novels purposefully drawing on his own life experience, under the pen name Michael Home. (During the 1940s he also published espionage novels under the Michael Home pseudonym.) Although his first detective novel, *The Plumley Inheritance*, made a limited impact, with his second, *The Perfect Murder Case*, Christopher struck gold. The latter novel, a big seller in both the UK and the US, was published in the former country by the prestigious Heinemann, soon to become the publisher of the detective novels of Margery Allingham and Carter Dickson (John Dickson Carr), and in the latter country by the Crime Club imprint of Doubleday, Doran, one of the most important publishers of mystery fiction in the United States.

Over the decade of the 1930s Christopher Bush published, in both the UK and the US as well as other countries around the world, some of the finest detective fiction of the Golden Age, prompting the brilliant Thirties crime fiction reviewer, author and Oxford University Press editor Charles Williams to avow: "Mr. Bush writes of as thoroughly enjoyable murders as any I know." (More recently, mystery genre authority B.A. Pike dubbed these novels by Bush, whom he praised as "one of the most reliable and resourceful of true detective writers"; "Golden Age baroque, rendered remarkable by some extraordinary flights of fancy.") In 1937 Christopher Bush became, along with Nicholas Blake, E.C.R. Lorac and Newton Gayle (the writing team of Muna Lee and Maurice West Guinness), one of the final authors initiated into the Detection Club before the outbreak of the Second World War and with it the demise of the Golden Age. Afterward he continued publishing a detective novel or more a year, with his final book in 1968 reaching a total of 63, all of them detailing the investigative adventures of lanky and bespectacled gentleman amateur detective Ludovic Travers. Concurring as I do with the encomia of Charles Williams and B.A. Pike, I will end this introduction by thanking Avril MacArthur for providing invaluable biographical information on her great uncle, and simply wishing fans of classic crime fiction good times as they discover (or rediscover), with this latest splendid series of Dean Street Press classic crime fiction reissues, Christopher Bush's Ludovic Travers detective novels. May a new "Bush public" yet arise!

Curtis Evans

# The Case of the Green Felt Hat (1939)

ON ITS EDITORIAL page a little over a century ago--September 13, 1914, to be exact--the *New York Times* primarily seemed preoccupied with gently censuring, under the headline "NOT A WAR OF EXTERMINATION," Britain's First Lord of the Admiralty, Winston Churchill, for dramatically avowing, in a speech at the London Opera House about the recent outbreak of war in Europe, "It is our life against Germany's. Upon that there must be no compromise or truce. We must go forth unflinchingly to the end." To the contrary, pronounced the *Times* breezily

> The end of the war will not be the end of life for either Germany or England. . . . When there is an end of fighting there will be peace in Europe without oppressively harsh terms. There may be a bit of territory transferred here and there, and bills of damages will be paid. But none of the belligerent nations will have its life choked out. The First Lord of the Admiralty will live to see British ships sail the seas proudly as ever. . . . Germany's manufacturers will go on making dyestuffs and underwear, and German professors will supply the world with an undiminished output of their dreadful systems of philosophy, each destructive of the others. . . . France will attend once more to her silks and her vintages, and Paris publishing houses will continue to supply the world with those delectable romances which are never omitted in the packing of a vacation handbag. Russian caviar will come to us again, and let us hope it will be cheaper. Doubtless, too, the Russian institution will make another of its periodical advances in liberalism, for which there is still a sufficient margin. Prophecy as to Austria might be premature, but we may confidently look forward to further agreeable light operas from Vienna.
>
> And the life of the people will go on in all these now unhappy countries very much as it has gone on in the past. . . .

In contrast with the hugely misplaced optimism with which the *New York Times* prophesied about the future of Europe after what we now call the First World War, which during its calamitous course and chaotic aftermath grievously altered and ended the lives of millions of people not only in Europe but across the world (including even the United States), the *Times* in another editorial page thought piece, "THE STIFF FELT HAT," wrote more sternly--though likely with the tongue a bit in cheek--about another vexing development in the second decade of the twentieth century: the rise of the soft felt hat. "Time was," reminisced the *Times* nostalgically, "when the ordinary man possessed two hats, not counting the silk topper laid away for ceremonial occasions and the cap worn for outing. With a straw [aka boater] in the summer and a derby [aka bowler] the rest of the year he was always in style." Yet now, the *Times* fretted, "there is a movement to discard the stiff felt hat altogether and substitute for it one of the objectionable soft hats of all shapes or none which the inconsiderate manufacturers and traders have forced upon the market. All the distinction they possess must be imparted by the wearer. In form, color and trimming they are symbols of a decadent age."

"The evil must be sternly faced," thundered the *Times*—sounding, incidentally, rather like Winston Churchill gravely addressing world war and the fates of nations. "Statesman and clergyman are victims of the soft-hat mania. The green felt, the plush hat, the soft hat with a fuzzy surface protect the skulls of eminent men. They are not only unsightly and forbidding; when you consider the transformation they have effected in masculine humanity, they seem positively indecent. A society for restoration of the derby hat cannot get to work too quickly."

With esteemed statesmen and clergymen alike bowing their heads to the dictates of fashion, however, it took more than the *New York Times* editorial page to upend the dominion of the green felt hat. In 1924 it figured centrally, if symbolically, in naturalized Englishman Michael Arlen's notorious Jazz Age bestseller *The Green Hat*, though in the novel the titular headgear is worn not by a man, but a woman, Iris Storm, the Bright Young

Thing who serves as the novel's iconoclastic central character: "It was bright green, of a sort of felt, and bravely worn, being, no doubt, one of those that women who have many hats affect *pour le sport*."

Fifteen years later, on the eve of another world war, one which was to prove even more devastating than the first, Great War veteran and green felt hat wearer Christopher Bush published his twentieth Ludovic "Ludo" Travers detective novel, *The Case of the Green Felt Hat* (1939), a classic village mystery which concerns the murder of Hanley Brewse, a crooked company director whose calculated chicanery lured thousands of innocents in England with money to invest into effectively throwing away much of their life savings. In Bush's novel, the green felt hat worn by the victim on the day of his death figures as a key clue in the investigation into his murder by Ludovic Travers, amateur sleuth extraordinaire, and his friends in the police.

*The Case of the Green Felt Hat* might well have been called *Busman's Honeymoon*, had not that title been taken already a couple of years earlier by Dorothy L. Sayers for her final Lord Peter Wimsey mystery, wherein Wimsey and his new wife, mystery writer Harriet Vane, honeymoon in a quaint English village and in between lengthy bouts of lovemaking solve a locked room murder committed in their own newly-purchased house. In *Hat* Ludo Travers and retired classical dancer Bernice Haire, with whom Travers fell most decidedly in love in his previous mystery outing, *The Case of the Leaning Man* (1938), have wed and are spending the first part of their honeymoon at a lovely country house in the vicinity of Edensthorpe, a thriving though secluded agricultural town. There the charming couple becomes good friends with another charming couple, Colonel Brian Feen, who happens to be the local chief constable, and Feen's wife, Laura. When Hanley Brewse--the despised corporate conman recently released from prison and settled, sporting both a beard and an assumed name, in the nearby village of Pettistone--is found shot dead in a burning shed, what is more natural than for Ludo to lend his friend Colonel Feen a hand, just as he has done so helpfully on three earlier occasions with another stymied provincial chief constable, Major Tempest, as detailed in *The Case of the 100% Alibis* (1934), *The Case of the Chinese Gong* (1935) and *The Case of the Missing Minutes* (1937)?

Bernice chips in as well to help solve the murder (even though she has no sympathy for that beastly Brewse bounder), when she can find spare time in between rounds of golf at the Pettistone course—playing golf seemingly being, along with gossiping and making bad business investments, the favored social activities of the Pettistone locals. Yet the case, which is made most difficult by the multiplicity of suspects who had unwisely invested in Brewse's now-bankrupt businesses and a plethora of impressive alibis, remains unsolved when Ludo's great Scotland Yard friend, Superintendent George "the General" Wharton, returning to London after a spot of official business in Shrewsbury, drops in to pay his respects to the newlyweds. Taking the ironic alias of Mr. Higgins ("Or my name is Higgins!"), the General in spite of himself is drawn into the investigation too, though he constantly protests that he must get back to London. Surely no criminal, however clever, can withstand the investigative duo of Ludovic Travers and George Wharton? When, however, that brassy modern young thing Molly Pernaby imparts the shocking news to the sleuths that she saw Hanley Brewse traversing the road to Edensthorpe doffed in his telltale green felt hat—this after, according to the medical evidence, Brewse had been, well, murdered—it does give the investigators pause seriously to think, as it should the readers too!

Rest assured, however, that order is eventually restored in lovely little Pettistone, which last we see through the charmed eyes of Bernice and Ludo as the couple, while departing the precinct in their car, look down from a hill on the peaceful English countryside:

> Edensthorpe lay in the valley beneath them, its smoke a faint mist in the morning haze. Away to the right was Pettistone, church steeple visible above the trees, and shimmering and greyly blue against the clear autumnal

light were the golf-course woods, and a glint of red which was the roof of a house.

[. . .]

Bernice was still looking back, and at last she sighed, and smiled.

"I shall always love Edensthorpe, and Pettistone. I almost feel I want to cry."

[. . .]

Then Travers shook his head, and as Bernice finished speaking, he was moving the car on again.

"Fields," he thought to himself. "Elysian fields, perhaps."

A month after the publication of *The Case of the Green Felt Hat*--praised by John Norris at the Pretty Sinister blog in 2012 as "a real page turner with some expert misdirection, a cleverly thought out crime with all its oddities and red herrings explained, and a couple of well-done surprises at the end"--Germany in March 1939 occupied the remaining independent portion of the Czechoslovakian Republic, in violation of the previous year's Munich Agreement, which British Prime Minister Neville Chamberlain, a man of rather a different mettle from Winston Churchill, had assured his nation would guarantee "peace for our time." To the contrary, sadly, less than six months ahead of the United Kingdom lay war—a war for the survival of the British nation, in which both Christopher Bush's life and his detective fiction would see major changes.

TO

DOUGLAS NEWTON

WITH GRATITUDE

"At the trial of almost the first, and certainly the shabbiest, of our long line of financial swindlers, defending counsel pleaded among other things for his client that he was a home-loving man and something of a musician.

"The late Edward Manifold, Q.C, who was prosecuting, remarked at once in a very audible aside that he presumed the instrument which the gentleman played and taught, must have been the tin-whistle.

"'Tin-whistle?' demanded His Lordship.

"'Yes, m'lud,' said Manifold suavely. 'His unfortunate clients certainly had to whistle for their tin!'"

LUDOVIC TRAVERS

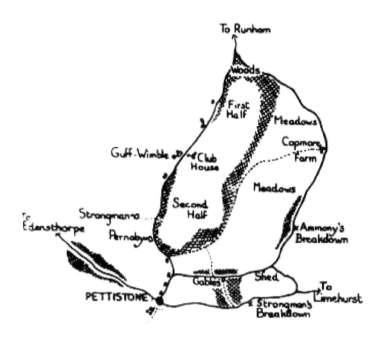

To Runham

Woods

First Half

Meadows

Copmore Farm

Guff-Wimble

Club House

Meadows

Second Half

Strongmanna

To Edensthorpe

Parnabys

Ammony's Breakdown

Gables

Shed

To Limehurst

PETTISTONE

Strongman's Breakdown

Roads \    Paths & Tracks '.     Woods ▦

# CHAPTER I
# BREWSE ARRIVES

A GOOD MANY months after the solving of *The Case of the Green Felt Hat,* Ludovic Travers happened to remark to his old friend Superintendent Wharton of Scotland Yard that if ever he wrote a detective novel he would begin with the words: "A shot rang out!"

"Why?" asked George Wharton bluntly and suspiciously.

"Oh, just to get the reader on tiptoe," Travers said airily.

Wharton grunted. "I see. And what would come next? A scream in the night, or some other damn' foolery?"

"Oh, no," Travers said. "Nothing so crude as that, George. I rather think I'd go on to show there hadn't been a shot at all."

"What the devil would you do that for?"

"Just to keep the reader still on his toes."

Wharton snorted contemptuously. "You're like some more I know. Give you a pen and a bottle of ink and you can do marvels. You can even reorganize Scotland Yard. Which reminds me. What about that Pettistone Case—the Green Felt Hat, as you call it? There was a shot there, wasn't there?"

"But I'm not thinking of writing about that," Travers said. "Besides, that case didn't open with a shot ringing out. That was what I'd call a nice, quiet, gentleman's murder."

Wharton grunted. "A damn' sight too much of the gentleman about it, if you ask me. That's why it was bungled."

"Bungled?" said Travers, and raised pained eyebrows. "A strange admission for yourself?"

"Me?" said Wharton indignantly. "I didn't handle the beginnings, did I? You were the one who knew all the ins and outs."

"Not quite all," smiled Travers. "But you're also forgetting that even I was considerably handicapped."

"How?"

"Well, torn between public duty and private consideration," smiled Travers. "Only real detectives, like yourself, are equal to solving murder cases on their honeymoons."

Travers might have urged quite a lot more: that Pettistone as he first saw it, for instance, was too drowsy and bucolic to make a man associate it with murder. And the Case of the Green Felt Hat was a kind of tail-piece to a whole series of unexpected things, not the least of which was his own marriage. There was no wonder that so confirmed a bachelor as himself should have had to stand a considerable amount of chaff when his engagement to Bernice Haire became public. Even George Wharton— the old General, as the Yard more familiarly knew him—trotted out and misquoted the ancient quip about Benedict, the married man. But Travers and Bernice had their revenge on a wide circle of acquaintances by getting married one late September morning at a little-known register office at a mightily inconvenient hour, with no witnesses but Bernice's sister Joy, and George Wharton himself.

The first part of the honeymoon was to be spent at Edensthorpe where a friend of Bernice had lent them a house, maids and gardener included. Edensthorpe, thriving agricultural town though it is, is itself secluded, and the house lay back from its country road with a view across undulating land that was charmingly wooded. House and district were ideal from the point of view of a honeymooning couple.

But Edensthorpe had other advantages besides being off the main arteries of traffic. Among its forty thousand people were few who could have heard of Ludovic Travers as an author, and probably none who knew him as an unofficial expert of Scotland Yard. Mrs. Travers could not possibly be connected with the famous classical dancer, Bernice Haire, and since the features of the newly married two had never been popularized by publicity, both could move about as humdrum and commonplace citizens.

A few days after their arrival, a letter came from George Wharton, enclosing a letter of introduction to a Colonel Feen, the local Chief Constable, who was an old acquaintance. George said he had business of his own at Shrewsbury and might drop in at Edensthorpe for a day or two on the way back. Mrs. Wharton's mother was ill, and with her in Scotland for a week or two at the least, it was fairly clear that George was thinking of a convenient holiday.

"What about putting him up for a few days?" Travers said. "Or had we better wait till he gets here and then see?"

Bernice thought the latter, and then they decided to call on the Feens that same afternoon. Bernice had a sudden alarm.

"I wonder if he's written to them!"

"Of course he has," Travers said, and then gathered what she meant. "You're wondering if George has told them we're two babes in the matrimonial wood." He smiled as he shook his head. "George can be the most tactful man on occasions. But you wouldn't mind, would you?"

Bernice's pale cheeks coloured rosily. "Of course not. But it does put one at rather a disadvantage."

"I think the secret's safe all right," he said. "There's only one little danger. You mustn't beam when you allude to me as your husband."

Bernice made a face at him. "Do I beam?"

"I most sincerely hope so," Travers said. "I'm always catching myself at it. Even before you married me, I began beaming all over the place."

The Feens turned out to be delightful people. Brian Feen was just over fifty, and so quiet in manner as to be almost unobtrusively gentle. Travers—always a shrewd appraiser—was of the opinion that if the need arose, the Colonel could be as quick, as competent, and even as aggressive as most. Laura Feen, much younger than her husband, wondered if Mrs. Travers played golf.

"I'm pretty bad," Bernice said.

"I'm perfectly dreadful," Mrs. Feen told her. "What about your husband?"

"He's rather good," Bernice said, and halted for fear of dangerous commitments.

"What's your handicap, Colonel?" asked Travers, plunging in to the rescue.

"A rather erratic twelve," the Colonel said.

"That's me to the life. Rather amazing, don't you think, that we should all fit is so well?"

It was decided that as far as golf was concerned, the most must be made of the fine autumn weather. The following afternoon was fixed for a round.

"I think you'll like Pettistone," Feen said. "It's not so crowded as our local course. Just a bit too exclusive, I sometimes think."

"Oh, no," his wife said. "If it weren't exclusive—expensive, if you like—it'd be overcrowded with all sorts of people."

"Far, is it?" asked Travers.

"Four miles," the Colonel said. "Pettistone's a very delightful spot, by the way. Lord Pettistone owns it, and he's selling no land for building on. If it weren't for that, it'd be a cheap and nasty suburb before you could say knife."

Later that afternoon Travers suggested to Bernice that they should have a look at Pettistone and the golf course. Before they played with the Feens, it might be as well to have some idea of the lie of the land. And very delightful land it turned out to be. Pettistone itself was little more than a hamlet, and its golf course lay well back from the Edensthorpe Road. Woods flanked the fairways everywhere, and Bernice sighed at the sight of them.

"My dear, it's going to be dreadful. Even if I hit the ball at all I know I shall be fascinated by those trees. All the time I shall be looking for lost balls."

"Don't you believe it," Travers told her. "A pretty wealthy lot this, as Feen hinted. Beautifully kept, and see those cars?"

It was the cars in the enclosure he meant, some of them of the size and rakishness that gulp down petrol, and two of them Rollses of a superior vintage to his own. Then as they came towards the village again. Bernice saw a tiny lane that led to the left, and thought it might go round that far side of the course they had not yet seen.

Travers turned the car in, then stopped. The lane came to an end at once, and there was nothing but a grassy track that skirted the woods.

"What about leaving the car here and stretching our legs?" he said.

Bernice was all for it. It was a lovely walk in the warm sun of early evening, with the woods on their left and the upland pasture on their right, and they went a good mile till the track switched up hill to a farm whose roofs could just be seen. As they walked back, Travers suddenly halted. Voices could be heard quite near, and there was the whack of a golf ball and the very swish of a club.

"Why, the course is only just through those trees!" Bernice said.

"I expect the woods thin out and then thicken," Travers said, and a few yards on pointed out a grassy ride that ran between the trees, through which there was no sign of sky to mark the nearness of the golf course beyond. Then they ventured along the ride to where there was a tumbledown wooden hut, and from there the course seemed only fifty yards or so away, for voices could be plainly heard again.

When they got back to back, Travers said he would try another way home, and he took the next turn to the left along a pleasant lane.

"But aren't we going right away from the village?" Bernice said, when the car had done a couple of hundred yards with no sign of a house.

"Rather looks so," Travers said. "But we'll ask this chap who's coming."

The man who was approaching had two black spaniels with him, and from the noisy way he called them to heel and the glare he gave at the Rolls, it was none too difficult to gather that he was something of a pomposity. He looked about forty and was massive in a gross sort of way: eyes puffed with good living, a couple of chins, and a complexion that was a study in purples and reds.

"Pardon me," said Travers, "but could you tell me where this road goes to?"

He gave a kind of snort. "Depends where you want to go to yourself. Well, back to the village. Take the first on the right, then. The other road goes to Copmore Farm."

Travers thanked him, and then the other suddenly turned back, as if on some impulse.

"I suppose you're not the new man who's coming to Gables?"

"Gables?" said Travers. "Never heard of it."

"That house on your right. Ought to have known, though. The garage'd have been too small for your car."

A nod and he moved on again, snapping at the dogs to keep them at heel.

"I don't think I like that man very much," Bernice said, as the car went slowly on. "That's the house he was talking about. There's the name—Gables—on the gate."

"Quite a nice little place," Travers said. "All on two floors, as the house-agents say."

He had stopped the car and, always as unconventional as they make them, was standing up and looking about him, though not at the house.

"Darling, what on earth are you doing?"

Travers nodded to himself as he sat down again.

"Trying to put two and two together. All the large houses we saw were near the golf course. If our pompous friend lives in one of them, then he's a fair way from home, and I should say that when he wants to exercise his dogs, he takes them on the golf course."

Bernice smiled bewilderedly.

"What I mean is, our friend—taking into account what he said to me—came down here especially to nose out something about the new people at this house."

Bernice laughed. "My dear, all that trouble, just to prove he's a busybody! I could have told you that myself."

"Telling isn't proof," said Travers knowingly. "The real fun is trying to work out the reason for things. You know: something curious happens and you put this and that together and work out why. Deduction, or theorizing."

"Like the geometry riders we did at school?"

"That's it. Except, of course, that twice out of three times you get the wrong answer. You try it for yourself sometime and see."

Bernice was frowning into the driving mirror.

"I wonder if I'd be wrong if I deduced those people were just about to move in here."

"But our pompous friend told us they were."

"But telling isn't proving," Bernice reminded him. "But do move on, darling. There's a furniture van coming just behind us."

"A furniture van?" He glanced in the mirror with: "Good Lord, yes!" and then grinned sheepishly as he moved the car on. So soon did they arrive at the fork that he overshot it and went on to the left, and as the road was too narrow to turn the car, it was not till they came to Copmore Farm that he was able to head south for the village again. In a minute the car was once more nearing Gables, and then the car had to be pulled up, for that furniture van was so across the narrow road that there was no room to pass. The driver said he would try to draw in on the verge. Two other men were already moving furniture, and a fourth—a clean-shaven, elderly man in black—seemed to be supervising.

"Looks like a family retainer," whispered Travers.

"I'd say he's one of a married couple," Bernice said.

Travers smiled. "You're not deducing things again?"

"Don't be too sure," she told him. "I think he's married, and his wife makes her own clothes."

Travers looked round to see if she were serious.

"But, darling, don't you see the dressmaker's dummy? That lay figure kind of thing, the far side of the van."

"So there is," said Travers and smiled sheepishly again. "I think I'll give up this deducting business."

Then suddenly he was breaking off and staring. His fingers went to his glasses—a trick of his when at a loss or on the edge of discovery—and then he was shooting back behind Bernice again. It was a man who had interested him: a short, dapper-looking man wearing a dark beard streaked with grey, who had all at once appeared through the gate of the house and now stood quietly watching the men at work.

But the driver of the van was signalling Travers to go through, and that was the last that Travers saw. But he slowed the car down and he was still shaking his head.

"You saw that man in the black beard?" he said to Bernice. "I know him; I'm sure I do, and I can't for the life of me think who he is."

"But how extraordinary!" she said.

Travers shook his head again. "It's on the tip of my tongue. I've seen him somewhere before. Where on earth was it now?"

"Darling, you'd better give up thinking, or you'll have us both in the ditch."

"Perhaps I had," Travers said ruefully. "Most exasperating, though. If I can't find out who he is, I shall be driven frantic. Aren't you like that when you can almost remember something and just can't?"

"It's hateful," Bernice said consolingly. "But why not find out from the agent who sold the house?"

"That's an idea," Travers said. "It'll probably be an Edensthorpe man. Pettistone's too small for a house-agent."

But just as he was in the suburbs of the town he remembered who the man was, and the realization was an amazing one. Then he knew he could not be right, only to know the next minute that he must be. Then on a sudden impulse he stopped the car. Would Bernice drive herself home and he would be along in a few minutes.

"I think I've discovered who that black-bearded man was," he told her. "I'll tell you all about it as soon as I get back."

It was Feen in whom he was intending to confide, and by a stroke of luck he found him at the local police headquarters. All Travers said was that he was anxious to know who had taken Gables. Feen rang up a local agent and in two minutes had the information.

"It was bought by a chap called Marlin; Percy Marlin," he said. "That any good to you?"

Feen still had his hand over the 'phone and Travers asked if Marlin could be described. When that information came, it fitted the man whom he and Bernice had taken for a sort of butler or indoor man.

"We've still not got it right," he said to Feen.

"I want to know who's the black-bearded man I just saw there."

"Wait a minute," Feen said. "I'll ring up Pettistone post office confidentially."

In another five minutes he had that news too. A letter was awaiting delivery to a man of the name of Hanley at Gables.

"Hanley!" said Travers triumphantly, and his eyes fairly bulged. "Then I was right."

"About what?" asked Feen quietly.

"About the identity of the man in the black beard. Do you know what his name really is? *Hanley Brewse!*"

It was Feen's turn to stare.

"It's true enough," said Travers, and nodded. "Marlin must be an old family servant and Brewse bought the house through him. Since he came out of jail he's grown a beard, and he's dropped the Brewse."

"Yes, but how'd you know him?"

"I gave evidence at his trial. You might say I helped to convict both him and Merrick Clarke."

"By jove, what a coincidence!" Feen said. "And what a sensation for Pettistone! It'll be all over the place in a couple of days. No end of Pettistone people came a cropper when Brewse went smash." He shook a dismal head. "Wonder what the devil made him choose to come to Pettistone, of all places?"

"The poor devil has to live somewhere," Travers said. "He's done his seven years and he's entitled to live his own life. Not that I'm sorry for him, mind you. I think he was a slippery rascal from the very start. Clarke was the one I sympathized with all along. He was Brewse's tool, and he didn't know it till it was too late."

"Didn't Clarke die in jail?"

"He did," Travers said. "About six months before his two years were up."

There was no more talk then because Travers said he would have to be going. Feen went with him to the street and his last remark was that there was a humorous side to the appearance of

Brewse at Pettistone. When Travers raised inquiring eyebrows, Feen said he would tell him all about it during the next day's golf.

Bernice was tremendously indignant when she heard the news.

"I think a man like Brewse ought to be deported as soon as he comes out of prison," she said. "Either that, or he ought to go somewhere right away from everybody."

"I don't see that he need come into contact with people," Travers said. "I very much doubt if he wants any publicity."

"But he was a scoundrel and a swindler."

"But, my dear, suppose he was. He's paid his penalty according to the assessment of the law. Besides, the world has a very short memory. The Brewse crash has been forgotten long ago."

"Yes, but think of all those he ruined—he and that man Clarke. People who lost their money won't forget. Every time they hear his name it will be just so much hurt."

"I know," said Travers. "That's the very devil of it. All the same, we've got to admit that Brewse has paid the price, and in a way I'm sorry for him if he's going to be hounded out of everywhere he tries to live."

"Well, my sympathies are with the Pettistone people," Bernice said, and she said it so vindictively that Travers had to smile. Then Bernice had to smile too, and in a few moments the sensational news was forgotten. In fact it was not till the next morning at breakfast that Bernice alluded to it again.

"Was that man Brewse married?" she asked.

"He was a widower," Travers said. "It was poor Clarke who was married. I never met his wife, and I don't expect she'd be very pleased to meet me, not that that's likely. After all, I suppose I was in some way responsible for his death." Then he smiled. "But you don't want to know that. You're bursting to tell me you were right about the man Marlin and his wife being a married couple, and the wife making her own clothes."

"Not bursting, darling," Bernice said. "Just humbly hoping for applause, that was all."

It was a lovely afternoon when the four arrived at the golf course. A fairish number of people seemed to be playing, and the two women decided to go off from the tenth. The Colonel and Travers found themselves on the first tee with a clear course ahead, except for two players who were just approaching the first green.

"That chap just taking his shot is Quench, the Pettistone vicar," Feen said. "An oldish man but very steady."

"The other fellow must have hit a long ball," Travers said.

"Look at the size of him," the Colonel pointed out. "His name's Strongman, by the way, which rather fits him. Lives in that house with a drive to it, just before you get here."

Travers enjoyed that round enormously. Pettistone might not have the peculiar charm of a seaside course but it was undulating, well planned and meticulously kept. And as his weakness was for hooking, the holes that lay along the wood had no terrors for him, though once the Colonel sliced pretty badly among the trees and after a couple of minutes' search the ball was given up for lost.

"A pretty hopeless business, looking for balls this time of year," he said philosophically. "In the winter, when there're no leaves on the trees, you can follow roughly where the ball goes, and that gives you some sort of chance."

"Had we better let these other people through?" Travers said.

But the two youngish men who had been coming close up behind were now looking for a ball of their own in the rough, and Travers and the Colonel carried on.

"Two of our best players, those chaps," Feen told Travers. "The younger one's Bob Quench, the vicar's son, and the other's a chap called Pernaby. He's been living here about six years now."

The round went on serenely till the sixteenth, when Travers's hook caused another search, and the couple behind were called through. Bob Quench waved a cheery hand to Feen as he passed. He was a good-looking fellow of about twenty-four or five, shortish but compactly built. His partner, Pernaby, whose thanks were more ceremonious, was a raw-boned man of about fifty with a greying moustache, and wearing glasses.

It was half-past four when the round ended, and after a clean up, the two came out to look for their wives. Travers casually noticed that of the two men approaching the eighteenth green, one was his pompous friend of the previous evening. The Colonel noticed him too.

"There's Guff-Wimble, our acting-secretary." He frowned to himself, then smiled maliciously. "Like to enjoy a little joke?"

"Every time," Travers said.

"Right," said Feen. "Remember what we were talking about last night? You watch what happens when I tell Guffy about Hanley Brewse."

The two players gave casual greetings as they passed and then the Colonel beckoned mysteriously to Guff-Wimble, who came across.

"Oh, Guff-Wimble, this is Ludovic Travers. Mr. Travers, this is Guff-Wimble, one of our local pillars."

"Mr. Guff-Wimble was good enough to be of service to me last night," Travers smiled.

The Colonel cut quickly in.

"What I wanted to speak to you about, Guff-Wimble, was this. Every one will know it in a day or two and if they don't you certainly will, so there's no harm in giving you the news before it gets out. You knew Gables was sold?"

"Why, yes," Guff-Wimble said in that blustering way of his. "The people are in already, so they tell me."

"Know who the new owner is?"

"Can't say I do. A chap called Marlin, so I was told."

"Then he's a figure-head," Feen said. "The man who's really bought it is—well, I'll give you fifty guesses."

"Dammit, how should I know?" Guff-Wimble told him testily.

"Well, it's an old friend of yours. Some one you'll recognize when you see him walking out. I wouldn't have told you otherwise."

"A friend of mine?"

"Yes." Feen paused for effect. "In brief, it's Hanley Brewse!"

Guffy—behind his back nobody called him anything else—stared with a goggle-eyed expression that Travers found comical in its bewilderment.

"But it—I mean—"

"I knew you'd be surprised," cut in the Colonel, "but you can take it from me it's true. He came out of jail three months ago, and now he's camped on your doorstep."

The other's face had been changing to purple indignation, and now he was spluttering with rage.

"But, dammit, it's an outrage! He can't live here. He'll have to go. Dammit, he'll have to be made to go!"

"Who can make him?" Feen asked calmly. "The man's got to live somewhere, hasn't he?" He half turned. "Still, I thought I'd tell you. See you again later perhaps. Mr. Travers and I have a couple of wives wandering about somewhere on this course."

A nod and he was moving off with Travers. Tea for four was ordered, and while they waited on the loggia for their women, he let Travers into the local scandal.

"Hope I didn't surprise you letting out that Brewse secret," he said, "but it couldn't have been a secret long, as you just heard. Also I couldn't resist getting one in on Guffy."

"Unpopular, is he?"

"Very much so. And he is one of the kind I particularly loathe. He's a nephew of Lord Pettistone who owns all this district, the course included, and he thinks it gives him proprietary rights. An interfering, pompous windbag—that's Guffy—and though you didn't enjoy the fun, perhaps, it tickled me to watch his face when I told him about Brewse."

"It certainly seemed to hit him in the wind," Travers said. "But what's the connection? I mean, with Brewse."

"I'll tell you," the old Colonel said. "Guffy used to be connected with a firm of stockbrokers. It must have been in some sleeping capacity, because he doesn't strike me as having brains enough for a respectable office-boy. Plenty of money, mind. His is that mansion place just across the road, almost in front of the pro.'s shop. Still, as I was saying, he was airing his stockbroking information when he came down here, which was about eight years ago. All the fools round here used to listen to him open-mouthed, principally because he was who he was, and I may say, he's a pretty nasty one to be up against. His great tips were Brewse's companies. He used to boast that Brewse was almost eating out of his hand, and when the local people began to make money out of Brewse, Guffy used to strut about like a public benefactor. London Consolidated, Lombard Trust—that was all you could damn' well hear."

Travers nodded. "I know. And what about when things were rocky? Did Guffy get his pals out in time?"

"That's the devil of it—he didn't. He swore blind it was all a deliberate scare to rig the market. Poor old Quench, who'd been hypnotized by him, lost practically everything, and has to make do on the living, which is only worth four hundred or less. His son Robert, who'd just gone up to Oxford, had to come home and loaf round till he got a job. As a matter of fact he was always fond of engines and that sort of thing, and I was lucky enough to fix him up with a big garage firm at Edensthorpe, and his father had sense enough to let him take the job. He's done very well, by the way. Coming in for a partnership very soon, I believe."

His hand fell on Travers's arm.

"See that girl there? That pretty girl in the yellow jumper. Walks like a thoroughbred, doesn't she. That's Molly Pernaby, niece of that chap we let through. Bob Quench is as good as engaged to her."

"A fine-looking girl," Travers said. "But about your pal Guffy. Anybody else here lose any money?"

"Only Mrs. Strongman." Feen said. "Strongman himself got out just right, so he told me. Mrs. Strongman was very bitter at the time, but I think she and Guffy are on speaking terms now. You can't afford to live in Pettistone and quarrel with Guffy. All the same, I never worried much about the Strongmans. It's poor old Quench I'm always sorry for."

Bernice and Mrs. Feen were approaching the ninth and the two men stepped down to watch the final stages. Mrs. Feen sank a ticklish putt and announced triumphantly that they were all square.

"The Colonel was too clever for me," Travers said. "He knows every blade of grass round here."

"Isn't it a lovely little course?" Bernice said.

"We really must come and play quite a lot."

That evening the Traverses agreed that they liked the Feens enormously. Bernice said that Laura Feen was an awfully good sort and most entertaining. Travers said the Colonel might not be George Wharton's idea of a copper, but he'd bet a fiver he was the best fellow in the world to work with and the kind who'd be popular with his men.

Bernice was playing golf with Mrs. Feen the following morning while Travers looked over the local antique shops. On the Saturday night the Feens were coming to dinner early and the four were to end the evening with a visit to one of the local picture-houses.

# CHAPTER II
# BREWSE DEPARTS

WITHIN FIVE MINUTES of receiving that astounding news from Colonel Feen, Anthony Guff-Wimble was exceedingly active. Like most of his self-satisfied and overbearing kind, he had a skin that was exceedingly tough, and the last thing that would have occurred to him was that since he had been responsible for the loss of Pettistone money, the less notice he now took of Hanley Brewse, the better for his own dignity.

The Rev. Norman Quench was the first to be approached.

"Are you busy to-night, vicar? Could you drop in for a minute or two?"

"Well, if it's not too late I'd be pleased to," the vicar said, and then somewhat nervously: "The fact is I have a meeting of the—"

"Eight o'clock suit you?" broke in Guff-Wimble, who saw Pernaby making for the gate and was afraid he might miss him. "Bring Bob with you, if he can come. Tell him it's most important."

But as Guff-Wimble made for the car park, he wondered if he should say anything to Pernaby after all. The Brewse crash had taken place before Pernaby's arrival in Pettistone, so he was not directly interested, and yet, when he came to think of things, Pernaby had always identified himself with everything that looked like being for the good of the club and village. And Pernaby was one of the few men for whom Guff-Wimble had any private respect, and whose good opinion he secretly cherished.

"I suppose you couldn't drop in for a few minutes to-night?" he said. "Something very important I want some of us to talk about. Quench is coming and I'm trying to get hold of Strongman."

"What time?" asked Pernaby in his usual laconic way.

"Oh, about eight. I told Quench eight, but he's never on time for anything."

Pernaby nodded, and the nod was so economic that it included in the same motion a hint to look to the left.

"There's Strongman, if you want him."

"Ah, yes," Guff-Wimble said, and made for Strongman who was going to the practice course to try some putts. Then he remembered he had not said quite enough to Pernaby, but when he turned, the laconic Pernaby had already gone. Strongman, massive, good-humoured and blond, reminded some people of an exceedingly amiable Great Dane. He said he'd certainly drop in.

"What about Gordon? Will he come?" Guff-Wimble asked.

Gordon was Strongman's son who was home on leave from the Sudan.

"I expect he will," Strongman said with his usual optimism. "If you really want him, I mean."

Guff-Wimble wasted no words on Strongman but retired to the strategic post of the office window in case there might be some momentarily forgotten somebody who ought also to be asked to the meeting at Great Panniers. Mrs. Strongman of course ought to be asked, but he had rather a fear of that most efficient and point-blank lady, and decided that two members of the family should be enough. Besides, if he asked Mrs. Strongman as, say the representative of one generation, then he ought to ask Molly Pernaby as the representative of the moderns. And not only was Molly Pernaby wholly unconnected with Brewse, but generally she was altogether unthinkable.

To Guff-Wimble's way of thinking, Molly Pernaby represented all that was most irritating, complacent and regrettable in the district's, and indeed England's, young women. She was wholly lacking in respect for authority—by which he meant himself—and there was one period, when he had been as usual voluntarily acting as secretary in the absence of Major Vimme, when she had been positively objectionable in the matter of improvements to the women's accommodation and course amenities. At the meeting she had been pointedly rude.

"You may have a handicap of two, Miss Pernaby," he had been forced to say, "but I hardly think that entitles you to interfere with the recognized traditions of this club."

"Is it a tradition of this club to be personal?" she asked him.

"When it's necessary for the good of the club, yes," he said.

Molly's face flared.

"Then for the good of the club I feel entitled to say that if its acting-secretary had taken the trouble to inspect the one available women's lavatory, he'd be far better informed."

That was the kind of thing of which Molly Pernaby was capable, and yet in his heart of hearts Guff-Wimble knew that she would have been the ideal ally in the matter of the ejection by some means or other of that unspeakable and barefaced scoundrel Brewse. But probably she would become an ally; her uncle was not the kind to reveal what was likely to be said at the evening's talk, but Bob Quench would certainly tell her everything, and it was his co-operation also that Guff-Wimble was most anxious to secure. After all, Bob Quench had lost most through that blackguard Brewse.

But there were no other local people whom Guff-Wimble was disposed to take into his confidence. The rest of Pettistone's inhabitants of any standing were what he regarded as the tottery kind—fogies who littered up the course and whose wives littered up the church. To bring in any one from outside the village was unnecessary and unthinkable. The matter concerned Pettistone alone, and the village—under proper leadership—was perfectly competent to handle its own affairs and set in order its own house.

And then suddenly Guff-Wimble thought of some one else—Charles Ammony, owner of the village garage and general stores. Of the people who had lost money over Brewse, the slimy Ammony was the one for whom Guff-Wimble had felt no sympathy at all. The fellow had thrust his fingers into something that was no concern of his and had got them badly bitten for his pains. He could see Ammony approaching him that morning, years and years ago, finger-flicking his hat.

"Excuse me, sir, but is it right what every one is telling me about this London Consolidated? I wouldn't have asked you, sir, only I happen to have a little handy money to invest."

Yes, Ammony had got his fingers bitten. He was the first man of his small Pettistone circle to invest money in stocks and shares, as he used to put it, and he was always boasting and bragging to his cronies about having money in this and that, and making a show with looking at the financial columns of the papers, which were gibberish to the general public. Then when the crash came, Ammony had been like a man demented. Never had Pettistone heard so much raving and shrieking, and he had even had the effrontery to force his way into Great Panniers and ask what about his money.

"Don't ask me about your money," Guff-Wimble told him in the presence of the summoned butler. "I'm not the custodian of your money. A man of your supposed sense oughtn't to have been such a fool as to put all his eggs into one basket."

But though Ammony had breathed out threatenings and slaughter and had found only a minor satisfaction in the justice which the law had meted out to Brewse, he had survived the jar to his own fortunes, and Charles Ammony—Grocers, Provision Merchants and Universal Providers—was now as flourishing as ever. Quite a useful ally, he might make, thought Guff Wimble, even if he was not the kind to invite to the evening's talk. An influential man, in his way, was Ammony, and he might do a considerable deal in the matter of a local boycott.

It was a quarter-past eight when the chosen five were all assembled in what Guff-Wimble was accustomed to call his snuggery, and the reasons that had brought them there were as widely different as their personal selves.

The vicar was a man of sixty; of medium height and stooping, with a thin, greying beard that gave him an air of frailty, though most who ever played a round with him soon found him far wirier than he looked. His face had a kind of peering expression which came from his deafness, and every one had grown accustomed to bellowing in his presence. His main reason for coming to that meeting was that Guff-Wimble was vicar's warden and capable of a florid generosity where the church was concerned, and in order to come, the vicar had scrambled most reprehensibly, as he knew, through the quarterly conference of the Bible Circle.

His son, Robert Keithmore Quench, had come because Guff-Wimble was a useful customer of the Edensthorpe firm and was talking about getting a sports runabout to ease the limousine. Bob, as his circle called him, was five feet six, charmingly mannered and humorously alert. At the moment he was taking ten days' holiday before the usual rush of work at the quarter's end.

The massive Strongman, lethargic and easy-going, had come because he had nothing better to do. Gordon, his son, had come because Bob, who was a friend of his, had rung him up and asked him to, otherwise nothing would have induced him to spoil an evening. He was as thick-set as his father, but shortish, like his mother, and with a face that the Sudan sun had tanned to an incredible brown His reticent manner gave him an air that some took for superciliousness. His leave, by the way, was up at the beginning of October and he was proposing to fly back to save a few more days.

Pernaby, six feet of raw-boned strength, moustache and hair a badger grey, was as monosyllabic as ever, and yet he had planned, if the need arose, to say a goodish deal. He had come principally because he was suspicious that the meeting had been called to form a nucleus in support of certain alterations—already vetoed by one public meeting—to the fifteenth hole; alterations which he shrewdly suspected Guff-Wimble would try to stampede through during the absence of Major Vimme, who was undergoing yet another operation to a leg that had been badly smashed by shrapnel in the war.

As host that evening Guffy had never been more effusive, and yet there was a strain of humility that was most unusual, and which Pernaby particularly found somewhat ominous in view of those suspicions he had all the time entertained. Perhaps that was why he was the most surprised when Guffy mentioned the real business of the private gathering. In the hush that followed the announcement and the mention of Brewse's name—and a shamed kind of hush it was—Pernaby's voice had such an artless surprise that the tension went at once.

"But who is Hanley Brewse?"

"My God! you don't mean to say you don't know who Brewse is?" Guff-Wimble said, and then cleared his throat. "I mean, it's pretty painful for me to say so, as things are, but I thought every one knew the scoundrel."

"Just a minute," Pernaby said. "You don't mean that financier who bolted and was caught and put in jail?"

Guff-Wimble smiled patiently. "I think you're representing him pretty mildly, but that's the man." The smile took on a certain bitterness. "A good many of us in the village have good reason for being acquainted with Hanley Brewse. I was pretty badly hit, and so were others, and though I was as much deceived as anybody, I've always considered myself as partly to blame."

A quick look passed between Bob Quench and Gordon Strongman. Guffy had never been heard in so apologetic a vein.

"You'll pardon me," broke in the vicar, who had been looking extremely uncomfortable, "but is this man Brewse a middle-aged man with a dark beard?"

"That's the man," Guffy said. "The beard's been grown in order that he shouldn't be recognized, and I believe he's taken the name of Hanley."

"Dear, dear," the vicar said. "And I met him to-day near the village, and shook hands, and hoped he'd be happy among us."

"There we are," said Guffy. "That's the kind of thing we've got to look forward to. Whatever he calls himself, every one will know who he is. I say it's an outrage for him to come here of all places. What we've got to do is get rid of him at the earliest possible moment. That's why I asked you gentlemen to this little confidential talk."

"But how can he be got rid of?" Strongman asked. "The house is his and no power on earth can shift him."

"Well, if we're going to take on a defeatist spirit like that, there's no more to be said. I was hoping that every one would recognize that he simply couldn't be allowed to go on living here. We know what Pettistone is and what it stands for, and I say that if that blackguard's name becomes connected with us— as it's bound to do in my view—the place is as good as done for."

"Old Ammony will be pleased," Bob said. "We shall have queues of cars coming through here at week-ends to have a look at Gables. You know what the curiosity-mongers are."

"But why should Ammony be pleased?" asked his father, hand still cupped round his ear as he strained to listen. "Didn't he lose a considerable amount of money too?"

Strongman chuckled amiably. Guffy was rather annoyed.

"I take it you're not being very serious. You don't want the man here, do you?"

"Want him here?" Bob was the least bit nettled at his tone. "I don't want him here any more than you do, and I take it that isn't very much."

"That's what we want to hear," Guffy said. "We none of us want him here." He cleared his throat again. "The meeting is open for suggestions, shall we say?"

Old Quench spoke first. He was feeling most uncomfortable about it all, and was wondering if there was anything his deafness had made him miss. Brewse was an event of an almost forgotten past, and he had schooled himself to acceptance and forgiveness. A persecution of Brewse—undesirable parishioner though he might indeed be—cut clean across such principles as turning the other cheek, forgiving them that had despitefully used you, and other vague but pacific injunctions that were suddenly harassing his mind.

"Do you think he would sell the house if he were offered a good price for it?"

"That's an idea," Guff-Wimble said. "What'd he give for it? Do you know?"

"Thirteen hundred was asked for it," Bob said.

"Thirteen hundred," Guff-Wimble said slowly.

"I don't want the place but it mightn't be a bad investment. What about you, Strongman? Would you like to buy it?"

"I'd have to think it over," Strongman said.

"I'd like to get rid of the fellow at any cost, but I'd have to talk it over with my wife. She's not going to feel any too pleased when she learns who he is."

"Exactly." Guff-Wimble said that rather quickly. Bob Quench cut in with an idea.

"He's on the 'phone, at least I think the 'phone's still there. What about ringing him up and sounding him?"

"Why not? Who's the best one to do it?"

"Why not you? He won't recognize your voice, will he?"

"Don't think so," Guffy said. "In any case I'll have a shot."

He looked up the number of the late owner and twiddled the dial. A moment or so and a voice was clearly heard.

"Hallo?"

Guff-Wimble grimaced at the company, and assumed his most impressive air. The gruffness in his voice was evidently intended as a disguise.

"Hallo. Are you the new man at Gables?"

"Yes."

"Would you care to entertain an offer for it? A really good offer?"

There was such a long silence that he was about to give another hallo, and then the voice was heard again. It was a dry rasping kind of voice.

"I'm sorry, but the house is not for sale."

"Not for a couple of thousand?" He winked at the company as if to assure them that so preposterous an offer was merely shrewd bluff.

"The house is not for sale."

"Any point in my coming round to see you? I say, is there—"

He listened, then looked round annoyedly.

"He's rung off."

A shrug of the shoulders and he was replacing the receiver.

"Well, that cock won't fight. What're we to do now?"

"If I might say something." Pernaby peered round behind his huge glasses. "Is this man Brewse going to make any real difference here after all? If there's any talk it'll be over in a few days, and I take it the very last thing he wants is to be seen in public."

"How'd you like to live in the same place with a fellow who'd swindled you out most of what you had?" Bob asked him.

"But, my boy, he's already been punished—"

"That's nothing to do with it, father. He's had a quiet time in a comfortable jail, but that won't bring people's money back, and, to put it bluntly, I'm damned if he's going to settle down for life to a nice comfortable time here."

"My views exactly," Guff-Wimble said.

But the few schemes that were put forward were none of them workable. A boycott by all local tradesmen would be useless, for Edensthorpe blacklegs would merely take advantage of it and their delivery vans would call at Gables. A public meeting of protest might or might not be supported, but in any case it would lead nowhere. Tarring and feathering, casually mentioned by Gordon Strongman, was a suggestion that old Quench sternly reprimanded, and he was feeling so uneasy at the turn things were taking, that he hunted for an excuse to be going.

"We'll call it an adjournment," Guff-Wimble said. "I propose we all think out ways and means and meet here again early next week. We may all think differently at the moment about the best way of kicking that blackguard out of Pettistone, but I know we're all resolved that he's got to go somehow. Even you will go as far as that, won't you, Pernaby?"

Pernaby shrugged his shoulders. "I've no personal grievance against the man, but will fall into line with anything reasonable that people want."

"That's how we all feel about it. Have another whisky before you go. You too, vicar. Help yourselves, gentlemen."

Gordon Strongman, who had hardly opened his mouth all the evening, whispered something to Bob as he poured himself a drink. When the party finally left, Bob, who had contrived to be the last out of the room, whispered something to Guff-Wimble who nodded. So interesting was that whispered communication that Guff-Wimble held Bob back by the sleeve and whispered in return, which was how Strongman came to notice that the two were up to something.

All five were going the same way, and walking, for the night was a fine one.

"Well, I've known Guffy do some pretty brazen things in his time," Strongman said in that languid way of his, "but I think to-night's was about his coolest effort. If it hadn't been for him in the first place, nobody here would have given a damn about Brewse."

"Gordon was only pulling his leg when he mentioned that tarring and feathering," Bob said.

"I really think the whole thing should be handled with great circumspection," the vicar hastily put in. "What's your private opinion, Pernaby?"

Pernaby refused to commit himself. He was too much of a newcomer and too much in the dark, as he said, to thrust his opinions on anybody, even if he had any. Strongman, as the party arrived at his house, asked them all in. The vicar had already mentioned an engagement, and the two younger men were off to Edensthorpe, but Pernaby went in for what was supposed to be a few minutes. It turned out to be well over an hour, for Strongman told him the whole history of the Brewse affair, as it had affected Pettistone. He even admitted that his wife might do something decidedly unbecoming if she heard that it was Brewse who was living at Gables.

"I like peace and quietness," Strongman said.

"The money's gone, as I've often told her, and what's the good of worrying? We're the hell of a long way off being broke."

"I'm surprised the vicar took the news so quietly," Pernaby said. "I've known him show quite a lot of temper at times."

"Bob's the dark horse," Strongman said. "He and Guffy were having a private pow-wow just before we left. I don't know if you've got any influence with him—through Molly, if you don't mind my saying so—but if you have, I'd just drop a hint."

"No hurry," Pernaby said. "The best thing to do is wait a few days and see how the whole village takes it."

That was on the Wednesday night. Next morning Colonel Feen happened to run into Strongman in Edensthorpe, and as the two were quite near Castle Row, they dropped into Harris's for coffee. Strongman re-imparted the news about Brewse, and Feen led him shrewdly on till he had heard practically everything about that little gathering at Guff-Wimble's.

On the Friday afternoon, Travers was playing golf with the Colonel. Mrs. Feen, with the object of extending Bernice's circle of acquaintants, had arranged a women's four with Mrs. Strongman and another friend, but that fourth called off at the very last moment, and Molly Pernaby, who happened not to have a game, made a fourth instead.

Travers heard all about the Great Panniers meeting from the Colonel, and though he was feeling himself uneasily responsible for the unpleasant time that looked like being in store for Brewse, yet there had been something decidedly amusing in Feen's account of the wordy futilities of that pow-wow at Guffy's house.

"You certainly seem to have started something in this peaceful parish," he said.

"It was bound to get out," Feen told him, "otherwise I'd never have mentioned it. Guff-Wimble would have spotted Brewse the first time he saw him. But the thing that's worrying me just a little is what Bob Quench and young Strongman may do. Pettistone comes under our jurisdiction, so to speak, and if they start any monkey tricks, they'll certainly be for it. Brewse is entitled to protection like any ordinary citizen."

"I don't know how I feel about it all," Travers said. "I must admit I can't help feeling the least bit sorry about Brewse. As we've said, he's paid what the law considers his proper penalty and now he's got to live somewhere." He smiled. "We've heard what the Pettistone men think about it all, and I'm wondering what the women are thinking. I shouldn't be surprised if our wives have heard all about it. As a matter of fact, Bernice, after her round, was even more hostile to Brewse."

"People are very bitter about it at Pettistone," she told Travers that evening. "Mrs. Strongman says if she meets him she'll box his ears." She smiled. "The Pernaby girl made me laugh. You know that matter-of-fact, direct way modern girls have? Well, when Mrs. Strongman talked about boxing his ears, she said, 'I'll come with you when you do it, and spit on his beard.'"

"Good," said Travers. "Let's hope Brewse doesn't spit back. What's she like, that girl?"

"I like her enormously," Bernice said. "She plays a marvellous game and doesn't put on any airs at all. Very jolly, too, and distinctly amusing."

"And Mrs. Strongman, what's she like?"

Bernice frowned. "Well, she's quite nice, but just a bit aggressive. Very much of a live wire, I think I'd call her. And I have an idea she'd rather have liked her husband to be the local magnate instead of that Guffy man."

"And what do you really think is going to happen to Brewse?"

Bernice nodded viciously. "I think he's in for what you'd call a remarkably thin time."

There was no Pettistone news on the Friday, perhaps because rain settled in just after lunch and lasted well into the early hours of the Saturday. The Traverses spent a kind of domestic day, with the Feens due for dinner and Bernice just a little on the anxious and fussy side. But half an hour before the arrival of the guests, she expressed herself as hopeful, if not altogether satisfied.

As a matter of fact the meal turned out to be an enormous success, and the Colonel and Travers were far too wary to be drawn into any partisanship over Brewse. There should have been no talk at all, but Mrs. Feen began it, and during the preliminary sherries when, after all, one must talk of something.

"I saw Molly Pernaby this afternoon," she said, "and she was saying that nothing had happened yet about that dreadful man Brewse."

"My dear, must we talk about him?" asked the Colonel patiently.

"Oh, but it's perfectly thrilling," Bernice said.

"Surely nothing ever happens in Pettistone, and now, when there is something really important, you're suggesting hushing it up."

"Drawing a discreet veil," suggested Travers.

"You must remember that the Colonel is in rather an ambiguous position. He represents the law and, after all, you know, there has been some rather—what shall we say?—unlawlike talk."

"I really don't see it." She smiled sweetly at Feen. "After all, the Colonel is a private citizen to-night and as much entitled to his share of scandal as any of us."

But dinner was announced and the talk turned to the picture-show to which the party were going. Travers had other tricks up his sleeve for drawing the conversation away from Brewse, but the occasions were unneeded, and never another word had been said by coffee time.

"There's no hurry," Travers said. "We've still got ten minutes and the seats are booked."

Bernice glanced at the clock, which said twenty-past eight. "It doesn't really matter if we are a minute or two late. I expect we shall have to sit through all sorts of things before the big picture."

"Terrible rubbish they put on sometimes," the Colonel said, and then the maid came in with the alarming news that he was wanted on the 'phone.

"Oh, dear," said Mrs. Feen distressfully, "I do hope it's nothing important."

"Is he often called away?" Bernice asked.

"Not often, but this *would* be the night when something happened. I remember once before—"

But Feen was already back, and the look on his face told that something was badly wrong.

"My dear, you haven't got to go?" his wife said.

"Afraid I have," he told the room generally. "And I'd like Travers to come with me if he will. You two go on alone. Perhaps you might come back here afterwards, in case we're late."

He was in his coat and making for the door.

"You really want me?" asked Travers, who had no idea what it was all about.

The Colonel clicked an exasperated tongue.

"I'm sorry. I ought to have told you. And, Laura, see that not a word of this gets out. There's a burning shed or something on that back road to Copmore Farm at Pettistone, and Brewse's body has been discovered in it."

# CHAPTER III
## BERNICE PROPOSES

Travers had already expressed his private views about the professional capacity of Colonel Feen, his absence of fuss and the efficiency of his department, and he was to receive confirmation at once. The Colonel's car, which had stood at the front door in readiness to take the party to the cinema, circled the town to the north and came out on the Pettistone Road.

"Any of your people out at the fire?" Travers asked mildly, all the pomp and circumstance of a Yard case in his mind.

Feen seemed rather surprised at the question.

"They told me everything's been done, so I suppose it has."

Rain seemed in the air and the night was pitch dark and gusty, and for the first mile or two the going was tricky and the Colonel had to keep his eyes on the narrow lane. When the wider road was reached he told Travers what he knew, which was not very much.

"Rather curious," he began, "that a thing like this should happen while you were here. George Wharton said he hoped I'd have a nice murder for you."

"You think it's a murder?"

"It sounds like it," Feen said. "All I know is that the man at Copmore Farm saw a blaze and rang up Edensthorpe at once. The Pettistone constable saw it too and discovered the body and rang us up. That's really all I know, except that our people ought to be there by now."

There was no glare in the sky as Pettistone was reached, but it was the woods that screened the fire for there was something of a glow as they drove along that lane which went past Gables. A few hundred yards farther on, and there was the fire, or what was left of it.

About a score of people stood watching in the lane, and a uniformed constable was at the field gate, keeping them out. The Edensthorpe fire engine was standing by. As the constable told Feen, the shed was a wooden, flimsy affair that had burnt down long before the engine had arrived. In fact, if the Colonel had no objections, the fire-brigade captain thought he might as well get back again.

The constable had been talking as he walked, for Feen was hurrying across the grass to the smouldering fire, Travers at his heels. The firemen were told they might go. Feen's right-hand man came up to report, and was introduced as Detective-Sergeant Reeper.

"Where's the body?" Feen wanted to know at once.

"Under that elm there, sir. Doctor Barnes is there."

"Ambulance been sent for?"

"It's here now, sir. Just in front of the fire-engine."

"Right," said Feen. "And what about the farmer? Where's he?"

"Standing by, sir. Haylock is his name, sir, if you wanted to know."

"He'll keep," Feen said. "Now tell me quickly in your own way what you gather has happened."

What Reeper said began to throw quite a different light on matters. It was the local constable—Corby—who saw the fire first, because by sheer luck he happened to be coming on his bicycle from the village in the direction of Copmore Farm. The fire was then well alight—or, say, nicely alight, as Reeper put it—but he had the gumption to look inside the cattle shelter in case anything might be there.

"Then he saw what looked like a pair of legs sticking out of that heap of manure," Reeper said.

Feen stared at him, then was moving nearer to the hot ashes that surrounded what looked like a black, unburnt heap of something. A fork stood handy, and Reeper, red-faced and perspiring, cleared some of the ashes away so that Feen could get nearer.

"It's pretty long manure," Reeper said, and by *long* he meant that it was more straw than dung. "Only burnt on the top, sir, as you see. Too moist underneath to get alight."

"I see, I see," Feen told him impatiently. "Go on with what happened."

"Well, sir, Corby pulled at the legs and out came the body, easy as pie, so he said. As he was doing it, there was Haylock arriving on his bike to say he'd seen the fire and thought it was something else and sent for the fire brigade on spec., so to speak. Then him and Corby put the body under that hedge and Corby biked off and rang us up."

Feen nodded. "Right. Then we'll have a word with Barnes? What's that light?"

"That's his torch, sir. He had plenty of light from the fire when we first got here."

"You clear all those busybodies off and then drive my car in and switch the headlights on," Feen told him, and moved off in the direction of the elm.

Barnes said he was making slow progress but he was of the opinion that death was due to a shot wound in the heart, and at quite close quarters.

"Body still warm?" asked Feen.

"Good Lord, no!" Barnes said. "He's been dead for hours."

Reeper was driving the car in and Feen broke off to direct the lights. Then he had the body moved near to the smouldering fire again so that ashes and manure heap and body were all in the full glare.

"What's this about him being dead for hours?" he asked the doctor.

"Well, he *has* been dead for hours, and that's all there is to it," Barnes told him.

"If you'll pardon me, just how are you determining it?" Travers asked.

"Rigor mortis and state of the wound," Barnes said, and wondered apparently what the devil Travers had to do with it in any case.

"I should have introduced you two," Feen said quickly. "This is Ludovic Travers."

The name apparently conveyed nothing to Barnes. "About the time of death," he said. "I know as much as a good many people about the fallacies of rigor mortis. All the same I'll bet either of you a fiver he's been dead for well over four hours, and you can call who you like in for referee."

"That's good enough for me," Travers said. "I expect you'll have good enough reasons when the time comes."

"By the way, Reeper," Feen said, "how did Corby know the man was Brewse?"

"It was a man of the name of Marlin who did the identifying," Reeper said. "Corby's got him handy."

"Do you still recognize him, Mr. Travers?"

"Quite well, even with that beard on," Travers said.

"Well, empty his pockets if you don't mind, doctor," Feen said. "The sooner you can get him away, the better. Bring Corby here, Reeper, will you?"

Corby was a young fellow, new to the district, but he made no bones about admitting that the real reason he was cycling up to Copmore Farm was to have a word with Haylock's daughter.

"Well, tell us everything that happened," Feen said.

"Well, sir, I saw the fire, like I told Sergeant Reeper, and looked in the shed and saw a pair of boots sticking out of the heap there, and—"

"Just a minute," Feen said. Travers was already looking at the dead man's boots and socks and trouser ends.

"They're scorched all right," Barnes said.

"Any actual burning?"

"No," Barnes said. "Very bad scorching on the right-hand side though."

"I take it the shed door was here?" Travers said, indicating the side nearest the road.

"That's right, sir," Reeper said. "I asked Corby that, and he said it was like a door in the middle of a wall. You know what I mean, sir. It was a wide door to let stock in, but there was wood each side."

"And when you tugged at the boots and the body came out, it was lying on its back?" Travers asked Corby.

"That's right, sir," said Corby, looking surprised.

"And the fire had started on what we might call the farm side, farthest from the village?"

"That's right, sir. So it had."

"Excuse me, sir, but how do you know all this?" Reeper asked. "You weren't here when it happened, were you?"

"Not in these," Travers told him with a glance down at the already spotted shirt-front. "All I assumed was that the fire began on that side because the wind lies that way. The heap's on that side too, just inside the door, and I gather the officer saw the boots sticking out as soon as he flashed his torch. Then if the right-hand side of the body's the one most scorched, the body must have been on its back." He smiled. "All very pretty but it doesn't get us very far."

"Well, you dragged the body out and then what happened?" Feen asked. "You needn't tell us about Haylock. We'll see him in a minute."

"Well, sir, I nipped along to the village, and just about two hundred yards along the road I met a man flashing a torch. I asked him who he was and what he was up to, and he told me his name was Marlin and he was looking for some one. I asked him who it was and he told me. I was in a hurry, as you'll recognize, sir, so I said if he was a man with a dark beard, he was lying up against where the fire was, and he was to go there himself and stay there, and I'd be back in a minute."

"Very sensible of you," Feen said. "Go and bring him here, and we'll hear what he's got to say. What about the pockets, Barnes?"

"Nothing but these," Barnes said, and displayed a handkerchief, pencil, penknife and some small change.

"Put 'em in an envelope and take 'em with you," Feen said. "If anything should happen to turn up, put it with them. In a minute or two you can get him away."

Corby was coming up with an elderly man in a raincoat beneath which could be seen black trousers. Travers recognized him as the one who had supervised the furniture unloading at Gables.

"Good evening," Feen said courteously. "What is your name?"

"Marlin, sir. Percy Marlin."

"You recognize this dead man here?"

He nodded his head sadly. "Yes, sir."

"Who is he?"

He shot a quick glance, hesitated, then moistened his lips.

"Mr. Brewse, sir."

"Hanley Brewse?"

"Yes, sir."

"Thank you, Mr. Marlin. What were you? Some sort of a servant to him?"

"Yes, sir. I and my wife were in charge of the house."

"I see. Tell us what's been happening to-day as far as you and your master are concerned."

Marlin made a gesture of helplessness.

"Well, sir, he went out early in the afternoon. He didn't say he was going, sir, because that wasn't his way, but I saw him going out of the front gate. Then when he wasn't in to tea, sir"—he anticipated the question—"five o'clock, that was, sir, I began to get a bit anxious. When he hadn't come in by dark I went to have a look for him. Then I saw a blaze, sir, and wondered what it was, and then I heard some one running, and as soon—"

"Running from where?"

"Well, sir, from what I afterwards knew was the fire."

Feen raised his eyebrows and gave Corby a quick look.

"You heard some one running. Well, what happened?"

"Well, sir, I saw the light of this officer's bicycle at much the same time and I thought I saw the man who was running slip into the hedge."

"But it was dark. How did you know it was a man?"

"Well, sir, I took it for granted it was a man. And I just happened to see something of him standing by the hedge as the bicycle light came along."

"And after you spoke to the officer, did you see or hear anything of him then?"

He shook his head. "As a matter of fact, sir, I was so upset at what he told me that I forgot all about him."

"Exactly." Feen nodded, rubbed his chin, then made up his mind. "Well, thank you so far, Marlin. Now you'd better get straight back home to your wife and make sure you're in if we happen to call later."

Marlin gave a little bow of thanks and moved off.

"We don't want the whole place cluttered up with people," Feen said. "Let's have Haylock here, Reeper."

Haylock was a middle-aged man in breeches and leggings. His evidence tallied exactly with Corby's. "Rather a risky business calling out the fire brigade for a shed, wasn't it?" Feen said.

"I didn't think it was my shed, sir," Haylock said. "I thought it was them two stacks of hay what stand in yon far corner, and I wasn't taking no risks."

"Wise man," Feen said, "Now about this shed. What was it made of?"

"Dry old oak and larch slabs, sir, and rough thatched, Just a shelter, that's all it was, so as the stock could get in in bad weather."

"How'd the manure get here?"

Haylock explained. A certain amount of litter-straw, if a cart came by handy, or rough mowings if there were any—was put in for the stock, and made a useful accumulation of manure with the dungings. Only a few days ago he had raked and forked it into a heap ready to take away, and he was intending to put clean litter down. That was a yearly job only, he said.

"Would it have burnt if the fire had got at it?" Travers asked.

The farmer shook his head. "I never heard of a dung-heap catching alight, sir, and I reckon you might call this a sort of young dung-heap."

Then all at once he was pulling at the heap with his fingers and holding up a good fruity handful.

"There you are, sir. Even if you'd lit a fire under it, I don't reckon it'd have burnt."

"We'll take your word for it," Feen said. "The funny thing is that whoever put the body here, evidently thought it would catch alight, otherwise why did he set fire to the shed?"

"I don't know nothing about that, sir," Haylock said. "All I do know is, no one couldn't have burnt that heap."

"But suppose there was paraffin or petrol on it?" Haylock grabbed another handful or two of the manure heap and smelt it, then pushed one handful under Feen s nose.

"There you are, sir. Do you smell for yourself. There ain't no paraffin nor nothing on that."

"Excellent," Feen said, and again was only too glad to take his word for it. "And what time was it when you saw the fire?"

"Just after eight, sir. Mr. Corby here will tell you, because I come straight down here as soon as I 'phoned."

"What was the time when you saw it, Corby?"

"About five to ten past eight, sir."

"Well, that's all right, Mr. Haylock, thank you. If we want you again, I know you'll be only too glad to help us."

Off went the farmer and Corby was sent back to the gate. Reliefs would be along very soon, and the whole area of the fire was to be kept under supervision till dawn, when there would be a thorough search.

"You might as well get along now," Feen told the doctor. "And what about calling Wilson in as well? You know what our coroner is, and we'd better have plenty of confirmation of whatever you have to say."

"I was going to suggest the same thing myself," Barnes said.

Off went Barnes and the body. Reeper had gone to 'phone for more men, and Feen and Travers stood looking into the last of that fire, with its embers glowing as the wind fanned them.

"A good job the brigade didn't splash water over all this," Travers remarked. "There'd have been the most unholy mess to work over in the morning, and all sorts of things might have been washed out.

"You mean blood?"

"Partly—yes. That is if he was killed here." He shook his head. "A bit early to begin theorizing."

"Yes," Feen said. "We might do worse than get along to Gables. Reeper ought to be back there by now."

Travers had a word with Corby as he went through the gate.

"How far down that heap was the body when you began pulling it out?"

"No distance down at all, sir. I could have pulled it out with one hand. One finger, if it comes to that."

"It looked as if it had been put there in a hurry?" added Feen.

"That's right, sir. Just as if some one had scrapped some stuff over it and hadn't had time to do the feet."

"Well, that's the end of Brewse," Feen said as the car moved off. "And a pretty queer end too."

"Yes," said Travers. "And it rather looks as if that Guff-Wimble conference might give us an idea or two."

"You think it's one of them?"

"I won't go half as far as that," Travers told him. "What I do think is, that you'll find the one who killed Brewse was some one whom Brewse relieved of quite a lot of money."

Just short of Gables, Feen drew his car clean on the verge and switched off the lights. The house stood sideways to the road, its front facing towards the village, and a small gate opened on a path that led to the front door. The garage had its separate gate at the back of the house, where there was also a tradesmen's entrance.

Reeper's car was already there and the three men made at once for the front door. Before Feen could knock, Marlin was opening it. The room into which he showed them was apparently the dead man's sitting- and dining-room combined.

"You would like to see my wife, sir?" he said to Feen. "She's still a bit distressed, sir. She hasn't got over the shock."

"I don't think we want her to-night," Feen told him. "Sit down yourself. We shan't keep you very long. Tell us, for instance, how long your association is with Mr. Brewse."

Marlin said his father had been butler to Hanley Brewse's father, and he had been with Brewse till the time of the crash.

"He came of a very good family, I believe," Feen remarked.

"One of the best, sir. But it didn't do me any good when I and my wife had to find new jobs, sir."

"You went through a pretty bad time while he was in jail?"

"We managed, sir," Marlin told him with a quiet dignity. "Then when he was released, we got in touch with him, sir, which is why we're here now."

"Any relatives, are there?"

"A son and a daughter, sir. The son went to America after the crash, and the daughter disappeared, so to speak, sir. I mean that she naturally didn't want people to know who she was."

"Well, she may come forward when she hears the news," Feen said. "Now tell us one important thing. Why did he choose this part of the world to come to?"

Marlin shook his head. "He was very bitter about it all, sir. He always said that if he'd been given time, he could have put everything right—"

"Yes, but what's that to do with my question?"

"Well, sir, I was trying to tell you that he was very bitter about it all. He came here, sir, so as to be out of the way of everything. He was a Lincolnshire man, sir, and his late wife was a Welsh lady. Then he had his country place near Winchester, sir, so what he did—he told me this himself, sir, and very bitter he was about it—what he did was to connect up those places, and London, with lines, and where they intersected he said he'd go, because it would mean he was the farthest possible distance from each one of them. Nobody would know him or be interested in him, he thought, sir."

"I see, and the lines happened to cross somewhere near here. And about this afternoon. When you saw him at the front gate, did you happen to notice which way he turned?"

Marlin said he had noticed him at the gate, and no more. As soon as he was through the gate he would have been lost to sight, for the hedges on each side were six foot, and Brewse himself was about five-foot six.

"What about telephone calls?"

"And, if you'll pardon me," added Travers, "Why did he keep the 'phone on?"

The 'phone was kept on so that tradesmen could be communicated with, and in many ways it would save leaving the house. In fact, it was an additional privacy. As for calls, Marlin couldn't be sure. The 'phone, as could be seen, stood in that very room where Brewse spent all his time. Mrs. Marlin was very deaf, and he himself had been busy getting house and garden a bit straight.

"Could you say if you heard him talking to any one, as if he was speaking over the 'phone?" Marlin said he knew the Edensthorpe library had been rung, and arrangements made about books, for the dead man was a great reader. Some jig-saw puzzles had been delivered, too.

"That doesn't get us far," Feen said, "and I remember you inferred that he was not the kind to talk over his affairs. But about to-night, and particularly that man you heard running from the direction of the fire. Did you catch a glimpse of his clothes?"

"Well, sir, since I spoke to you, I've been thinking, and I seem to remember he had on a raincoat. A light-coloured coat it must have been, and that's why I saw it when the bicycle lamp happened to shine that way."

"Could you possibly judge where he was when you saw him?" Travers asked.

"I might perhaps, sir."

"I seem to remember there's a wide ditch running along that hedge," Travers mentioned to Feen. "And there's been quite a bit of rain recently."

Feen caught his point and got to his feet at once.

"Will you come with us, Marlin, and have a shot at remembering just where he was? Your wife won't mind being alone?"

Marlin went off for a quick word with his wife, and then was ready. Reeper was moving ahead to get his bag from the car, but he stopped almost at once.

"What was that, sir?"

"What was what?" hissed Feen in the dark.

"A funny noise, sir," came back Reeper. "Like something scampering about."

The four listened intently, then Feen shook his head.

"Probably the wind. It's making enough noise."

"It may be a cat, sir," Marlin said. "We've been troubled with them already."

The four moved on. About two hundred yards along the lane, Marlin halted.

"Somewhere here, I think, sir. I know there was a bend."

The four drew over to the left-hand side of the road, and while Feen worked with Marlin's borrowed torch, Reeper concentrated on the ditch which was soft and damp though free from surface water. Within fifty yards of the beginning of the search they came to a place where the weedy grass that skirted the ditch had clearly been trampled down, and it was not too hard to make out the very place where the man had squatted while the bicycle passed.

But when the ditch bottom was examined, there was something at which Feen was really excited. Two footprints were perfect, and there was a particularly fine one of a shoe that had been heavily pressed into the ground while its owner leaned forward to get a grasp of the thin beech-hedge to pull himself through.

"Rubber shoes with a patterned sole," Feen said. "Golf shoes, most likely. Pity this hedge wasn't thorn. He'd have scratched his wrists and hands."

Reeper wriggled through the gap to see if he could trace the way the man had gone, but the grass had been grazed by stock and though there was plenty of dew, the night was too dark to follow the line of retreat. But the sergeant had everything in his bag, including a bottle of water, and the footprints were soon filled with plaster.

"I'll keep an eye on them till they're ready," he told Feen. "By the time you get here in the morning, sir, they'll be beautiful."

Another quarter of an hour and the Colonel's car was on the way back to Edensthorpe. It was well after eleven and Travers had been growing a bit anxious, but it was the Colonel who had suggested ringing up from Corby's headquarters and advising the women to turn in to bed.

"What do you make of it all?" he asked Travers as soon as they started back.

"Nothing much yet," Travers said, and shook his head.

"Murder's a damnable business," Feen said, "but all that Guff- Wimble hanky-panky ought to do us a bit of good. We can make no bones whatever about asking the whole boiling to give a remarkably detailed account of their movements for just what times we consider fit."

"And on the face of it, there was only one motive for murder. It looks any odds on one of Brewse's former clients having done him in."

"Well, we've got plenty of time," Feen said. "Nobody's going to run away and nobody's got to be looked for."

"I wonder."

Feen gave him a quick look.

"Just that matter of the fire," explained Travers. "Might it or might it not have been accidentally lit by some tramp? If I judge rightly, Pettistone is between two workhouses—Edensthorpe and Limehurst. Also the hobo gentry love camping out at this time of year, and I gather that that shed would have been a good doss-down—manure included."

"But a tramp would have seen the body. Corby saw it as soon as he flashed his torch."

"Well, put it like this." Travers, as a theorist, was easy to start and hard to stop. "The body's under that manure heap where the murderer hid it. He would have hidden it, wouldn't he? He'd scarcely have stuck it in with the feet poking out. Very well then. The tramp lights his usual fire to boil his tin, and then wonders what about bedding. He begins raking over that heap and finds quite a lot of long, dryish stuff that hasn't too fruity a smell. Or, if you prefer it the other way, he thinks the smell too fruity, and abandons the job, but before he does so, he happens to have uncovered the boots. What does a tramp like better than a spare pair of boots? So he uncovers some more, then takes to his heels as though the devil is after him. He doesn't want to be mixed up with dead men in manure heaps. Perhaps he'd also seen that his fire had set the side of the shed alight too."

"Yes," said Feen, but none too enthusiastically, as he remembered those clear prints in the ditch. "But do tramps wear shoes like golf shoes that leave serrated patterns?"

"It's conceivable," Travers said. "Tramps are always begging at doors for old shoes. These might have had good soles but split uppers."

"But why did he run *towards* the village? You'd have expected him to bolt to open country."

But Feen knew Travers far too little to imagine he would be stumped by objections as paltry as that. George Wharton was always making bitter remarks about Travers's readiness to theorize about anything at the shortest possible notice.

"You and your theories!" he once remarked to Travers. "When Gabriel's horn goes, I can just see you. Out you'll pop and you'll polish those glasses of yours, and give a good listen, and then remark to all and sundry that the hunting season must have started again."

"Then why not two people?" Travers now said.

"The tramp, and another—the other being one of the Guffy conspirators. By the way, you can find out about the fire and how it really did start. Surely one of the big companies has one of its men at Edensthorpe?"

"As a matter of fact I know the very man," Feen said. "I don't like waking him up at this hour of the night, but I'm afraid he'll have to be up at dawn in the morning."

"There we are then," said Travers cheerfully. "If he determines the fire was started with, say, paraffin, then we can rule out our tramp. I don't think petrol could have been used, do you? It's risky stuff."

They were in the outskirts of the town, and he asked to be set down somewhere near the house. Feen seemed rather surprised, especially after having cleared the way for Travers to make a night of it.

"You can tell me everything in the morning," Travers said placatingly. "I'll be out independently; soon as it's light if I can manage it."

His key was in his pocket and he was intending to creep warily up the domestic stairs, but as he came in sight of the house, there were the downstairs lights still on. Bernice had actually prepared a cold snack, and coffee was warm on the trivet of the electric fire.

"A ministering angel thou," quoted the gratified Travers.

"I simply couldn't go to bed," Bernice said. "I had to hear all about it."

Travers confidentially imparted the more thrilling details, and deftly avoided awkward questions. At the tail-end came the news that he must be off again at dawn.

"Well!" said Bernice, with an indignation that was a delightful pretence. "So I'm to be a—" She frowned. "I mean, something like a golf widow."

"A sleuthing widow," Travers said helpfully.

"That's not very good," she said, "but it will do. I'm to be a sleuthing widow and when I ask questions, I'm told it's all desperately secret and confidential."

"Not too confidential," hinted Travers.

"Well," she said resignedly. "I suppose you'll have to help poor Colonel Feen."

"He's rather expecting it," Travers said, "and I'm scared stiff he should expect too much."

"But George Wharton told me you were wonderful."

"George Wharton's the world's prize humbug," Travers told her. "Also I'm not going to lend Feen a hand after all—at least, not in the way he thinks."

Bernice stared, and he chuckled at the disappointment in her look.

"Why do you think I'm getting up at dawn and on a Sunday morning?"

Bernice shook her head.

"This is the idea," he said. "I want to be back here for breakfast, long before Pettistone is up. Once people there get the idea that I'm even a comic detective, Othello's occupation will be gone. Now, if every one can take me for an ordinary citizen and a golfer on holiday—well, then that gives me a chance, and you won't have to be a sleuthing widow."

"Darling, you're wonderful!"

"I only hope you're right," he told her.

But Bernice was already looking wide-eyed with another idea.

"But why shouldn't I be able to help! I know quite a lot of people at Pettistone already."

It was his turn to stare, and his fingers were suddenly fumbling for his glasses.

"Do you know," he said, "I'm beginning to think, that's a really magnificent idea."

# CHAPTER IV
# SABBATH MORN

TRAVERS HAD ANNOUNCED that he had the gift of waking at any time he chose, but it was Bernice who woke him that Sunday morning and said she was sure it must be getting near dawn. Travers put on his glasses and verified the time as five o'clock, and then decided to get up in any case though it was an hour before it would be light.

As he drove along through the darkness of that none too warm autumnal morning, something he had wondered over-night occurred to him again: why Bernice should after all be prepared to let hostility to Brewse so far lapse as to volunteer help in discovering his murderer. What did not occur to him was that Mrs. Feen had remarked that there had never been a mur-der case at Edensthorpe during her husband's time, and that it would be a gaudy feather in his cap if he could get his man. She had remembered in time to add how fortunate it was that Mr. Travers should be at hand, and what a queer coincidence it was.

"The fact of the matter is, I believe Ludo murdered this man Brewse himself," Bernice said. "Husbands will do anything when it's a question of their hobbies."

But deprecatory though Bernice might be, she was deter-mined that Ludo should come out of the affair at least as well as the Colonel. As for her confidence, it went beyond the wifely. Though she might quote George Wharton as principal refer-ence and testimonial, there had been one occasion—an occasion indeed, out of which their engagement had arisen—when his perspicuity and powers of deduction had terrified her, happy though the ultimate outcome had been. Which was, perhaps, why she still preferred to think of his theorizing as the fascinat-ing game which her own first attempts had found it.

Dawn was in the sky when Travers drew the Rolls in by the field gate. Feen had already arrived. Reeper was there too, and some dozen men in all were having a meal of sorts which the Colonel had brought in his car.

"That's Pollfax, looking at the fire," Feen told Travers. "He's an assessor for the Midland and Metropolitan. We'll have a word with him as soon as I get these men started."

The extra men had come to help in the search of the neigh-bourhood of the fire, and above all Feen was hopeful of finding the empty shell.

"He was definitely shot then?" Travers asked.

"At point-blank range and clean in the heart," Feen said. "The bullet ended up against a back rib. A hefty lump of lead, out of a Colt, I'd say. It's already on its way to your experts."

"Anything more definite about the time of death?"

"Yes, both doctors are agreed," Feen said.

"They say he was shot between three and four o'clock. Those are the limits both ways, and they say they've taken every possible likelihood into account."

"Including the one that the manure heap was wet and therefore hot?"

"Yes," Feen said. "They've even thought of that. Heat might have affected rigor mortis but it wouldn't affect the state of the wound, or his stomach content. Marlin was rung up and we were told when Brewse had lunch and what he had. A bit gruesome, but damn' good evidence."

He got the search going, then came back.

"Before we have a word with Pollfax," Travers said, "there's something I'd like to put up to you." Feen was delighted when he heard the scheme and he called Reeper over at once.

"Mr. Travers is not supposed to have anything to do with this inquiry," he said. "He's going in a few minutes, and nobody's to know he's been here. He's just an interested party—"

"A curious bloke might be better," suggested Travers. "Pokenose was one of my nicknames at prep. school."

"Well, we'll put it as a friend of mine who was naturally curious," Feen said. "Tell Corby the same. And remember it's particularly important."

"It might help," suggested Travers, and gravely tapped his skull, "if you hinted to Corby about—"

Reeper grinned. "I know, sir. Just a screw loose somewhere."

"That's right," Travers said. "One screw only will do."

"Well, discovered anything yet?" Feen asked Pollfax.

"I'm getting ideas," he said.

"This is Mr. Travers, a friend of mine."

"You in this line?" Pollfax asked.

"Lord, no," Travers told him. "I'm just a nuisance whom the Colonel was too polite to snub."

Pollfax nodded as he went down on one knee, and began stirring some of the ashes with his finger.

"This is the only thing that interests me so far. See this lot of ash, and then this? Notice any difference?"

"Something fishy?"

"I think so. Paraffin, or I'm a Dutchman. I can't tell you for certain before to-morrow."

"That's soon enough for me," Feen said. "Help yourself to as much as you want."

Pollfax grubbed about for a few more minutes and then left. Feen and Travers began an examination of the manure heap, as far down as to the easily verifiable depth to which the body had been put. Handful by handful the heap was scanned for traces of blood, and after half an hour's work there was never a sign.

"As a matter of fact there was hardly any seepage of blood," Feen said. "I don't know if you noticed the waistcoat, but there wasn't a stain bigger than a half-crown. I just thought there might be a chance, that's all."

"Since I'm not coming back here, I'd rather like a plan of the shed," Travers said. "We can see the foundations fairly clearly. It doesn't matter about the height."

Feen had a two-foot rule and Travers took measurements. Distances were roughly stepped out, and from the shed door to the gate was thirty-five yards. Then he asked if he might have a word with Corby.

"One thing I particularly want to know," he said. "Don't give me the kind of answer you think I want. If you don't know, just say so and there'll be no harm done. It's about that body when you began to pull it out. Which way did the legs lie? Parallel with the side of the shed, parallel with the front of the shed, or

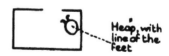

"What about the sound of the shot?" he said.

Feen said that inquiries would be made, but he was dubious about results. For one thing, the district was an agricultural one and a shot was the last thing to be noticed. And if Brewse had been shot inside the shed, the sound would have been naturally deadened.

"You think he was killed here?" Travers asked.

"Don't you?"

Travers shrugged his shoulders. "It's a capital spot. On a lonely lane, and the same lane where Gables is. Tall hedges to shield it from the road, and nice recesses to have a private talk in. All the same, if Brewse was killed here, then there's something badly wrong."

"And what's that?"

"Well, his body was hidden in the heap. So far, so good. It was a Saturday and farm-hands don't work on Saturdays these days, so the murderer was fairly sure the heap wouldn't be removed. But if he knew that much, then why was he such a fool as to think the manure heap would burn? They say every man's a gardener by instinct, and every gardener loves making fires and burning rubbish. Let's go further and say that every local man—including all our likely suspects—is a gardener. It doesn't make sense, isn't that so? And even if he were such an agricultural and gardening fool as to imagine the manure heap would catch fire and burn, he still couldn't have been such a certifiable lunatic as to imagine the fire would be big enough or hot enough to burn that poor devil Brewse, hide, hair, bones and all."

"Then why not go back to your own theory that the fire was an accident, and never was meant to burn the body?"

"Why not?" said Travers. "But if Brewse was killed here, why did he come here? Did he take a walk for exercise, and was he killed on the spur of the moment by some one who saw him by chance? Hardly likely, I think. People don't just happen to have heavy revolvers on them. Very well then. If he wasn't here by chance he was lured here by design. Which reminds me that I ought to be slipping away. Why not have another word with Marlin in case he can suggest anything about the luring away? There might have been a letter or a note, for instance."

"That sounds a good idea," Feen said. "We might as well look through Brewse's room while we're there."

"Marlin's had the free run of it," Travers pointed out. "He might have removed anything if he wanted to. Yet I don't know. He strikes me as a genuine old chap. What do you think?"

"I don't think there's any vice in Marlin," Feen said. "All the same, you never know. Which reminds me of something. Those casts are handy if you want to have a look at them before you go."

The pattern of those golf shoes had come out clearly, and it seemed extremely likely that inquiry at the professional's shop or in Edensthorpe might discover the owner, unless, as Feen ruefully remarked, that the owner was aware that prints must have been left, and had burnt the shoes already.

"What size do you make them?" asked Travers, who was busy making a drawing. "Nines or tens?"

"We can find that out later," Feen said. "They're certainly the shoes of a fairly big-footed man, if that's any help."

"By the way, do you know what Brewse actually weighed?"

"I've got it here somewhere," Feen said, and consulted his notebook. "Just under ten stone fully dressed. A hundred and thirty-eight pounds, to be exact."

"I remember he was a dapper little fellow when he stood in the dock," Travers said, and then had a sudden idea. "By the way, what became of his hat?"

"I've been wondering that," Feen said. "Either he went out without one, or else it got burnt. Marlin would tell us if he did have a hat, and what sort it was."

Travers took the Colonel in the Rolls because he said he would like to walk back for a leg-stretcher, and it was he who let out the exclamation as Travers slowed down the car at Gables.

"Hell's bells, what's that!"

Travers looked up and then was gaping too. That whole end of the house that faced the road, unbroken except for two small windows on the ground floor, was presenting the most amazing sight.

## THE GABLES CINEMA
(Hanley Brewse, proprietor)

NOW SHOWING

## <u>CONVICT 99</u>

The enormous letters had been well spaced, and the lines had been painted alternately in yellow and black—colours which stood out startlingly well on the faint pink of the brickwork. Huge broad-arrows covered the rest of the wall and made a kind of background.

"A pretty foul sight," Travers said, and shook his head. "I don't think very much of it do you?"

"Neither cleverness nor decency," Feen said.

"Just dirty hitting below the belt."

"Young Quench and his pal?"

"I'd hate to think so," Feen said. "Still, what might have seemed very amusing and thrilling at night, looks damnably cheap and nasty this morning. Whoever did it certainly had a nerve. That was the noise we heard here last night when we came out."

"Just a moment," Travers said, and was all at once polishing his glasses. "Whoever did the job has never had a view of it. The very first thing he or they think of this morning will be how the job's turned out and what it looks like. What about my slipping back and bringing one of your men? If he lies doggo in that thick hedge across the road, he could spot any Peeping Tom."

"That's a thundering good idea," Feen said, and then, before Travers could make a move, old Marlin appeared.

"Good morning, gentlemen," he said. "I thought I heard voices."

Then he caught sight of the end of the house and his mouth gaped. A moment, and his face had reddened, and he was shaking his head. Travers feared for a moment he was going to weep. Feen clapped him on the back.

"Pay no attention to that, Marlin. Just the work of some young hooligans. Let's go into the house. One or two things I'd like you to tell me."

He nodded to Travers, who slipped back to the meadow in the car. Reeper reported that nothing whatever had as yet been found. In spite of the rain, the ground was hard and there was never a footprint.

It was Mrs. Marlin who admitted Travers to the house when he came back. She was a plump, kindly looking soul, and must have been rather handsome in her young days. Travers found her even more deaf than he had thought, and bellowed so loudly that Marlin came out with something of a smile and ushered him into the room.

"Not much progress," Feen said. "I have induced Marlin to lay a formal complaint, though, about the damage to the wall. That gives us a chance."

"This the hat?" Travers asked, and picked up the brown felt hat from the table.

"No, this is the twin of the one he went out in," Feen explained. "He had two of these hats, bought apparently at the same time, one green and one brown. Unlined, as you see, but the maker's name on the sweat-band."

"Any notes or letters?"

"Two letters, both on the evening he got here, so Marlin tells me. Each looked like a private letter."

"No sign of either?"

Feen indicated the grate. "There was a fire here in the evenings. Brewse found it a bit chilly."

"Who would be likely to write to him?" Travers asked.

"I couldn't say, sir," Marlin said.

"Where'd his money come from for you to buy this place, and to live?"

"Some friends started a fund just before he came out," Feen explained, and got to his feet. "I gather also that there's some sort of allowance from his children. It's getting latish, by the way, so perhaps we'd better have a look round the side of the house."

Marlin showed them round. The ground was everywhere so hard that no marks were left but of dropped paint, though there did seem in one place to be the faint prints where a ladder had stood.

"It must have been an extending ladder," Travers said. "The ordinary kind would have left a sharper edge. What is the ladder here?"

"There isn't one here," Feen said. "Whatever ladder was used was carried here."

Travers raised his eyebrows. "That sounds helpful. How long would it have to be? Eighteen foot in all, or less?"

Feen drew back and calculated the height by the courses of brickwork. Sixteen feet would have done it comfortably, he thought, which meant an extending ladder of two nines at the most.

"Now don't you worry in the least about this filthy wall," Feen said to Marlin as they were going. "On Monday morning I'll have a man here to attend to it, and if decent-minded people here aren't highly indignant in the meantime, then I shall be very surprised."

"Doesn't this lane fork off to the village?" Travers asked when he was in the car.

"That's right. A hundred yards or so past the fire, you can turn off right to the Limehurst Road."

"Why not hop in then and let me take you back after all?" Travers said. "We can have a quick talk and I can circle back through the village. I'd rather like to have a look at the lie of the land round here."

Nothing had happened at the scene of the fire, but they had their brief talk there. Feen said he thought things were working out very well so far. That painting business, for instance, was not unlucky. Whereas it might be nasty work letting Petti-stone know that one of its inhabitants was wanted for murder, it would be easy enough to arouse a certain indignation against that vulgar eyesore on the wall of Gables, and every one ought to consider the finding of the perpetrator as something in the best interests of the village.

"While we're looking for one thing, we'll be looking for another," he said. "What everything really amounts to is that everybody has to have two perfect alibis—one for the hour between three and four when Brewse was shot, and another for the time when the fire was started. For the latter one we can make a perfectly genuine pretence of looking for the painter, because the painting was done round about the same time."

"And not only that," Travers said. "Once the painter, or paint-ers, are found, they're off the murder list. Whoever thought of that method of driving Brewse out of the village, couldn't have been the one who killed him. There was the devil of a risk in do-ing that painting, and whoever was doing it wouldn't have run that risk if he'd also been connected with murder."

Feen nodded. "I'd say it's a certainty that the painter didn't know Brewse had been killed. There must have been some won-dering, by the way, when you and I appeared at Gables last night when the painting was going on." He suddenly stared.

"If you were recognized, that's going to queer the pitch."

"I doubt if I was," Travers said. "As soon as the cars drove up, you bet your life the painter scuttled into hiding through that shrubbery. We spoke in whispers, too, if you remember."

"I think you're right," Feen said. "One of the first things I'm going to concentrate on is finding the owner of an extending lad-der, and when I've found it, I'm going to have a good look at it."

Travers wanted to know just how Feen would like him to help.

"The golf course is your stamping ground," Feen said. "You and I don't appear together from now on. We can always com-municate through the station 'phone, and I might slip round to your place in the evening."

"About golf. Is the week-end a very crowded time?"

"On the Saturday, no. That seems odd to you perhaps, but this is an agricultural district, and Saturday is market day at Edensthorpe, so everybody's pretty well engaged. I'd say the locals have the course very much to themselves on Saturday, but Sunday—that's different. The course'll be absolutely crowded to-day. The locals rather avoid it on Sundays, I believe."

"I thought I'd hover round and listen to gossip," Travers said. "And will you ring up Guff-Wimble for me and ask if he can fix me up with some games now you're likely to be busy?"

"I'll make it my business to see him this morning," Feen said. "It'll be a first-class excuse to call. Any particular person you'd like a round with?"

"The vicar, on Monday," Travers said promptly. Feen raised his eyebrows.

"Oh, I've nothing against him," Travers explained. "I thought he'd help to kill a few birds with one stone. Through him I might get a line on his son, and so on to the Pernaby girl, and then on to her uncle." He held out his hand. "Well, I'd better be moving along. If you ring me up, you'll always be told where you can get hold of me. If I go out anywhere, I'll leave word with the maids."

Feen strolled back with him to the car.

"Bad luck about not finding any letters at Gables or getting a line on 'phone calls," he said. "I thought that luring business would have been our best approach if only we could have got some sort of start."

"You can't trace any calls to and from Gables?" Feen shook his head. "Automatic system here, the same as at Edensthorpe."

"A pity," Travers said. "But did Marlin say anything at all about Brewse's exercise? Was he proposing to take a regular walk?"

"I gathered he wasn't proposing to take a walk at all, except after his evening meal," Feen said. "He took the one walk down to the village for a quick look round, and Marlin said he hadn't left the house since. All he did was to read, or do jigsaw puzzles all day, and the telephone was right against his ear."

"I'll wager that this is what happened," said Travers, always ready with a theory. "He was proposing to take regular walks, and he thought no one was aware of his identity. As soon as he got here he took a walk to the village, and then he didn't go out again. Why? Because when the insufferable Guffy rang him up and made that ridiculous offer for the house, he guessed at once that Pettistone knew him, and wanted to get rid of him."

Travers was feeling on quite good terms with himself as he moved the car on. At the fork he turned right and soon found himself at another junction. A right turn again and he was in a wideish road which he knew must be the one that went to Lime-hurst. It was more of an avenue than a road, so closely did its trees cover it, and on the right, through a gap in the woods, he just caught a glimpse of a path that seemed to lead in the direction of Gables.

As he neared the village he slowed the car to a crawl. On his right was the church and, alongside it, what would be the vicarage. Then the church bell began to toll, and he guessed it was for early Communion at eight o'clock. On the left was a line of petrol pumps and a garage, and alongside it a shop—or rather two long shops in one—above which was the painted sign:

# CHARLES AMMONY

## GROCERS PROVISION MERCHANTS
## UNIVERSAL PROVIDERS

Thoughts began to run through the head of Ludovic Travers. If the sign proclaimed the man, then Ammony was as much a pomposity as Guff-Wimble. A painted sign, and a painted sign on the end of Gables. Ammony's sign had been recently repainted, and, doubtless, as a universal provider, he sold paint. The church bell still tolling. Probably old Quench pulling the rope himself, and Quench was a man who had lost most through Brewse. Vicars might be human, but unhappily in the whole history of native murder he could recall only one cleric who had committed it.

But the car was already almost through the little village, and he quickened speed for home. Bernice had been up for an hour, she said, and the house smelt of a breakfast which was ready for the table. Travers ate an enormous meal, and between bites let out as much information as would probably be in the next morning's papers. Bernice said it must have been thrilling to work on the scene of the crime.

"Not so much as you'd think," he said. "I'm far too squeamish to make a first-class sleuth in any case."

"Squeamish?"

"Well, thin-skinned if you like. Detective work is only spying on a smaller scale, as it were. Take myself, now Feen wants me to help. I've got to act as if I've nothing to do with the police, and I shall have to tell a good many lies. If we're both lucky, some one may get hanged, and that's not always a cheery thought to end a day's work with, especially when you're of the private opinion that the murderer was badly up against it."

"Well, I think it is thrilling. I'm thrilled even to think I'm going to do anything."

He smiled. "But you're not. You're going to be passive—like me. You back up what lies I'm forced to tell, and you do nothing but listen."

"But, my dear, that's not very exciting."

"You took me for better or worse," Travers said. "I don't remember any mention of excitement. But take a concrete instance of what you can do. Suppose one of your friends at Pettistone begins to question you about me, and trying to find out if I really am connected with the police. Wouldn't that be valuable information?"

"Well, yes, I suppose it would. But don't I ask any questions at all?"

"They also serve who only stand and listen," Travers said hastily. "Other people will do the talking. The very last thing we want to do is to appear too interested in anything, except in the case, as a case. But to take another example. As I told you—in the very strictest confidence, by the way—we want to know where certain people were between three and four in the afternoon, and at eight o'clock at night. If Mrs. Strongman, we'll say, volunteers the information that she or her husband was at a certain place at those times, then she'll probably have a reason. That'd be valuable information."

Bernice was frowning. "Yes, but—" She hesitated. "Need the same person be affected by the same times? I mean, couldn't there be two people?"

"How do you mean?"

"Well, Mrs. Feen told me, frightfully confidentially, about that meeting at Mr. Guff-Wimble's house—"

"The devil she did!" said Travers.

"Well, darling, she did. What I was thinking then, was that all those people wanted to get rid of the man Brewse. Suppose one of them did kill him and then was terrified at what he had done. He might have confessed to one of the others, and the other one might have said, 'Never mind. I'll get rid of the body for you, if you're too scared to do it yourself.' And that would be the one who tried to burn the body."

Travers's fingers were fumbling at his glasses.

"That's an idea. All the same, the two times still hold. If a man can prove an alibi for both times, that includes either of the times."

"I didn't think of that," she said. "But what are we doing this morning, Ludo? It looks perfectly heavenly outside."

"You choose."

"No, darling—you."

"No, you. It may be your last chance before you assume your widow's weeds."

She laughed. "Very well, then. What about golf?"

"Well," he said, with a pretence of grave consideration. "I have an idea that Pettistone won't be playing much golf this morning. I rather think it will be at church."

"Church? Then why shouldn't we go to Pettistone Church?"

His hand had shot up by way of warning.

"Bernice Travers, don't say it would be lovely, and we ought to go."

"But why not?"

He smiled. "Because you're thinking precisely the same thing as I am."

# CHAPTER V
## TRAVERS SEES DAYLIGHT

PETTISTONE CHURCH, with its enormous churchyard, and, still farther beyond it, the vicarage and its gardens, lay in the angle made by the golf-course lane and the main road. Instead of parking the Rolls in the very handy space along the churchyard wall in the main road, Travers went to the left in the direction of the golf course, and found a parking-place a hundred yards or so along the lane. What he had noted was that there were two paths to the church porch, one from the lane and one from the road, and it was the former which was likely to be taken, when they came out of church, by the people he was most anxious to meet.

Travers was looking really distinguished that morning, and Bernice was enormously proud of him. It takes length to set off a suit, and his six-foot three was the very thing for the summer grey, the grey Homburg hat and, for a touch of colour, the light and dark blue of the tie. Bernice was wearing what he would have called a something in red and black, but it went superbly with her dark hair and eyes and the lovely pallor of her face.

The bell was at its last tolling as they entered. Travers steered Bernice to a back pew, and was just in time to avoid the ushering forward of a short man with a moustache whose ends were carefully waxed and stuck out like twin needles. But the short man, who had darted forward at their appearance, saw them provided with books.

From that back pew, Travers could note who was at church and who was not. Guff-Wimble was there, and he thought he recognized Molly Pernaby, sitting between a woman in fluffy grey, and a man who was probably her uncle. He recognized Strongman, too, and imagined the woman with him was his wife, but the son, Gordon, was not there; nor could he see anything of Bob Quench.

The congregation was quite small, even considering the size of the village, and the service and sermon turned out so uninspiring that he could hardly wonder. The vicar read his sermon, and was so unskilful in concealing the fact that Travers waited hopefully for the moment when he should lose his place altogether and be forced to come to a merciful halt. Then he wondered if that nervy, fussy method of delivery were his usual one, or whether he was disturbed that morning and not his ordinary self.

The last amen was said, the organ switched from a sugary *pianissimo* to the gurgling forte of a march, and the congregation began to move out. Travers, who had chosen that back pew with yet another design, lingered out his paces, and it was as he stepped from the porch that he heard behind him a voice he recognized.

"Why *must* Guffy wear that ghastly tie? I was almost ill in the plate."

There was a sh! but as it came, Bernice turned. She also had recognized the voice. Molly Pernaby's tone changed dramatically.

"Good morning, Mrs. Travers. I never dreamt it was you. What did you think of our church?"

"I thought it was a lovely old place," Bernice said. "You know my husband, do you?"

Molly smiled at Travers and said she'd seen him on the course. Then she introduced her aunt, Miss Pernaby, and her uncle. Pernaby, looking more gaunt and loose-limbed than ever in his formal black, was the very image of his sister, who also was tall and angular.

"Are you great church-goers, Mr. Travers?" she asked.

"Of course they're not," Molly said. "Nobody is, nowadays."

"But, my dear!" protested her aunt.

"Well, everybody here would much rather be playing golf," Molly said.

"Do you play, Miss Pernaby?" Travers asked.

She smiled and shook her head. The smile made all the difference to her face. The set hardness went, and revealed a kindliness and a sense of humour.

"I'm afraid not," she said. "I'm merely responsible for a house with two people who're golf fanatics."

The Strongmans came by then, and there were more introductions. The massive Strongman, shambling as ever, looked rather uncomfortable in his church garments, and reminded Travers of an amiable bear on an invisible leash. Mrs. Strongman, whom he was seeing at close quarters for the first time, was everything that was opposite—short, slim, and almost alarmingly alert. What she had to say and there was plenty of it, was fired as if from a gun.

"Not much of a sermon, do you think?" she said to Travers, and, before he could say a word: "The vicar really gets worse than ever—poor man. So rare to find what you might call a sporting vicar who can preach at the same time, don't you think?"

"Is he always as jerky as that?" Travers cut in. "My dear man, you don't know him. I think this morning he was rather better than usual, if anything."

"How's the golf going?" Bernice asked her, and with that the group somehow began forming itself into male and female.

"How'd you get on with the vicar on Saturday?" Strongman asked Pernaby, and Travers pricked up his ears.

"Just beat him," Pernaby said. "Gave him three bisques and just won on the last green."

"Was that in the morning?" Travers asked. "Saturday afternoon," Pernaby said. "Very few people on the course, by the way. We didn't start till well after two, and we were back in the club-house at soon after four."

"That's the quickest round the vicar's done recently," Strongman said. "I wish he'd move like that when he plays with me."

Pernaby grunted, then asked Travers how long he was staying at Edensthorpe. Travers said it might be another week or ten days.

"I saw you playing with Feen," Strongman said. "He's a pretty sticky customer to beat."

But the party had arrived at Travers' car, and Strongman moved forward with quite an unexpected agility to open the door for Bernice.

"You must come to tea sometime," Miss Pernaby was saying.

"You must come and see us too—both of you," added Mrs. Strongman.

"I'm expecting to be rather at a loose end nowadays," Travers said. "I'd been relying on Feen for my golf, but he let me know this morning that he's likely to be busy." His voice took on a due gravity. "I suppose you've heard about the murder last night?"

"Murder?" said Pernaby, and stared. "Here, unfortunately," said Travers, and shook a sad head. "That man Hanley, at Gables. Hanley Brewse, he is really, so they tell me."

"Brewse!" Strongman was gaping. "Murdered, you say?"

"Last night, so I gather," Travers told him. "Mind you I don't think Feen would be pleased if he knew I was passing this on, but there was something about a fire, and his body in it."

Then all at once there was a kind of moan, and a quick stirring on the path. Things began so quickly and were over so quickly that Travers, his view obscured by Strongman's bulk, never knew quite what had happened, but it looked as if Miss Pernaby had either almost fainted or had been about to faint. Pernaby was holding her, and Molly was saying something in a quick, agitated voice.

"I'm all right, my dear." Miss Pernaby was smiling wanly. "Just a bit frightened, that's all."

"But there was nothing to be frightened at!" Molly was telling her, and then Mrs. Strongman was there, and Bernice was getting out of the car.

"She's all right, aren't you, dear?" Molly said. "She wasn't at all well yesterday. I had to go into Edensthorpe and fetch her some powders, and it was rather a shock hearing about—about anything so dreadful."

"Do let me drive her home," Travers said. "You're sure you're all right, Miss Pernaby?"

"It was silly of me," she said, and was smiling wanly again. "I've not been feeling very well lately, and perhaps it was rather a shock. It's all right, Arthur. I'm absolutely all right."

Pernaby let go of her arm. Molly took it, and smiled meaningly as she began leading her on.

"I think we'll be getting along now. Thanks awfully, Mr. Travers, but I'm sure she'll be all right."

"See you during the week perhaps," Pernaby said to Travers, and with a good-bye to the Strongmans, moved hastily on.

"Very blundering of me," Travers said to Mrs. Strongman. "I ought to have known the news would be upsetting to any one who'd been unwell. Most thoughtless of me."

"Grace Pernaby's a martyr to headaches," she said, and smiled grimly, "but I'm the one who ought to have felt faint. I shouldn't be surprised if somebody doesn't say I had something to do with killing him." She caught Travers's smile of polite surprise. "It isn't amusing, I assure you. You've no idea what a hotbed of scandal this place is. Just because the man swindled me out of my money—"

"Mr. Travers doesn't want to hear all your troubles, my dear," Strongman said. "But you weren't pulling our legs in any way, were you, Mr. Travers?"

"He really was murdered?"

"He certainly was."

"And last night, you said?"

Travers shrugged his shoulders. "Afraid I know only as much as I've been told." He held out his hand. "Good-bye. See you both during the week, perhaps. We might be able to fix up a game."

The car was through the village before Travers put his question.

"Well? What do you think of things?"

"I thought that fainting attack was extraordinary," Bernice said promptly. "Who is the Miss Pernaby? I get rather confused over them."

"I haven't a notion. I take it she's Pernaby's sister. She's the very spit of him. The niece, Molly, must be a daughter of their brother, who's presumably dead."

"Miss Pernaby's name is Grace, I do know that," Bernice said. "She and Mrs. Strongman seem to be very close friends."

"About that fainting attack," Travers said. "Most unexpected, as you said. She looked to me as strong as a horse."

"I wouldn't say that, Ludo. She looked very dark under the eyes, just as if she'd had a very bad time with headaches."

"That may be. Also it may be possible for some one in this twentieth century to feel faint at the mention of murder—but I doubt it."

"Especially after living with a niece like Molly," laughed Bernice. "I'm sure murder's a very proper subject compared with some of the things Molly talks about."

"A queer question about all those people," Travers said. "I wonder precisely how snobbish they are. That seems a pretty good test of character. If you and I, for instance, had rolled up here in an old two-seater and looking as if we had to count the pennies, do you think every one would have been quite so friendly?"

"I think Molly Pernaby would."

"And somehow I think Pernaby would." He smiled. "In other words, those seem to be the only two we like."

"I don't dislike Mrs. Strongman," Bernice said, and then remembered something. "I heard what Mr. Strongman was doing yesterday afternoon. Grace Pernaby said something—I forget what it was—and Mrs. Strongman said her husband was stranded with the car yesterday afternoon and had to send the chauffeur back to the village for a spare wheel, or something." She frowned. "I didn't catch anything else. Oh, yes, the chauffeur was a young man they're trying. Grace Pernaby seemed to know him."

"Back to the village," Travers said reflectively. "That would be to Ammony's garage probably." He nodded. "To-morrow I'm going to make an excuse for a talk with Ammony. And talking about alibis, Pernaby and the vicar were playing golf yesterday afternoon. Quite a good tussle, from what I heard. If Feen should have managed to fix me up with a game with the vicar in the morning, I may hear more about it."

"But what is there to hear about it?" asked Bernice. "If they were playing a round of golf, isn't that an alibi?"

"Don't know," Travers said. "The question is, did they play a whole round, right on from start to finish. They might have knocked off half-way round, at the club-house, on some excuse or other. I mean, one might have said to the other, 'Do you mind waiting for ten minutes or so? Something I've got to slip back home and do, and I won't keep you waiting longer.' You see the point? Each man could justifiably say he had spent the afternoon at golf." He nodded to himself. "There're two kinds of alibis that I've learned by hard experience to recognize. Those you can bust and those you can't. I've got to know a considerable deal more about that round of golf before either Pernaby or the vicar is struck off the list."

"But you said you liked Pernaby!"

Travers smiled soberly. "Liking doesn't count. I've liked all sorts of people, but that wouldn't make me go back on my job. I liked Merrick Clarke, as I was telling you the other day, but I helped to send him to jail. Since he died there, it might even be said I helped to kill him. And what about George Wharton? Don't you think he's helped to hang many a man whom he had at least a liking for?"

Bernice said she would stay in the garden that afternoon and read. Travers, who proposed putting in an hour at the golf club, promised faithfully to be home for an early tea.

He found the course crowded, as Feen had hinted, but as he had had no intention of playing, the fact disturbed him little. Two or three customers were in the professional's shop, but he waited till they had gone.

"Golf shoes, sir? Certainly, sir," the pro. Said. "What size?"

"Elevens," Travers told him, adding an extra size to make reasonably sure they were not in stock. The pro.'s face fell at once.

"Sorry, sir. I only keep eights and nines. They're the ones we're nearly always asked for. I can get them for you in a couple of days."

"I'm afraid that'll be too late," Travers said, and had a look at a pair nevertheless. Then a customer came in and he examined the pattern of the soles. It was quite a different design from that of the footprints in the ditch.

"These the only kind you sell?" he asked.

"The only kind, sir." He expatiated on their merits and their popularity with the members. Travers listened courteously then bought a box of balls by way of solatium.

The next visit was to the secretary's office.

Guff-Wimble was smoking a post-prandial cigar and toying with various papers on the desk. Travers was greeted most effusively. Most decidedly it would be an advantage for him to take weekly tickets for himself and his wife.

"Very glad you can both play here," he said. "We shan't need any introduction in your case, either. Feen introduced you originally. By the way, didn't I see you and your wife at church this morning?"

Travers admitted the fact. Something in his tone made Guff-Wimble confidential. He had to go himself—vicar's warden, and all that—but it was a rather dreary business. And all the time he was talking, Travers knew the words were coming from behind a screen. Guffy had something on his mind, and, sure enough, he ultimately came to it.

"You've heard about this perfectly bloody business? About the murder?"

Travers nodded gravely. "Feen let me know. That's really why I shall be at a loose end this week. Of course, he may have the luck to catch the one who did it, and then he'll be free for golf again."

"By the way, he saw me about you, and asked me to fix you up to-morrow." There was a queer note of inquiry in that last remark, but Travers merely nodded. "He said you were on the steady side, so I fixed you up with old Quench. Ten o'clock, if that suits you."

Travers said he was grateful, then spiked Guffy's guns by asking if Feen had let out anything about the murder. Not that he was interested, except out of sheer curiosity.

"He didn't tell me a thing," said the obviously disappointed Guffy. "My own idea is that this isn't what you'd call a local job. It's ridiculous on the face of it. It was bad enough having that black guard Brewse in the place at all—the wrong kind of publicity, if you get me. What's the place going to be like now?"

"That sort of notoriety soon blows over," Travers assured him. "But who do you think did it?"

Guffy waved an airy hand. "Fairly obvious, don't you think? Somebody he ruined found out he was here, and that's all there is to it."

"Yes," said Travers. "That sounds a very brainy idea. All the police have to do is work through the list of those he did ruin, and find out if any of them were this way yesterday."

"Precisely," said Guffy, and rose. "By the way, I wonder if you and your wife would come to dinner with me one of these nights. A bachelor establishment, but I'll ask one or two people in."

Travers said he would be delighted, and that was the end of the interview. Once outside the door, Travers was polishing his glasses and blinking away owlishly in the sun. Guffy had been wearing a pair of *black* shoes, the size being tens. But he would never have worn black shoes with mustard-coloured plus-fours if brown had been available. Moreover the black shoes had something of a resurrected air about them, and they were certainly not the kind that Guffy had worn that morning in church.

"If I were betting," Travers was saying to himself, "I'd risk a fair sum that Guffy was the man in the ditch. After he got through the hedge he had to go across a meadow that still had a good crop of grass on it, and was wet with dew. His shoes got soaked and couldn't be worn this afternoon, so he put on the old black ones instead. To-morrow morning his man will have the brown ones back to their polish. I wonder?"

A minute or two and he was making his way to the car park. It was so crowded that his own car had had to be run off the gravelled square and was standing with others on the grass that led to the rough off the first fairway. Travers contemplated the spot for some considerable time, then walked round the spaces between the various cars. Then he made for a whitish stone which was lying on the gravel. The stone was put on the grass and he trod it firmly in with his heel.

Next, Travers took out his number six and his putter and made his way to the acre of practice ground which lay between the road and the tenth fairway. It was deserted, as he anticipated, but after half an hour of approach work, he became aware of two people watching him from the comparative seclusion of the club-house loggia. Molly Pernaby, in brown skirt and jumper, was one and the other he was almost sure was Bob Quench. A few more shots and Molly came sauntering over alone, and she was in time to see Travers scuffle one along the ground.

"Do you do those off your left toe or your right?" she said.

"It all depends," said Travers craftily. "You show me how you do them."

She pulled a couple of balls from her pocket and borrowed his club. Her first effort took the turf an inch too soon and went ten yards only.

"Oh, damn! Not having my own club, I expect."

The second effort was a beauty and dropped like a stone near the pin.

"Good!" said Travers. "I must try a few of those."

She watched a couple of efforts, and said that soon he'd be doing them every time. Then, most casually, she mentioned her aunt.

"By the way, Aunt Grace is awfully upset about that exhibition she gave this morning. She feels a frightful fool."

"She oughtn't to feel that way about it," Travers said. "How is she now?"

"Absolutely fit. She often has those turns, you know. Anything brings them on. Yesterday she was frightfully ill. Sick headache and all that, and she'd run out of powders. I had to go into Edensthorpe in the afternoon, and she spent the day in bed."

"Rotten things—headaches," Travers said, and once more addressed his ball. Something else was trembling on her tongue's tip and he wondered if it would stay there. But it came.

"That was a beauty. Pretty foul for the village, this murder business, don't you think?"

"Murders are not very nice things wherever they take place," he told her. "And I shouldn't like to be at this particular moment in the shoes of the one who did it."

"But Brewse was an awful swine—so everybody says."

"Even swine have certain rights," Travers told her dryly. "For one thing, they can't be killed except in a licensed slaughter-house."

That rather puzzled her. Something else hovered for a moment, but never came.

"Well, I'll be pushing off now. We must make up a mixed foursome next week with your wife."

Travers said he would love it, and that was that. Out of the corner of his eye he saw her go right across the seventeenth fairway, and when he shifted a point or two south, he caught sight of Bob Quench with her over by the edge of the woods at the fourteenth, and the two seemed to be walking aimlessly, and talking.

Travers set off for home, and as he drove he communed with himself in that cheerful, introspective way of his.

"I had an idea she'd look me up, and she did. I knew she'd mention her aunt—and she did, though I was careful not to refer to her myself. And why did she take all those pains to tell me about the aunt's ailments? Was it to lead up to the fact that Aunt Grace spent the afternoon and evening in bed? If so, what the devil has that got to do with the murder? And did Bob Quench put her up to coming over to me? If so, what information did she get out of me?"

There Travers shook his head. As far as he could remember, he had revealed nothing, and then he recalled something which he had learned. For what it was worth, Molly Pernaby had been at pains to tell him that she herself had an alibi for the Saturday afternoon!

But surely she could not have been mixed up with the murder? Had she given the information then on behalf of Bob Quench? A possibility certainly that must be noted. And then Travers wondered what it was that was an uneasy background to his own mind, and in the same moment knew. Too many people were providing themselves with alibis, and, in the course of the first few hours before inquiry had really commenced. If things went on at the same rate, the bottom looked like falling out of the case, and Feen might after all have to work along the lines that the egregious Guffy had so airily suggested.

As soon as tea was over, Travers rang the police and asked for enough plaster of Paris for two mixings. Feen was called to the 'phone and said he would bring it at once himself.

Travers had not the slightest intention of withholding information, but he was certainly not prepared to buoy Feen up with impossible hopes. All he reported was that he had several vague ideas, and that he was hopeful on the morrow of finding out the identity of the man who had crouched in the ditch.

"I've been thinking something," Feen said.

"George Wharton's due to-morrow and I rather expect he'll be staying with us." He saw Travers's surprised look. "Were you expecting him to come to you?"

"Lord, no," Travers said. "He was very vague about it all when he mentioned it, and we've done nothing in the matter."

"What I was thinking was this," Feen said. "He'll probably be seeing as much of you as of us. What I'm getting at is that you and I don't want to be seen about together, so George can be a kind of errand-boy between the pair of as." He gave something like a wink, "It that doesn't interest him in this business, then I'm pretty badly wrong."

"I doubt if he'll lend a hand," Travers said. "George is a stickler for the proprieties."

"I'm not so sure," Feen told him. "Anything happened with you to-day?"

Travers reported the little there was, and Feen had very little too.

The vicinity of the fire had been thoroughly searched and even the ashes had been sifted, and nothing helpful had been found, though, as a matter of fact, he had never been at all hopeful of finding the empty shell. Bob Quench and Gordon Strongman had come past Gables in Bob's sports car just as the church bell ceased ringing in the morning, and according to the watcher behind the hedge, they had not glanced notably at the painted house.

"When they turned up at the meadow," Feen said, "they said they'd heard about the fire, and they were absolutely staggered when I told them about the murder. Either the surprise was genuine or it was a masterpiece of craft."

"Did you mention about the house?"

"Oh, no," Feen said. "I left it to them and they didn't mention it. That's the unusual thing. They couldn't have helped glancing at the house as they passed, and they must have noticed it, even if they hadn't a hand in it."

"Yes," said Travers. "They daren't mention it for fear of losing their nerve. I saw Guffy, by the way, and he said you'd seen him."

"I saw him all right," Feen said. "And I let him do all the talking. He was very ready with suggestions."

"I know," Travers said. "Some one whom Brewse ruined had tracked him down, and so on."

"That's it. And I'm not worrying. When I've something to work on, then I'll act, and not before. The more talk and gossip there is, the better I shall be pleased."

"What about to-morrow?"

"The inquest first," Feen said. "That'll be merely formal, but I've taken care to see that none of the Guffy gang is empanelled. Then I'm plastering Pettistone with bills, offering a reward for the discovery of the persons or person who defaced that house. I'm also inquiring about paint, and, very cautiously, about the ladder."

"A sound programme," Travers said. "I'm playing golf with old Quench, as you know, and I may learn a thing or two. And that's all that's happened to you?"

"That's all," Feen said. "Except perhaps that Corby tells me that some one or other rang up his landlady at about a quarter-past eight and said there was a fire in Copmore Lane. That shows some one was about near Copmore Lane last night. And it couldn't have been the man in the ditch."

It was a casually imparted piece of information, and apparently of no great import, but Travers's fingers were fumbling at his glasses. All that day ideas had been filtering through his mind, and now he had the one connecting clue that he had needed. For the first time there were many things—and vital ones—of which he was absolutely sure.

# CHAPTER VI
# LABOUR IN VAIN

THE MONDAY MORNING brought the expected letter from Wharton, and, as Feen had hinted, it was not with the Traverses that he was staying, though he hoped to see a good deal of them. A Whartonian quip or two about the honeymoon was evidently intended to show that in staying with the Feens, George had a knowledge of the fitting.

The chuckling Travers had just passed the letter over to Bernice, when the 'phone went. Feen now also had a letter and was announcing the same news.

"He thinks he'll be here about tea-time," he said.

"And we'd like you both to be here. Four o'clock suit you?"

"We'd love it," Travers said. "And you're still hoping to rope him in?"

"I'm betting the trouble will be to rope him out," Feen said. "All the same I'm counting on you to lend a hand. Plenty of soft soap used to be the recipe for George."

"It still is," Travers told him amusedly.

Another interesting thing that Travers saw on the breakfast table was the flaring headline of Brewse's murder across the front page of a newspaper. Reporters from town would already be hurrying across England to reach Pettistone in time for the inquest, and probably some would be there at the moment, taking pictures of Gables and interviewing the locals.

Travers decided to change his plans. He would be at Pettistone soon after nine o'clock and Bernice could come on at her leisure with her partner, Mrs. Feen. Then in the half-hour before it was necessary to start, he read what the three papers had to say about Brewse, and the murder. The one piece of possibly new information was that nobody had been aware of the part of England where Brewse had settled. The sum collected by sympathizers and friends had been given him in cash, and it rather looked as if it had been expected he should go abroad. Bernice remarked on that.

"Isn't that just what I said?" she told her husband triumphantly.

Travers shook a sad head. "The most tragic phrase in the language. One that's wrecked more homes than all the others put together."

"What is?"

"'I told you so.'"

"Yes, but I did tell you so."

Travers gave a humorous shrug of the shoulders. "Now I come to remember it, so you did. And before I forget it, what about calling on Miss Pernaby this morning, and asking how she is?"

He was slightly behind schedule when he left, and he went by that back road which he and Feen had taken on the Saturday night, and he drew up before Ammony's garage. A small delivery van, with Ammony's name on it, was standing there, with a mechanic attending to it and the driver watching. There was evidently an argument going on, and Travers, having an idea the mechanic was the only one on duty, drew near to listen.

"Well, I think it's the petrol feed," the driver said.

The mechanic was exasperatedly pointing to the carburettor as Travers asked what was wrong.

"It's the filter choked again, sir, that's what it is," the mechanic said.

"I tell you it's the feed pipe," the driver told him. "The boss said after he blew through it she went as right as rain."

"When was this?" asked the helpful Travers.

"Saturday afternoon, sir, and she's been all right ever since, till just now."

"Just a minute," said Travers. "What sort of country did Mr. Ammony drive her in? Hilly or flat?"

The question made no sense, as he was well aware, but his manner was so serious and hopeful that both men had to make pretence of seeing his point.

"Only up to Copmore," the driver said. "I was going up there, and he said he'd go himself. I reckon he wanted to see Mr. Haylock about something."

"Copmore Farm would be rising ground," Travers pronounced. "I should try the feed pipe again and see what happens. But you might put me in ten gallons first."

The mechanic went. Travers tackled the driver who, he imagined, would now be on his side. "Mr. Ammony often drives his own vans?"

"Not once a month, sir, only I reckon he wanted to go there and thought it'd be the quickest way."

"And didn't I see this van in Copmore Lane on Saturday afternoon?"

The driver grinned. "I wouldn't be surprised. He reckoned he was tinkering about with it for best part of half an hour. I expected him back at half-past three, and it was gone four when he rolled up."

Travers nodded and went on to the mechanic, who was turning the wheel of the old-style pump.

"You didn't say what kind you wanted, sir, but I reckoned you'd want this as you'd drawn up here."

"That's right," Travers said. "Some of these cheaper petrols sometimes let you down. And, by the way, didn't Mr. Strongman have a breakdown on Saturday? Some one or other was telling me so."

The mechanic snorted. "I wouldn't call that a breakdown, Darn carelessness, if you ask me. You wouldn't believe it, sir, but what do you think? Out he goes with Tom Jewry—that's the one used to be in the gardens and who he's trying out for chauffeur—and when he gets about a mile along the Limehurst Road, a tyre goes flat. Out hops Tom to put on the spare, and the spare's as good as flat. Then he looks for the foot-pump, and where do you think it is? At home, in the garage!"

"Then I take it Tom isn't chauffeur any more," smiled Travers.

"Oh, I don't know, sir. Mr. Strongman's not a bad boss. He made Tom hoof it all the way back here with the spare, and he sat in the car and waited. We didn't half pull Tom's leg when he got here. Sweat? I His face was running."

"Well, he learned something," Travers said, and handed over a note in payment. A tip out of the change seemed likely to be a good investment.

It was still not half-past nine when he reached the course, and the car park was deserted. Monday was always a slack morning, and the locals had no need for an early start. But though there was plenty of room on the gravel, Travers drew the nose of the car up to that soft place in the grass which he had marked with the white stone, and then proceeded to make the spot more damp by draining his radiator. Then he backed the car and drew in again with the bonnet on the near side of the sodden grass.

A few minutes' wait and he caught sight of Guff-Wimble. At once he was examining the engine, feet well clear of the soft spot. Guff-Wimble received a cheery wave and came across.

"Something gone wrong?"

"I'm not sure," Travers said. "I thought I'd better drain my radiator and make certain. I can always fill up again here."

"A bit sticky here, what?" Guffy said, and drew back gingerly to firmer ground.

"It is rather," Travers said, and began screwing up again. "Still, I can fix this up at any time."

He strolled with Guffy as far as the corner of the club-house. Guffy asked if there was much excitement in the village. The blasted papers, he said, were full of the murder.

"Things were quiet enough when I came through," Travers said. "What time's the inquest?"

"About eleven. They've got that blighter Ammony on the jury." He stopped with a look that was somewhat sheepish. "You're a pal of Feen's, though, aren't you?"

"Not too much so," said Travers meaningly. "Why?"

"Well, between ourselves, I think it's a scandal. He's prejudiced."

Travers, anxious to get back to the car, cut hastily in with hints that showed the Ammony history was reasonably well known.

"Ah, but that's not all," Guffy said. "I saw Ammony myself on Saturday morning and he was saying some remarkably compromising things. He'd learned that Brewse was—well Brewse, and he told me point-blank that he'd have him out of the village. Several people heard him."

"He's a bit of a hot-air merchant, so they tell me," Travers said. "Still, we shall know more later. I'd better be getting ready for the vicar, by the way."

And he had to hurry, for if Quench was a punctual man, then he would be appearing in less than ten minutes. So Travers mixed the plaster and filled in Guffy's footprints, which looked, if anything, too deep. But the shoes he was now wearing were brown, and they had seemed still to be slightly off colour as if not wholly recovered from their soaking. Then he backed the car again and ran it forward till the drying plaster was well beneath. By the end of the round, the casts should be beautifully set.

Quench was five minutes late, but most apologetic. The fault was his son's, who had driven him up in the sports car with Gordon Strongman. Travers was formally introduced to the two.

"Something the matter with your car, is there?" Travers said.

"We probably left a piece or two of the works out on Saturday," Gordon said. "We spent the whole afternoon taking her to bits. A filthy job it was, too."

"You did it yourselves?"

"Bob's a perishing genius," Gordon said. "He even had the differential scattered all over his garage floor."

The vicar was one of those players who refuse to be brisk, whatever the need and occasion. Not only was his walk leisurely, but each stroke had its couple of practice swings, and Travers had a suspicion that a fraying of his opponents' nerves was no small factor in the reputation he had acquired of being a mighty hard man to beat. But Travers was not the kind to be ruffled, and the vicar's leisure gave opportunity for talk. Yet there was one unexpected drawback. He had been unaware of the vicar's deafness and he was soon finding that hollering into his ear was a trying business.

Then in time came a reference to Pernaby, whom Travers said he knew.

"He just beat me on Saturday," the vicar said, with a rueful shake of the head. "I had him when he lost a ball and we were all square, and then somehow nothing seemed to go right." He clicked his tongue. "I've only beaten him once, and I really thought I was going to win."

"What's his handicap?"

"He's four but he ought to be lower." He shook his head again. "A perfect afternoon for golf, too. I always play so badly in a wind."

"But didn't I see you in the club-house soon after three on Saturday?"

The vicar looked surprised, then gathered that there was an innuendo, and smiled.

"We neither of us need any Dutch courage, I fear. As a matter of fact I did think of leaving my number two in my locker as we passed—I was playing so badly with it—but I thought it would be cowardly, and we went straight on." Another rueful shake of the head. "I wish I had, I topped badly with it at the sixteenth and that really ruined my last chance."

At the end of the fourteenth the vicar was two up, and at once he was most genial and helpful. He was a shortish driver himself, as Travers must have remarked, he said, but though he was taking the safe way round, Travers was such a long hitter that he advised him to take a chance and carry the trees, and so reach the green in two shots.

"Our friend Pernaby is one of the few who always do it," he said, "and I'm sure you're driving as far as he does."

What he forebore to add was that the fifteenth was the hole at which Pernaby had come to grief on the Saturday afternoon, and that in his heart of hearts he was hopeful of Travers doing the same. Travers, always something of an adventurer, swung lustily.

"I believe you've done it!" the vicar said, if with a touch of regret. His own ball had been placed cannily to the left, from where he was hoping that a good third might get back the sacrificed stroke. Travers was hopeful, too, and sure enough, his ball sailed well over the trees and was lying nicely teed.

So the vicar found himself only one up again a state of affairs which it was Travers's policy to rectify. A foozled shot or two, and at the sixteenth the vicar was dormy two, and in high good humour. He and Travers bellowed their way along the fairway of the seventeenth, talking about Brewse, the murder and the inquest. But there was nothing mentioned which Travers did not already know, except that the vicar had actually seen from the window of his upstairs study that evening, what he afterwards knew was the glow of the fire. So busy had he been over the final draft of his two sermons, however, that he had paid little attention.

"I expect you're pretty lonely there sometimes?" Travers said, and wondered how he would take it.

"I am," he said. "But I'm used to it. A man of my age, Mr. Travers, learns to make his own amusements."

"Didn't I see your boy at Edensthorpe on Saturday night?"

"You probably did," he said, and shook his head again. "He was out somewhere, I know. Young people never seem to stay longer in the house than is necessary for meals. Very different from my own young days.

The match ended on the seventeenth green, and the vicar was highly delighted with his win. He even thought that when Travers knew a little more about the course, the result might be the other way.

"I'm a poor man nowadays," he said, "and golf is my one relaxation, and it happens to be a cheap one. If things had been different—"

"You might have been a worse golfer," Travers ended for him, and Quench chuckled at the aptness. He tried, in fact, to fix a return match for the near future. Travers mentioned a wife, and hinted at engagements beyond his control.

It was after one o'clock, and the casts of Guffy's soles had set superbly. By the time the car radiator had been filled, Bernice was ready to go. Travers said would she go back with Mrs. Feen after all, as there was something he still had to do, and could they call at the police-station on their way and hand in a small parcel. By the time Bernice was home, he hoped to be home himself.

All he had in mind was a sight of the famous Charles Ammony, and he was to be lucky. Ammony himself, who was probably relieving an assistant during lunch, was at the counter, and he was the man with the pointed moustache who had been so officiously helpful in church. Travers summed him up as oily and unctuous and not to be trusted an inch.

"*Good* morning, sir," he said, and bowed the invitation to the order.

"Have you any really good chocolates?" Travers said. It was a spur of the moment choice.

"We have some very good boxes, sir. You staying here, sir?"

"More or less," Travers said.

Ammony began producing boxes, and he was talking all the time.

"All the excitement over, sir. Quite a lot of people here, there were. Some from London, so they tell me. I never saw the Parish Hall so crowded. That's where the inquest was, you know."

"What happened?"

"Not a lot, sir." The chocolates were momentarily forgotten.

"I happened to be on the jury, so I heard all, as they say. What surprised everybody was that he was killed in the afternoon." His head went cunningly on one side. "What do you think about that, sir?"

"What do you think?" countered Travers.

Ammony gave a knowing look. "You don't tell me that, sir. People don't go murdering people in broad daylight, not up anywhere like Copmore Lane."

"Who said he was killed in the afternoon? The doctors?"

"Doctors!" Ammony said, and with infinite scorn. "There's some things they know, sir, but a lot they don't. Now I knew a man who the doctors all gave up. . . ."

Ten minutes went by and Travers was at last able to ask the price of a box that looked likely.

"That one, sir? Five shillings, sir, and you'd be asked six for it in Edensthorpe."

Travers paid him and said there was no need to wrap it up. Ammony thanked him effusively. "If you should be thinking of settling in the district, sir, I should be delighted to have your custom, sir. We may look old-fashioned but you'll find we're up to date, and always ready to oblige."

"I don't doubt it," Travers said, and then caught sight of the extending ladder that stood near the counter of what was apparently the ironmongery department.

"That looks a good ladder. What's it extend to? Twelve foot?"

"Ah, sir, there you have something out of the ordinary." He was brisking round at once. "A local product this, sir, made by one of our tradesmen. Now this patent here. . . ."

Travers had let himself in for another two-minute exhibition of salesmanship, but the only interesting part came at the end, when the persuasive Ammony remarked that every one in the parish had bought one.

"The vicar got one?"

"Yes, sir. I sold him a ten foot; extending to eighteen, that is."

"The golf club got one?"

"No, sir, but Mr. Guff-Wimble has."

"Good. And what about Mr. Strongman?" Ammony chuckled. "He's got a nine-foot, sir."

"Right," said Travers. "We'll take it that all God's children got ladders. One of these times I might buy one myself."

"Delighted to supply you, sir." He followed the customer out to the road, and then darted forward to the car and had the door open. "Permit me, sir."

"Thank you," Travers said. "You didn't tell me, by the way, what the jury's verdict was at the inquest?"

"No verdict, sir." He threw his chest out. "We were adjourned, sir, for a week to-day."

Travers nodded, then as his hand went forward to the lever, he caught sight of what looked like one of Feen's bills on a board in front of the shop. Ammony followed the direction of his look.

"They're offering a reward, sir, about that painting some one did on that wall at Gables. I suppose you haven't seen it?"

There was a smirk that left no doubt where his sympathies lay.

"As a matter of fact I did catch a glimpse of it," Travers said. "Not a very charming sight, do you think, to see that poor devil Brewse's name on his own house, now he's dead?"

"Perhaps you're right, sir," said Ammony, face sobering. "All the same, you know, sir, they do say that all's fair in love and war."

"That's one way of putting it," Travers told him dryly. "It might make a bit of unpleasantness for you, though, if by any chance you happened to sell the paint that did it."

Ammony shook his head. "I'm not worrying about that, sir. As a matter of fact, in confidence, I don't mind saying I've been asked about that already. 'Not guilty, m'lord,' I told the gentleman. 'And, what's more, sir,' I said, 'you can't hold me responsible for what I sold, even if I sold it—which I didn't.'"

"A sound argument," Travers said, and at last could move the car on. That he was late was pretty certain and he was travelling fast when he overtook a car about a mile short of the town. The car was vaguely familiar, and then he knew who the driver was and slowed down ahead.

"Morning, Sergeant. Where've you come from? The inquest?"

Sergeant Reeper said it was more like afternoon, and he had been clearing up after the inquest.

"Anything fresh?" Travers wanted to know. "Not that I know of, sir. Only that we had the report on the fire, and they reckon it must have been started off with paraffin. Mr. Pollfax thinks the whole of that side of the shed nearest the wind was soaked with it. Probably a two-gallon tin."

Travers, whose whole ideas about that shed had been built round the idea of a deliberate fire, gave the necessary look of astonishment.

"You on to anything yet, sir?" Reeper asked.

"Not absolutely definite," Travers said. "I did manage to take a pair of casts this morning which I'm hoping may be interesting. The only trouble is, if they're whose I think they are—I mean, that man who crouched in the ditch—then we're up against another little problem. I think I've also found out that four of the men who were at Guff-Wimble's place that night have quite good alibis, but I'll go into that with the chief later. . . ." He held out his hand. "Now I must be pushing along. I saw that man Ammony, by the way, just now, when I happened to go into the shop. I rather gathered you'd been interviewing him, too."

Reeper grinned. "What'd you think of him, sir?"

"Not a lot," Travers said. "He's the first grocer who's made me believe the old yarn about sanding the sugar."

"He's a slippery one is Charlie," Reeper said. "I've known him for twenty years. A rare one to get on, though."

"I've no doubt," Travers said. "Which reminds me that I must be getting on, too."

An apologetic Travers arrived home half an hour late. Bernice said it didn't matter in the least. With tea at the Feen's the afternoon would be a domestic one.

They talked about their rounds of the morning, and Travers could be excused for dwelling rather long on that one great drive of his when he had emulated the pros. and saved a shot at that doglegged fifteenth hole. Bernice was the least bit complacent, too, having beaten Mrs. Feen by four and two.

"By the way," Travers said, "just how much does the Colonel let her know?"

"About what's happened?" Bernice said. "I don't think he tells her anything. We were talking about it casually, and she spoke as if she never took any interest in what concerned his work."

Travers smiled. "Which shows what married life can ultimately degenerate into. Still, I think you and I must be most careful to copy the Colonel. I mean that Mrs. Feen mustn't have an idea that you're collaborating. Which reminds me of something. It may or may not become public, but that shed where Brewse's body was found was definitely burned down. Set alight with paraffin in fact, and what I'm thinking is that whoever did it wouldn't have walked boldly into a shop with a two-gallon tin and openly bought two gallons. In other words, who would be likely to keep quantities of paraffin? The village has electric light, so people don't use oil lamps."

"That's easy," Bernice said. "I can tell you all about that."

Travers gaped in astonishment.

"But it *is* easy, my dear," she said. "It's just one of those things women always talk about. Electric light is most expensive there and people hardly use it for power, so nearly every one has an oil-cooker as well as an electric one, so I gathered. Then I asked how they bought the oil—Mrs. Strongman, it was, who happened to be talking about it in the club-house—and she said a man came round twice a week, and she had a ten-gallon drum. Then some other woman said she had the same."

"Very interesting."

"Yes, and this morning when I got Mrs. Feen to call at the Pernabys, I discovered that they use an oil-cooker, too. Grace Pernaby told me it was most economical compared with electricity."

"Better and better. And how was Grace Pernaby?"

"Very well indeed. Most upset about what she referred to as the scene she made."

"But why are you shaking your head?"

"Was I?" She smiled. "Perhaps I was. It does seem rather sneakish after all, to find out things about people and tell tales."

"I warned you."

She laughed. "Now who's saying, 'I told you so'?"

"I admit it," he said. "All the same I can sympathize with what you say. I've generally had to be sneakish with people I didn't care twopence about."

"That's just how I feel," she said. "Now take Grace Pernaby this morning. I really felt I liked her quite a lot. There's something appealing about her. What it is I don't quite know, unless it is that she strikes one as just a bit forlorn. I mean, she looks tough and masculine, and you find out she isn't."

The 'phone bell went and he nipped across to answer it.

It was Colonel Feen, reminding Travers of tea, and the time as four o'clock. Travers said he would be early as he had certain things to report. "And about those casts I sent you. Any luck?"

"I don't know how you got them," Feen said, "but it must have taken some doing—"

"They were what we wanted?" cut in Travers.

"Unfortunately, no," Feen said. "But we happened to have a bit of luck ourselves. I got to Pettistone early on account of the inquest, and Bob Quench and young Strongman had their car in the road and something had gone wrong with it. They were taking the vicar down to the course to play with you, and he was waiting about, so he came across to me and we stood talking for a bit.

"Reeper noticed he'd been standing on a lovely soft spot and took an impression for luck. We checked up not long ago and there isn't a doubt. Old Quench was the one who was in the ditch on Saturday night."

# CHAPTER VII
## WHARTON HAS A LOOK

WHEN TRAVERS turned up at the Feen's for tea, he had still not quite recovered from the shock of the discovery that the Rev. Norman Quench was the man who had crouched in the ditch that Saturday night, and as soon as an opportunity presented itself, he put one small objection.

"What I can't get over is that Quench was running. He's the last man you'd expect to run."

"Put it this way," Feen said. "He certainly was the man, and he certainly did run, which means he saw something that scared him badly. All the same, I've seen Quench run. He plays cricket occasionally still, and he's surprisingly spry between wickets."

"When are you seeing him?" Travers asked.

"That's one thing I was going to talk over with you," Feen said. "I'd rather like to see the whole crowd who were at Guff-Wimble's that night. I dropped in on Guffy this afternoon and told him he'd laid himself open to considerable suspicion by asking all those people round to his house, and I said the sooner he and the lot of them could show a clean sheet, the better for all concerned."

"How'd he take it?"

"Like a lamb. Most anxious to help, and all that. So what I'd like to do is to reassemble that meeting, as it were, and hear what they've all got to say. They'll all jump to that and then I can get an individual statement from each."

Travers told him what he had discovered about the alibis of the vicar and Pernaby for the Saturday afternoon, and those of Bob Quench and young Strongman. Before he could get to Strongman himself and Ammony, Laura Feen came hastily in from the garden and said a car had drawn up past the gate. It was George Wharton, who had been half over the town, he said, following the directions given by its misbegotten inhabitants. Every one was delighted to see him.

If Bernice Travers had described Grace Pernaby as likeable because of a certain forlornness of appeal, then George Wharton should have been the most likeable man in the world.

There was his vast weeping-willow moustache, for instance, to give him something of a henpecked look, and the antiquated spectacles to impart an old-fashioned, disarming simplicity. Nothing pleased him better than to play the role of a harassed but discerning father of a family, and women, as he would boast in his expansive moments, were so much putty in his fingers. Travers had never ceased to find him a source of delight, and he had for him an enormous affection and no little respect. His snortings, his gruntings, his deft hypocrisies and his joy in showmanship were the rich colourings of a ripe and fruity personality. As Travers once said, George Wharton was no drawing-room miniature, and the Royal Academy would never be perfect till Belcher had put him on its walls.

In his off-duty moments, the old General could be the very best of company, and few were better at an anecdote. Bernice, somewhat on tenterhooks for fear he should make some incautious reference to the newly married, was happier when the drawn out meal was over. Wharton was following her and Laura Feen out to the garden when Travers drew him gently back.

Wharton looked surprised for a moment, then guessed what was in the wind.

"Just a few minutes at the feet of Gamaliel" Travers told him. "That's all we ask of you, George."

"You've read about everything in the papers?" added Feen.

Wharton said bluntly that he'd read damn-all. He'd seen that Hanley Brewse had been murdered, and he'd stopped in Edensthorpe and bought a special edition, to find out what had happened at the inquest. It was obvious that, off-duty or not, he was now expecting to hear the really important things which were being kept back.

"By the way, didn't you know Brewse?" he asked Travers.

"I was a director of one of his earlier companies—Royal Invested," Travers said, "but I got out months before the dirty work began. I had some dealings with Merrick Clarke, too."

"I never thought Clarke got a square deal," Wharton said. "He was a catspaw, it ever there was one. Still, that's neither here nor there. Let's hear all about Brewse's murder."

Before Feen had hardly begun, he was asking for a map of the Pettistone district. Feen had had the foresight to provide a large-scale one, and Travers had one he had drawn himself to supplement that plan of the shed.

"Mind if I take a few notes?" Wharton said speciously. "I'll be away and gone in a day or two, but I'd like to be able to follow things in the newspapers."

"I hoped you'd slip along and have a look round for yourself," Feen said.

Wharton's hands were raised with such horror that Travers knew he would be at Pettistone before the light was gone.

"You know I can't do a thing like that," he said. "It'd be more than my job was worth, or my name's Higgins." He snorted. "A nice state of affairs—a Scotland Yard superintendent poking his nose into other people's business when we haven't been officially called in? Dammit, some one'd be asking questions in Parliament!" He grunted. "Still, that's no reason why I shouldn't take a few private notes."

In a quarter of an hour he knew most of what there was to know, and all pretence of personal disinterestedness had gone.

"What about the bullet?" he said. "What expert evidence have you had on it?"

"It was fired by a .38 automatic," Feen said.

"I rushed it up to your own expert on Sunday morning."

"Anybody in that district known to own one?"

"That'd be too easy," Feen told him dryly. "But what we guess is this. We're an agricultural district as you know, but we're an important railway junction at the same time. All sorts of criminals drop off here and try their hands when they've been shifted on from elsewhere. I refer to cheap crooks like ringing-the-changes men, and hotel swindlers and a confidence man or two. Last year we had a burglary epidemic and Pettistone was included, and there was one case of robbery with violence. We collared the chap ultimately, and he got seven years and the cat."

Wharton nodded. "I see. And everybody in Pettistone rushed off and surreptitiously provided himself with a gun."

"I suspect as much," Feen said. "I actually heard one man boast of the fact, though I can't repeat it as evidence."

Wharton grunted again. "Well, if you were to ask me for my immediate views, they'd be these. You're trying to find local people with a motive. Hanley Brewse came to where he thought nobody would know him, and it turns out he dropped into a regular nest of his old customers." He looked at his notes. "There's the big noise of the district, the Guff-Wimble man, who swanked about having inside knowledge and induced everybody to invest his money. The local vicar lost a packet, so did a Mrs. Strongman, and the grocer, Ammony. The vicar's son had to leave Oxford, which Mr. Travers, as a Cambridge man, ought to be the last to consider a motive for murder. And Mr. Travers also added the information that a Miss Grace Pernaby was so staggered at the news of Brewse's murder that she swooned in her tracks."

Travers clapped gently. "Splendid, George, splendid! But now the irony's all over, just what are you driving at?"

Wharton chuckled. "Well, take this meeting at Guff-Wimble's house. There wasn't anything desperately secret about it, and one of the men made no bones, Colonel, about telling you what had happened. That's right, isn't it? Very well then. There's no particular exaggeration in calling the meeting a public one. Everybody in Pettistone was likely to know of it sooner or later, and yet"—Wharton paused to wag a dramatic finger—"and yet after that public announcement of an intention to drive Brewse out of the village, one of those people actually murdered Brewse." He shook his head. "To my mind, the thing doesn't hold together."

"After that expression of hopeful optimism, may I say something?" Travers said. "Guff-Wimble, the Quenches, the Strongmans, and the Pernabys may all have been fools if they had anything to do with murder after knowing they'd be the first suspects, but doesn't the fact remain that they've still got to be regarded as suspects? You're telling us it'll be easy to wipe them off our list. That's good hearing, but they still can't be wiped off till their movements have been inquired into."

"I never suggested anything else," Wharton told him indignantly. "All the same, I'll put one other question. Do you think that because some one lost money years ago that that'd be a sufficient motive for murder? At the time it might have been, but I ask you. People forget a whole lot in six or seven years, whatever they feel at the time. Murder's a queer thing to bring your mind to, and it isn't only the act of killing that you've got to think about. It's that other little affair at eight o'clock in the morning, when you take a short walk to a long drop." He grimaced as he shook his head. "That's what makes a possible murderer think. That's what gives him a queer feeling round his collar."

"There's a lot in that," was all Travers said, in spite of a dozen objections at the tip of his tongue. "But going back to Gamaliel, how would he be handling this case if he were in charge of it?"

"If you mean me," said Wharton, "I'd be doing what you're doing. I'd make sure of every suspect even if I didn't think he was more than a million to one chance. And I've nearly always found this. The more people you talk to, the more likely you are to hear of somebody you've never thought of at all."

"You'd work along the lines of the two alibis?" asked Feen.

"Of course. Make dead sure where everybody was between three and four o'clock. I don't think that eight o'clock alibi matters quite so much, but it might be handy. If you could be so lucky as to find the missing hat and the gun, that wouldn't do you any harm. Scour the whole district for them."

"Wait till you've seen Pettistone," Feen said. "Scouring the district won't look so promising."

"I'm seeing no Pettistone," Wharton said with a snort. "I'm here on a breather and I'm liable to be called away at any time."

Travers smiled. "You shall be taken in a nice comfortable car, George, and your name, if you like, shall be Higgins. If you don't think that's safe, then the Colonel will fit you up with some false whiskers."

The 'phone bell went while he was speaking, and he went across to take the call. It was for Feen, his station sergeant speaking.

"A Miss Molly Pernaby is here, sir, and wants to see you. I told her you were out but she won't leave a message. She's still waiting."

"Something private, is it?"

"She didn't give me any idea, sir. I shouldn't be surprised if it's to do with you-know-what."

"I see." The Colonel thought for a minute. "Well, tell her I'm at home and see what she says. I'll hold on."

Wharton and Travers were told what was happening, and then the sergeant was speaking again.

"All right, sir. She said she'd come round."

"Now what ought we to do?" Feen asked the room. "I'm practically sure it's nothing to do with golf or she'd have rung me here."

"Let's assume it's something unimportant," Travers said. "That'll give Mr. Higgins and myself a chance to hear. And why not be admiring your roses? They're quite near the gate. Stoke up your pipe, George, and look domestic."

Feen went off to warn the women, who were to appear only if the occasion demanded it, and by the time he was back near the gate, Molly's little car came snarling up.

"You'll have to get that exhaust seen to, young lady," the Colonel told her. "This is an old friend of mine, Mr. Higgins; Mr. Travers you know. I'll go and find the womenfolk—"

"Please don't," Molly said. "I'm only staying a second. It's something to do with the murder and I thought it was my duty to tell you."

"Something you've discovered?"

"Well, not exactly. It was about the inquest. Everybody says that man Brewse was killed in Copmore Lane at half-past three, and he couldn't have been."

Feen stared. Travers's fingers were at his glasses, and Wharton was peering over the tops of his antiquated spectacles.

"I saw him myself just before four o'clock, and he was nearly two miles along the Edensthorpe Road."

Feen's eyes narrowed. "Which way was he going?"

And so to the proof. It was three o'clock when she left Pettistone to fetch the headache powders for her Aunt Grace, and it was four o'clock when she got back. The hour was accounted for by shopping of her own, and she also remembered that she saw Mrs. Feen in the town that afternoon and had a few words with her.

"Higgins, would you mind finding my wife and asking her what time it was?" Feen said. "You mustn't mind us making a thorough inquiry, Molly. It's absolutely essential we know to within a minute or two what time it was when you saw him. And, by the way, are you sure it was Brewse you saw?"

"Of course I'm sure," she said.

"Well, I'm sorry to be such a nuisance, but how did you identify him? To the best of our knowledge he left his house only once before he was killed."

She smiled. "That was when I saw him—the morning after he got here. A smallish man of rather slight build, with a dark beard—"

"What clothes was he wearing on Saturday afternoon?"

"A greyish suit and a green hat—a felt hat. I remember the hat because you don't often see a green hat."

Wharton came back with the information that Mrs. Feen thought it was round about three when she met Miss Pernaby.

"There you are!" Molly told Feen. "I told you it was. Then I did some of my own shopping and got my car out of the park, and I was held up twice by traffic lights."

"The whole thing's determined by the time at which you reached your house again," Feen said. "Can anybody else prove it was four o'clock?"

"Yes, Aunt Grace can. I reminded her—asked her, I mean— just before I came here."

Feen rubbed his chin. "Well, that sounds pretty conclusive. Still, there's one thing I'm afraid I've got to ask you to do. You must come with me to the station and view the body."

"The body!" She was staring, and it was frightenedly.

"Nothing to be alarmed about," Feen said. "You must have a quick look and sign a statement that he was the man you saw. You'll see only his head."

She was moistening her lips and her fingers were fidgeting.

"I shall go with you," Feen went on, "and it'll be nothing to terrify you. Merely a quick look at a dead man's face."

"I'll go too, if it will help," Travers said. "You come as well, Higgins."

"A capital idea," Feen said. "I'll go in Molly's car and you two can catch us up at the station. Afterwards I shall have to drive out to the spot where he was seen."

Travers told Wharton all he knew about Molly Pernaby.

"A nice-looking young lady," Wharton said, and Travers somehow had the idea he was thinking of something very different. And he made no other comment till the station was reached.

"A back way, is there?"

"Round to the room they're using as a mortuary," Travers said. "There's Feen at the door."

Molly was waiting in the ante-room and most of her nervousness seemed to have gone. Wharton made her smile when he peered about him and remarked, "So this is a police-station, is it? Doesn't look at all a bad place to me."

"Now we'll get this job over," Feen said. "I'll go first."

Brewse lay in his coffin, for the funeral was to be the following afternoon. Feen pointed, and spoke quickly.

"Is that the man you saw?"

Molly looked, and it was surprising how long she looked.

Perhaps it was relief that held her, for the face of the dead man was as placid as in sleep.

Then she nodded quickly, and was turning away.

The whole business had taken no more than a minute. Molly, still somewhat subdued, said the ordeal had not been anything after all, and Feen must have thought her a frightful idiot.

"Everybody isn't going to know about this?" she was soon asking with much of her old casualness.

But Feen was busy typing the statement form, and in a minute she was signing it. Then she repeated the question.

"Well," he said, "we may have to call you as a witness at the reopened inquest. Otherwise no one shall know a thing about it."

"You mean I shall have to stand up in that room—"

"A mere nothing," broke in Feen. "It'll all be over in a couple of minutes."

She was suddenly looking most indignant. "If I'd known that, I'd never have come. I asked Corby if they let anything out when people had any information about anything and he told me it was always confidential. I think it's mean of you."

"Who's Corby?" put in Wharton.

"Our policeman, and you can ask him if you like, Colonel Feen." She shook her head angrily. "I've never even said a word to a soul, not even to uncle, and he'll be furious when my name's in the papers, and everything."

"It's no business of mine," said Travers, who saw a chance of ingratiation, "but it doesn't sound to me as if Molly—you don't mind my calling you Molly?—as if Molly's getting a square deal."

"I certainly wouldn't like to see my daughter's name in the papers in connection with a man like Brewse," added the pious Wharton. "Not that it's any business of mine either."

"Well, if you all feel like that about it, we'll see what we can do," Feen said, tumbling to the idea. "Now we'll go and see where it was that you saw him. Thank you two for coming, by the way. I may get a chance to see you later."

"Oh, but you've got to get back," Travers said. "We'll come along too, and then you can come back with us."

"You two are a couple of parasites," Feen told him. "Still it'll save me driving my own car. Come along, Molly."

It was exactly two miles from Pettistone where Molly halted. She knew the spot, she said, because of the nasty bend where she always slowed.

"Much traffic on the road, was there?" Feen asked.

"Hardly any," she said.

"You met or passed nobody you knew?"

"Not a soul."

"That's a pity," he said. "I'd hoped we might be able to check up that way. And what about getting your aunt to verify the time you got home as four o'clock?"

"I doubt you won't be able to do that without giving Molly away," Travers said.

Another couple of minutes and Molly was speeding on towards Pettistone.

"And where now?" asked Travers.

"Home, I think," Feen said. "It's a pity Wharton won't go the other two miles and have a quick look, now we've got so far."

"Oh, I'll look at anything," said Wharton nimbly. "I don't often get the chance to ride in a real gent.'s car."

"Now I call that very friendly," Feen said,

"Go straight on through the village, Travers, and round to the fire, then we'll come back past Gables."

At the scene of the fire the landscape was as pastoral and silent as it had always been. Wharton had a quick look round and took in the lie of the land with Travers's map and plan in his hand, and he was graciously pleased to admit that looking for a gun and a hat would require more than the police force of the whole county.

Travers slowed the car at Gables where there was little to be seen. Feen had had the side of the house photographed and all that day a man had been busy painting over the disfigurement. Then Travers made a deliberate mistake at the fork and turned towards the golf course, but it was no matter, as he said, and Wharton might as well see everything while he was on the spot. So the whole circuit was made to Copmore Farm and by Gables again, and dusk was in the sky when at last they drew up at Feen's house.

But when they walked in, there was a surprise, and all the excuses were unneeded. Laura had left word that she and Bernice had suddenly decided to go to the first house at the pictures, that they would be in by eight o'clock, and that there was cold supper in any case.

"Let's go and find it," Feen said. "You'll stay Travers?"

Travers said he'd have a drink but nothing else. Feen went off to 'phone and came back with the results of inquiries at the chemist's and the shoe shop where Molly Pernaby said she had been. Both confirmed the purchases but could not be more explicit about time than "about three to half-past."

"Saturday's market day here," Feen explained to Wharton, "and most of the shops are bung full. Still, I think we can take it that her story's confirmed."

"One thing I ought to mention," Wharton said, "and that is that when I asked Mrs. Feen about the time she saw that young lady, she said it was just before three. I said was she sure, and she said she wasn't, but it wasn't later than three."

"I wouldn't pay much attention to that," Feen said. "Laura's about the most forgetful person I ever knew, and, between ourselves, the most obstinate. What I mean is, if she gets the casual idea she saw Molly Pernaby at a quarter to three, the Twelve Apostles couldn't make her change her mind."

"The whole thing's the very devil anyway," Travers said. "If Brewse was seen two miles on the way to Edensthorpe at five minutes to four on Saturday afternoon—and it seems as if he must have been—then he must have been killed within a minute or two of being seen."

Wharton glared. "What're you grumbling at? It looks to me if you've been handed evidence on a beautiful silver platter and now you're not satisfied."

"The trouble is, the evidence conflicts," Feen said. "The medical evidence is that he was killed before four o'clock. Between three-thirty and four are the limits each way."

"Medical evidence!" Wharton snorted. "Don't tell me. Stomach content and all that gibberish! Did they know what his digestion was like? Stomach content!" He snorted again. "And your doctors say he might have been killed at four o'clock, don't they? Even if they don't you can't get away from facts. He was seen on that road just before four, and therefore he couldn't have been dead at half-past three. That's your medical evidence for you!"

"There's one other thing," Travers said. "Didn't Marlin say he left the house early in the afternoon?"

"I got him to narrow that down to about three o'clock," Feen said.

"Then that's all right," Travers said. "He might have taken an hour to walk the three miles. Also you'll be bound to find some one in the village who saw him walking through."

"He needn't have gone through the village," pointed out Feen. "There's a back lane that comes out clear of the village on the Edensthorpe Road. Let me mark it for you on your map."

"Yes, but how did Brewse know that?" asked Travers. "He'd only been in the village once."

"Well, as I see it," Feen said, "if he was killed two miles along the Edensthorpe Road, he was lured there by somebody who took good care to give him explicit directions how to avoid the village."

"But the only one who knew him was Guff-Wimble!"

"I still don't see what you're grumbling at," broke in Wharton. "That place where the young lady saw him is all turns and it's all woods. That's where he was killed—where the woods are—and it oughtn't to be too big a job to search. There's where you'll find the hat, and you may find the gun."

"Then why shift the body?" asked Feen. "Why take the trouble to lure a man to a certain spot—where there was every likelihood of his being seen—and then run the risk of moving the body elsewhere? That road's busy till dark on market days."

Wharton raised a pontifical hand. "Facts. You can't get away from facts. If you want theories, apply to Mr. Travers here." He chuckled. "He's the world's prize theorist. He'd probably tell you that the man who lured Brewse out on Saturday afternoon, merely took the gun as a precaution and didn't intend to kill him. The killing arose out of a quarrel, or something of that kind."

"Which still wouldn't explain why the body was moved," retorted Travers.

"Well," said Wharton, with that peculiar brand of complacency he could assume on occasions, "I may be getting old and past my best, but I think I could find a remarkably good explanation of that. In fact, I don't know that I couldn't find one that was a stone certainty."

"And what is it?" asked Feen quickly.

"Give me time," said Wharton. "I said I thought I might. Ask me to-morrow morning, and if I can't fix you up, then my name's Higgins. Really Higgins."

Feen said that sounded reasonable. The search of the Edensthorpe Road should be put in hand at once, he said, and he was almost of the mind to see all the Guff-Wimble gang that very night if Wharton wouldn't mind. The sooner he had their statements, the better he'd be pleased.

Wharton gave a hypocritical clearing of the throat. "I'll go along with you for company, if you like."

"You'd better take these notes with you," Travers said, and gave Feen a quick wink. "Just a few jottings I made this afternoon. Those alibis I was telling you about, and a special reference to Charles Ammony, who, as I think I told you, sells ladders for a pal of his."

"When you're interviewing that list of suspects," Wharton said, "you might let an old hand give you one tip. Don't move a muscle when they tell you lies. A liar's the copper's best friend—provided you've spotted him."

"I see your point. It gives you a hold over him."

"That's it," Wharton said. "I always reckon that liars have put me exactly where I am."

"Always remember that the Colonel's somewhat handicapped compared with yourself," Travers said.

"Oh?" said Wharton. "And how's that?"

"Well, if it takes a thief to catch a thief, it takes a good liar to catch a liar."

Feen laughed. "I call that damn' disrespectful."

"Not a bit of it," Travers said. "No man's a hero to his own apprentice. But about to-morrow. Perhaps I'd better ring up after breakfast and see what's going."

They saw him off at the gate, and as Travers said good night to Wharton, he supposed Wharton wouldn't like to tell him what he had meant by that hint that he had known why the body had been moved.

"Ask me to-morrow," Wharton said.

"But I shall know for myself before to-morrow," Travers told him amusedly.

"What's that?" asked Wharton.

"What I said. In fact, I'm now beginning to think I've known it for some time. Still, I don't want to damp your fireworks, George, so I'll tell you what I'll do. To-morrow morning I'll write down what I think and we'll see how it compares with your startling revelations. The Colonel can be umpire. If you like, I'll bet you a new hat I'm as near the truth as you are."

"Make it a new suit," said Wharton, "and the bet's on."

# CHAPTER VIII
## WHARTON IS INTERESTED

BEFORE TRAVERS COULD ring Feen the next morning, Wharton turned up, bringing some notes of the over-night interview with the Guff-Wimble gang. A private note was inside. Feen was likely to be all over the place that morning, so would Travers keep Wharton amused and at the same time get him more and more interested in the case. One more little effort at persuasion, thought Feen, and Wharton, alias Higgins, would be in it up to the neck.

Wharton had a few words with Bernice and then asked Travers why he had come out so strongly on the side of Molly Pernaby over the question of her appearing at the reopened inquest.

"If it comes to that," Travers said, "you backed me up."

"I thought you wanted backing up," Wharton said indignantly. "It all sounded so flagrant to me that I thought you must have had some idea behind it."

"What's all this about Molly Pernaby?" Bernice asked.

"George doesn't know you've married a philanderer," Travers said. "Molly Pernaby and I are going to be great friends. As a matter of fact, while you and Feen were otherwise engaged, George, I fixed up a round of golf with her for late this afternoon."

"Lady, you have my sympathy," George said.

Bernice laughed. "I've got my own methods of retaliating. I'm playing golf myself this afternoon."

"There must be something in this golfing game," Wharton said with a shake of the head, "though I could never see it. What is it? The exercise?"

"Take him out to the practice course this morning, Ludo," Bernice said. "I think it will be sinful if he spoils a lovely morning like this talking about nothing but murders."

"You needn't worry about me," Wharton said. "I'm finished. I'm on holiday."

"Then off you two go to the garden," Bernice said. "You can smoke your pipes and pretend you're reading the paper."

Wharton did read the paper and Travers went through Feen's notes.

*Precis of Interviews.* Please return via Geo. W.

I rang Guff-Wimble at seven-thirty and suggested a meeting at his place at eight-thirty, and gave him the list for him to 'phone. He was to report to me if anybody was unable to come. Just before eight he rang back to say that Bob Quench and Gordon Strongman were otherwise engaged. Wharton suggested a bluff, so I told him they were to be there or I'd come and fetch them here. Both were there when I arrived.

Those present were the original meeting: Guff-Wimble, Rev. Quench, L. M. Strongman and his son Gordon, Robert Quench and Arthur Pernaby. Wharton was good enough to accompany me, and I also took Reeper, and we were all well acquainted with those notes you let me have.

"I told them all, principally for Strongman's peace of mind, that their original meeting was public knowledge, and if they wanted to save gossip they'd better provide themselves with clean sheets and make that public, too. I said that while the statements were not actually official, I should regard very seriously any attempts at prevarication or concealment. I thought it best also to remind them just what murder was, and what my own powers were, and I said I would make no bones about having any of them before the Coroner to give any subsequent statement on oath (Geo. W.'s hint, that!). If any of them did not wish to mention his affairs in front of the others, he might speak to me privately afterwards.

ANTHONY MONCRIEFF GUFF-WIMBLE.

Said he was doing secretarial work at the golf course between the hours of three and four. "In the secretary's room all the time?" I said. He said he was out on the course some of the time, whereupon I thought it best to remind everybody again that we were engaged on a very serious inquiry and I wanted no ambiguities. No innocent man, I said, should be afraid of disclosing his every movement, particularly as it was in the strictest confidence.

Then he said he had been looking at certain of the greens on the second half of the course, which had been giving trouble. I asked if he had witnesses, and he said both Quench and Pernaby remembered seeing him at the twelfth, and he could also get the Davidsons to say they'd spoken to him at the seventeenth. I said that sounded good enough but I should have to question Colonel Davidson. It should be done most tactfully, and I took advantage of that opportunity to tell them all that any of their witnesses would have to be confidentially interviewed.

Bob Quench, rather pettishly I thought, asked if that was necessary, and wouldn't it make talk. I told him that was a strange objection, seeing that the original meeting at that very house had laid them all open to the very kind of gossip I was trying to counteract.

As for the 7.30 to 8.30 hour, Guff-Wimble was then at dinner and his butler and other indoor men could prove it.

REV. NORMAN QUENCH.

Said that for the afternoon hour, he and Pernaby were in the middle of a round of golf and were never out of each other's sight. He was very voluble in his own particular way, and went on to say that he had tea in the club-house afterwards with Pernaby and his niece. Then I wanted to know about the evening hour. He said he was alone in his study, which is upstairs, and was following his habit of going over his two sermons for the next day.

I said, "Were you in the room the whole time?" whereupon he looked distinctly uneasy. Bob Quench got as far as: "Surely you're not insinuating that my father would—" when I spoke to him pretty sharply. I was doing the talking, and I'd thank him to speak only when spoken to. Then his father said he might have come down for a leg-stretcher. "In the garden?" I said, and he seemed relieved, and he dodged the question, with: "Just a bit of exercise," and smiled fatuously round at everybody with the platitude that all work and no play, etc. Having got him where I wanted him, I left it at that.

ARTHUR PERNABY.

Said Quench and Guff-Wimble had already accounted for his afternoon movements. As for the evening, he was alone after half-past seven, for his niece was out and his sister had been in bed all the afternoon and evening with a very bad headache. If he remembered rightly, he practised putting on the drawing-room carpet and he read a book, and he added in that blunt way of his that he had no proof and he didn't give a damn what inquiries I made. He did remember that he went up to his sister's room at eight o'clock and asked how she was.

ROBERT KEITHMORE QUENCH.

Was interchanging glances with Gordon Strongman all the duration of his examination. Said he and Gordon had been over-hauling his car all the afternoon, and did not finish until half-past four, when they left the vicarage garage and had tea in the vicarage. As for the evening, he said he would see me privately about that, and then he asked if he could make a personal state-ment. I said why not.

The statement was that if any one thought he had any griev-ance about having had to leave Oxford, then they were wrong. Whatever he might have felt and said at the time, he now knew that Brewse had been in some ways his best friend. He might never have done so well for himself as he had done, and Oxford would actually have been a hindrance.

I said, "Are you inferring that it was a good thing for your father that he lost all his personal fortune?" He said he wasn't bringing his father into anything but was stating a personal case.

GORDON STRONGMAN.

Said Bob Quench had already proved the afternoon alibi, and I agreed. Then he said his evening alibi was connected with the statement Bob Quench would be making privately, and might he also make a personal statement.

The statement turned out to be that he was proposing to re-turn to the Sudan by train to Brindisi and boat to Alexandria, instead of flying all the way, and that would mean his leaving next Thursday morning.

I accepted his arrangements as nothing unusual, though they struck me as very much of an attempt to bolt. What I did tell him was that it was his own business, and I should have to know his precise whereabouts in the event of his having to be called back to England as a witness. That took him rather aback, but he made no comment.

LANCELOT MATTHEW STRONGMAN.

Said he started off at a quarter-past three on Saturday afternoon to visit a friend named Ritch at Limehurst He was driving his big car and was taking with him Tom Jewry, who'd worked for years as second gardener and whom he was trying out as chauffeur. A mile along the road a tyre went flabby and he drew the car in on the verge by which time it was nearly flat. Jewry got out the spare and it was flabby, too, so he was told to pump it up, but when he looked for the pump it wasn't there. Strongman said he was furious and made Jewry trundle the spare all the way back to Ammony's garage, and it was four o'clock when he returned.

"What were you doing all that time?" I said "Cussing generally," he said, "and studying my A.A. book to pass the time." He added that he afterwards went on to Limehurst and was back at six o'clock. The punctured tyre was found to have a nail in it.

Bob Quench chipped in again and asked if he might say something in corroboration. The fault about the pump was his. Mrs. Strongman had asked him to look at her own car on the Friday evening, and he had had reasons to borrow the big foot-pump from the other car—hers had only a hand-pump—and he had neglected to put it back.

As for the evening hour, Strongman said he was alone from seven-thirty, as there had been early dinner in order that his wife might go into Edensthorpe to the pictures with the Davidsons. As near as he could remember he had listened to the wireless, and the maids could probably prove it had been on, since his set had a speaker connection with the kitchen.

I expressed myself as satisfied, and, subject to certain provisos I'd already mentioned, each might consider himself as finished with. Every one then left except Bob Quench, who was to make a further statement. I thought at the time that Gordon Strongman was also staying on, and I was distinctly annoyed when I found that he had left, and for reasons which you now see.

Bob Quench said he didn't see why Molly Pernaby's name should be brought in, except in the strictest confidence, but he and she had met soon after dinner. They had spent some minutes in the garden of her house and later had taken a walk, and it was about ten o'clock when Molly was back in the house.

I said that was absolutely satisfactory, provided that Molly confirmed it, but how did it affect Gordon Strongman?

"Oh," he said, "he came round just before eight, knowing where I'd be, and proposed going to the pictures, but Molly and I weren't keen, so he stayed for a bit and then went."

"Yes, but where?" I said. "He said your statement would cover his movements."

He then said it wasn't till eight o'clock that Gordon left him, and he thought that was good enough. Then he winked, and said the rest had better be understood. Gordon had certain private affairs of his own he didn't want broadcast. I asked bluntly if he meant some girl, and Bob said he did, though Gordon hadn't divulged her name even to himself.

I was not more than five minutes with him and when I thanked Guff-Wimble and went out to my car with Reeper, the vicar was there, and he volunteered the information that he was waiting for Bob, who was driving him back. I formed the distinct impression that he was on the point of confessing something, which the presence of Geo. W. and Reeper was preventing, so I took the bull by the horns, as it were, and I said this: "I've rather got the idea you've remembered something you ought to have told me. If you have, you can tell me about it to-morrow."

I should also add that when I said good night to Guff-Wimble, I had the idea he had something on mind, too. I leave you to form your own ideas about all the above. I am seeing Ammony first thing to-morrow (Tuesday) morning.

One other thing which absolutely bewilders me, in spite of Geo. W.'s views on medical evidence, and you needn't mind telling him so. I saw Barnes only a few minutes ago and he insists that death took place not later than a quarter to four. He said they took a third opinion, and with three pieces of evidence to go on—I take it he meant rigor mortis, state of wound, and stomach content—he'd defy any authority to think otherwise. I asked why he'd mentioned four o'clock at all, and he said if he hadn't, then the Coroner would have been sure to prate about human error, and mentioning three o'clock to four o'clock was making a handy sort of foot-rule for all concerned.

PS.—Geo. W. will give you his private views on that set of interviews. Shall be seeing you later. B. F.

Travers made a note or two then smiled over at Wharton.

"Well, what do you think of the Guff-Wimble gang?"

Wharton snorted. "What I told you from the beginning. I said there wasn't a motive, didn't I? All those people are people of position. Why should they want to kill a man because of something that happened years ago?"

"Then what about the vicar? You said you loved liars? Well, isn't the old boy a liar?"

Wharton grunted. "So he may be, but he didn't kill Brewse. If you ask me, he was in that lane on Saturday night because he was trying to screw up courage to go and have a personal interview with Brewse. Then he saw the fire and got the wind up."

"Maybe you're right," Travers told him. "But any ideas about the rest of the party?"

Wharton shrugged his shoulders. "What sort of ideas?"

Travers smiled. "You're being very difficult for a man on holiday."

"Difficult? What d'you mean by difficult?" He snorted again. "What's the good of having ideas about people with alibis? Every man-jack's got an alibi, hasn't he?"

Travers smiled mysteriously. "There're alibis and alibis."

"Oh?" said Wharton. "And what's wrong with them? Pernaby's and the vicar's are perfect, aren't they? So are everybody else's for that matter."

"That we shall have to see about," Travers said, and Wharton shot him a look. "But what's your idea about this new medical evidence that Brewse was not alive after a quarter to four?"

"Ah, that," said Wharton speciously. "When I said I didn't rely on medical evidence too much I didn't know everything that Feen has got down in those notes. It's only a question of a few minutes anyhow, and that Molly girl may have been a bit out in her times. She seemed a bit too confident for my liking."

"Even if she were ten minutes out," Travers said, "that still doesn't make it fit."

"Well, suppose it doesn't?" Wharton said. "Suppose Brewse was killed at a quarter to four, and Molly saw him alive at ten minutes to. What's the answer?"

"A lemon," said Travers flippantly.

Wharton refused to smile.

"I'm asking you what's the answer. You ought to know one answer. It's something in just your line. One of those theories of yours in the—what's the word?—in the fantastic style."

"I still don't know," Travers told him. "And I shouldn't call it fantastic exactly. If a man was definitely dead at a certain time and then was walking about five minutes later, I'd call it miraculous."

Wharton chuckled. "Well, it's a feather in the old man's cap to beat you at your own game. But what about this? If Brewse was dead at a quarter to four, then he was dead, and that finishes with Brewse. Facts, that's what we're dealing with—facts! Therefore, Molly Pernaby didn't see him at all." He leaned forward, wagging a dramatic finger.

"She saw some one else. *Some one dressed in his clothes and hat and wearing a dark beard*"

Travers stared. "Good Lord, yes!"

Off came his glasses, and then he was staring again.

"But why? How would it help?"

"Don't know," Wharton said. "In the first place it's something clean out of my line, and in the second it isn't my business to work it out."

"Yes, but George, there's no reason why we shouldn't look at the elementary implications." The glasses that were being replaced suddenly stopped short an inch from his nose. "Good Lord! there's something else. Work out that theory and one conclusion is that Brewse wasn't killed at all but some one very much like him!" Then he shook his head. "But it couldn't have been that. I recognized Brewse, and Marlin couldn't have been deceived, and the dead man did have a real beard."

Wharton was chuckling again as he got to his feet.

"Well, you can't say I haven't provided you with food for thought. And now what about this golf you were talking about? I don't know that I wouldn't like to try my hand."

Bernice could not be induced to accompany the pair, but she lent Wharton a niblick and putter. Travers provided a pullover to give the old General something of a golfing air, though he was perfectly convinced that it was Pettistone that was attracting him, and not golf.

"Isn't this man Ammony, whom I haven't seen, a grocer or something?" Wharton asked as they were nearing the second milestone.

Travers told him all he knew. Wharton shook his head.

"He's not the sort of chap to have been lugging an automatic around. And much as I hate to keep harping on it, you and Feen can think what you like, but I still think there's no motive. You don't kill a man because he took your money six years ago."

Travers had been slowing down, and soon he spotted a couple of men moving along the edge of the wood.

"Feen's men still at work," he told Wharton. "It doesn't look as if they've had any luck so far." Wharton kept his eyes about him as they neared the village, and he made a note or two in his book when Travers began pointing out where various people lived.

"Neither Strongman nor Pernaby seems to have been ruined," was his comment. "Damn' fine houses, both of them, and so was the one I was in last night, so there's three you can strike off your list, or my name's Higgins. What should any of them want to murder Brewse for?"

They made their way to the approach course where Wharton was duly initiated. A lucky shot or two and he was saying that the game was easier than he thought. Travers gave him a stroke and played for a penny a hole, and in half an hour the General had lost fourpence, but chiefly because he was all the time staring about and asking who was this one and that. It was he who spotted Quench again, playing a round with Guff-Wimble, and also caught sight of Strongman, playing with some stranger.

"A powerful chap that," he said, and pursed his lips till his moustache looked like the storey of a pagoda. "He's the one who had the car breakdown isn't he?"

Travers had to smile. It was typical of George to discard a man indignantly at one moment, and at the next assume a cherubic ignorance of the fact. And then in a few moments he was suggesting a little ride round.

"Go right round, the way you took last night," he said, and Travers obliged. But the General's real objective was the Limehurst Road, and as soon as the car turned into it, he was wondering if the marks of the wheels of Strongman's car could still be made out on the grass verge. Travers obliged again by sidling along on the wrong side of the road.

"That looks like it," Wharton said, and there, sure enough, were the marks of two wheels.

Wharton looked about him, then began to walk in the direction of the village. Within a couple of hundred yards or so he came to a stile on the right, and a path through the woods which Travers deduced could lead only to somewhere near Gables. "That breakdown struck me as a rather unusual occurrence," Wharton said. "Suppose Strongman was the man who lured Brewse out to the Edensthorpe Road, mightn't he have told him to come this way? And mightn't he have been watching in the car to see if he really came?"

"But he couldn't have taken his own car three miles on and killed him," Travers said.

"I'm not so sure," said Wharton dourly. "Let's move on to that road that Feen said went round the back of the village."

It was a lane that lay clear of the village on the left, and after a semicircle which had no house save a small farm, came out, as Feen had said, well along the road.

"This seems to be the way that Brewse came," Wharton said. "Might as well push on home now we're so far. I feel a bit guilty leaving Mrs. Feen alone like this—not that it's my fault. I come down here for a holiday, and you go dragging me half over England."

"Sure you wouldn't like to go back and run your eye over Charles Ammony?" asked Travers dryly.

But Wharton resisted the temptation and they pushed on for home. Feen was standing on the verge as they neared that second milestone.

"I saw you go by," he said, and by the tone Travers guessed that something had happened. "I didn't stop you because we'd nothing to report. Now we've got this."

It was the green felt hat, found in the wood not far back from the road, and handy for a gappy part of the hedge.

Travers and Wharton had a look at the spot and noticed for themselves the distinct marks or movement in the rather scanty undergrowth between the young oaks.

"It's all too dry for footprints," Feen said, "but we're going to work over every inch for signs of blood. I doubt if we'll have the luck to find the gun."

"Why not come back with us?" Travers said. "Leave your own car here and George can drive you back in his. Besides, he was going to tell you why the body was moved from here to that shed."

Feen got in. Wharton made no protest about the afternoon, but Travers was remarkably suspicious when he began talking in that gentle, paternal tone he would adopt on certain occasions.

"Some of those alibis you were dished out with last night, Colonel, aren't worth the paper you wrote them on. You let Mr. Travers here get his microscope to work on 'em. He's one of the best alibi breakers I ever ran across." He nodded at the amused Travers. "When he theorizes, that's when you'd better take to your heels, but if he tells you he's busted an alibi, you can take it from me it's busted."

"What's the idea of the adulation, George?" Travers said, and then smiled. "I think I know, though. It's that bet of ours. You were trying to draw the talk away from it, and now we've reminded you, you'll probably want it cancelled."

"I'd like to make it two suits," Wharton said belligerently.

Travers felt in his breast pocket and passed back an envelope to Feen.

"I'm with you, George. Seconds out of the ring. Your turn to lead. Just why was the body removed from that wood where we've just been?"

"Don't rush me," Wharton said. "And remember that I've only your own version to go by as far as concerns that manure heap where the body was found."

"No hedging," Feen said. "He knew the conditions when he made the bet, didn't he, Travers?"

"All right," said Wharton virtuously, "I'll do my best. What I say is that the body was moved so that it could be found. The shed was set fire to so that some one would see the body. Whoever set fire to the shed knew that the manure would actually protect the body. He wanted the body found intact. And why?"

"It's all in the envelope," Travers told him. "Oh, is it," said Wharton, for once in his life somewhat taken aback. "Well, why did he want the body found intact?"

"Answer your own questions," Travers said. "It's your turn first. All you've got to do is to let me know when you're finished."

"Have it your own way," Wharton told him. "I say the murderer wanted the body found intact because he wanted the police to know the precise time of the murder, *for which he had a perfect alibi:*"

"Never shake your gory locks at me," Travers said. "I still keep telling you it's all in the envelope."

"Damn the envelope!" Wharton glared back at Feen. "Open the damn' thing and let's hear what he's got in it."

But when the reading was done, and he made his comments, his voice was the coo of a dove.

"Well, I must say there isn't a lot of difference in the two versions."

"I'd one advantage over you, George," Travers said. "I knew that as soon as that fire was well alight, some one rang up Corby, the Pettistone policeman, and said there was a fire. That was the murderer, and Feen says Corby's landlady couldn't identify the voice except that it was a man's. That was pretty plain evidence that the murderer was making sure the body was found."

"Yes," said Wharton. "I wasn't aware of that, as you say. Perhaps we'd better call it all square."

But there was something just a bit too placatory in his tone and Travers guessed he had had some new idea. In a moment he was hearing it.

"I don't know that the bet is off. If you'd given me time, instead of throwing that damned envelope in my teeth, there was something I was going to add. What about this? Take a look at your own plan, and suppose you're leaning on that field gate. You look too, Colonel. The legs of the body were so placed that they were visible in broad daylight!"

"To tell you the truth, George, I noticed that myself," Travers said, "but I thought it too footling to write down."

"Footling!" glared Wharton. "It's as good a piece of observation as I've come across."

Travers was slowing down the car in the main street.

"The trouble is this, George, that there was no point in making the body visible by daylight when it couldn't have been moved till after dark."

"Oh, yes, there was. The murderer hadn't thought of lighting the fire and he hoped the body would be seen on the Sunday." His face was lighting with an idea. "You tell me if I'm not right, Feen. Don't all the courting couples in the village go that way on a Sunday, and wouldn't they have seen the feet?" He glanced round as the car came to a halt. "What're we stopping here for? Going to buy yourself a hat?"

"I'm going to buy you one for a consolation prize," Travers said. "Not because you've won the bet or anything like it, but because I think it'd be rather better than having to listen to any more of your specious arguments."

"I'd have paid up if I'd lost, wouldn't I?"

"Heaven help us—yes," Travers said and winked back at Feen. "And I tremble to think what I'd have looked like, George, if I'd ever worn the reach-me-downs you'd have bought me. Well, are you coming to choose your hat, or are you not?"

"Well, if you insist," said Wharton, and followed him unblushingly.

Bernice wanted to hear all that had happened, and Travers told her most of it.

"I love George's little antics," he ended. "I always feel I'd like to have him stuffed. And I wager that before this week's out he'll be taking full charge of this case and Feen and I will be carrying out his orders."

At three o'clock the two were due for golf. Travers, in one of his adventurous moods, was slaughtered by Molly Pernaby, even though she played from the men's tees.

But what interested him was how from time to time she would bring the talk round to the murder, and his affectation of indifference seemed only to make her the more communicative. She announced, for instance, that Feen had had some people on the carpet the previous night.

"You don't mind me talking about Feen?" she said.

"Lord, no," said Travers. "I simply love scandal"

"This isn't even scandal," she said. "I think Feen's an old woman. As if anybody here could have murdered Brewse. By the way, I shouldn't wonder if he has me on the carpet, too."

"You?"

"Not me exactly," she said. "He seems to have an idea Bob Quench wants inquiring into. As a matter of fact, Bob Quench was with me on Saturday night."

Travers raised inquiring eyebrows.

"Yes, we spent a delightful time in the garden."

"In the dark?"

"Of course. Why'd you say that?"

"I don't know," said Travers lamely. "I merely wondered what you'd be doing all that time in the garden—still in the dark."

Molly sniffed contemptuously. "My dear man, what do people do in the garden in the dark?"

"Lord knows!" said the ingenuous Travers, and left it at that. It was not till some time later that he began to wonder something else. Had that volunteered information perhaps contained a really big truth? Molly Pernaby and Bob Quench had doubtless spent the dark hours in the garden. But whose garden?

None had been mentioned, and it had been left to himself to conclude that the garden was the one belonging to the Pernabys. But there was also a garden at Gables.

# CHAPTER IX
# THE FORGOTTEN MAN

THE MORNING BROUGHT a letter from Joy Haire, Bernice's sister. Joy, diseuse and mimic—impersonator seems nowadays to be the fashionable word—was often summed up as a combination of Ruth Draper and Florence Desmond, which was something of a libel on all three parties. Joy had neither the grand, consummate artistry of the one, nor that stage and screen limitation of selection which makes the devastating repertoire of the other. Her shows were always a series of five minute glimpses, and her repertoire was as fresh and unexpected as her unusual self.

It was her voice that had the amazing range, and there were rarely more than a few deft touches to indicate the victim's character. The Chancellor of the Exchequer oozing his way into the confidence of the British public over the wireless; the She Secretary of the Library League, trying to arrive at the book of the month; two navvies, discussing the day's racing prospects; a lady novelist nobbling a critic—those were all in that farewell show she gave with Bernice when the elder sister retired just before her marriage.

As for those private turns which the public never heard, Travers had good reason to remember a representation of George Wharton and himself, arguing about a lost collar-stud. Travers had, in fact, not only a tremendous admiration for his young sister-in-law, but a profound respect in which there was always a definite disquiet. Not that he was in any way alarmed at the prospect of Joy's accompanying Bernice and himself on that tour in Italy with which they were proposing to round off the honeymoon. Travers, the married man, felt himself newly and most satisfactorily equipped for dealing with a sister-in-law of any sort.

Joy's letter said she would like to come down on the Saturday, and if the Italian tour could be put forward a few days, she would be grateful, as she was considering a most advantageous contract which might mean being back in England a week earlier than anticipated.

"What do you think about it, darling?" asked Bernice.

Travers began polishing his glasses. "I'm rather pleased in a way. I was just beginning to feel rather unhappy."

Bernice looked at him wide-eyed. He smiled.

"Not what you think. What I was going to say was that I was feeling rather unhappy about this detective business. It all seems so very unfair to you. Here we are, supposed to be by our two selves—"

"My dear, you did frighten me so. But why's it unfair to me?"

"Well"—he hooked the glasses on again—"you're being subordinated to all this murder business, and all the time I'm feeling most horribly guilty. Yet I don't want us to let Feen down, if you know what I mean. He and his wife have been extraordinarily kind to both of us, and I'd like to do what I can. He's the chap I'd like to see put up a good show and get some credit."

"But I want you to help Colonel Feen."

"Sure?"

She kissed him. "My dear, of course I'm sure. And I do love to see you enjoying yourself"

"Well, that's all right then," said Travers. "A few more days and we'll be leaving here, as Joy wants us to."

Bernice was frowning away to herself.

"You know, darling, I don't think I'm as keen as I was on finding out who killed that dreadful man Brewse. I don't mean I'm not keen about you finding out, because I really am desperately keen, and I'd love you and the Colonel to settle it all—"

"And George Wharton?"

She smiled. "Yes, and George Wharton, to settle it all before we go away." She shook her head and smiled puzzledly. "I don't know quite how to explain. I think it's after playing golf with Mrs. Strongman yesterday afternoon."

Travers smiled a polite inquiry.

"You see, she told me heaps of things I didn't know. About that poor vicar man losing all his money, and other people too. She lost no end herself, though she blames Guff-Wimble for that. She was really very embittered about it all."

"I rather think most of Mrs. Strongman's grievance lies in the fact that she lost her own money," Travers said. "If she has to go cap in hand to Strongman every time she wants a fiver, that wouldn't make her sympathize with Brewse."

"But surely you don't sympathize with him!"

"Not to the extent of being blind to your point of view, and Mrs. Strongman's. Whoever killed Brewse—according to that point of view—didn't do anything so terrible after all." He shook his head. "The trouble is that Feen—and Wharton and myself— can't look at things in quite that way. Feen can't pick out only the nasty murderers, though I dare say he'd very much prefer it, as I should!"

His fingers went to his glasses again, and then fell.

"I suppose Mrs. Strongman didn't happen to say what she was doing on Saturday afternoon?"

"Let me see." She frowned. "She said her husband went out— yes, that's right. Her husband went out and her son was out with young Quench, so she treated herself to a nap in her room."

"Very sensible too," Travers said, and then the maid came in with an envelope. It was from Feen and he looked quickly through the two typewritten sheets.

"Feen would rather like to see me at ten o'clock. It'll probably be quite a quick business."

"My dear, you mustn't be so apologetic," she told him. "I'd love you to go. We can have our game this afternoon instead."

Travers stoked his pipe and began a study of Feen's latest report.

INTERVIEW WITH QUENCH, ETC.

*Please return direct.* B. F. Many thanks for your brief note of yesterday evening, re the discrepancy in the evidence of B. Q. and M. P., with regard to their movements on the Saturday night. I talked things over with Geo. W., and as there was still half an hour of daylight, and there was something I was hoping to see out at Pettistone, I rang Molly up and asked her to meet me just outside the village. As she'd already been told W. was merely a friend, he preferred not to go with me. She was there and this is what took place.

I told her Bob had quoted her as evidence of his movements on the Saturday night, and she made no bones about spinning me the same yarn as she spun you. Then, unfortunately as I now think, I disregarded Wharton's ruling re the handling of liars, and asked her to explain how it was that Bob had said that he and she had gone for a long walk. She never turned a hair. You know that cool way of hers, and how she'll look you clean in the eye. "Bob's the most frightful fool about things"—I think those were her exact words—"and ridiculously old-fashioned. He'd hate to admit that we spent a couple of hours in the garden. He'd much prefer to say we were wandering about the roads arm-in-arm like the gardener and the second housemaid."

"But whose garden were you in?" I said, and I was sure that upset her equilibrium for a moment. Then she smiled most amusedly. "Our garden, of course. The vicarage garden's simply lousy with ants. Would you like to come and see just where?"

I said that was all, and she simply shot her car back to the village. The idea was obviously to get on the 'phone to warn Bob and reconcile the two tales, but I thought I'd forestall her and see Bob first, so I shot on too—to the vicarage. There I had the very bad luck to find that Bob was out, and his father didn't know where.

We had a minute or two's talk in general, and I was just going to ask him about his ladder when he blurted out that there was something he'd like to tell me. He'd been most distressed for days and couldn't sleep—I must say he didn't look like that to me!—and he had to ease his conscience. So up we went to that study of his and this was his tale. I may say straight-out that I believe it, but you may think otherwise.

At about a quarter-past five on the Saturday afternoon, Quench was called up on the 'phone by Brewse. I asked him how he knew it was Brewse and all he could say was that the man said he was Brewse, and the matter of the conversation seemed to confirm it. Brewse said he had been made aware that he had unwittingly come to live in a part of England where there were people who had suffered by his own financial disasters, and he was prepared to make such local and personal restitution as lay in his power. He was proposing to begin with Quench, who, his informant had said, was one of the worst sufferers. But the matter would have to be a very close secret, for if a living soul got wind of the restitution, then Brewse's life would be hell.

He proposed therefore that Quench should meet him after dark, ten-past eight being the time suggested, in the lane past Gables, at a shed near the road. There they could have a brief preliminary talk. Quench, who expressed himself as having been quite taken aback, agreed, and vouched for the necessary secrecy.

Just before eight o'clock on the Saturday night then. Quench made his way towards that shed. He was in time to see the fire and to see by the light of it Corby carrying out the body. He says instinct told him something was badly wrong, and he at once made his way off. He was lucky to glance back and see the light of Corby's bicycle, and he also heard Marlin's steps, and he crouched in the ditch during their brief talk.

I asked why he hadn't reported everything to the police and he had a whole lot of answers ready which you can guess for yourself. I cautioned him and said I'd be along next morning at nine to take a statement. He's pretty badly scared, by the way, and might be a useful source of information.

For instance, I asked him about his ladder as soon as I'd dressed him down, and he was most abject and helpful. It was dark but he got his torch and took me to the old stable where it was usually kept, though warning me that I couldn't use it as it had been broken when it fell down from a plum-tree in August, and he had always forgotten to ask Ammony about having it repaired. Then as soon as we clapped eyes on the ladder, he was even more abject. The ladder had been repaired! I took the torch and examined it closely, and found it had also been cleaned down. If there had ever been any paint on it, it had all gone, and there wasn't even a whiff of the turps or whatever it was that had removed it. I told him I should want the ladder and he was too much under my thumb at the time to ask any questions. I also took a length of rope and lashed the ladder along my car. Am having it examined by an expert to see if there are any traces of paint that escaped the washing-down.

So much for old Quench. If you believe his yarn, and Geo. W. certainly does, you'll see the problems that are raised.

I thought, by the way, that I'd kill another bird with the same stone, so I saw Ammony and told him I'd like to see him at Edensthorpe in the morning at ten o'clock. He struck me as decidedly perturbed and I thought it best to leave him so, and I gave him no information at all. If you would like to be present at the interview, there is another room opening out of mine, and we can leave the door open.

We didn't find the gun. No disappointment, as I'd never quite hoped for it. No sign of blood anywhere either, but Barnes warned me there'd be little likelihood of that. Am now organizing a house to house inquiry in the whole of Pettistone in the morning, to see if anybody did happen to see Brewse on his way through or round the village that afternoon.

Hope to see you here for the Ammony interview. If you can't get here, keep these notes safe till you see me. Thanks for what you've done re Geo. W., who's with us now, I think, for all he's worth, though still Higgins.

B. F.

Travers walked to the police-station and was there in time to see Feen and Reeper returning from taking old Quench's statement at Pettistone. Reeper had also set going that house to house inquiry in the village in case anybody might, after all, have caught a glimpse of Brewse on the Saturday afternoon.

Wharton, as a complete stranger, was thinking of lending a hand in that.

The three were no sooner in Feen's room than Wharton came in with the news that Ammony had arrived.

"He's a bit early," Feen said. "See that he waits for a minute."

Then he was handing Travers an opened envelope and its letter, with a "Have a look at that. Don't worry about prints. It's got none on it. Our friend Higgins has seen it, by the way."

Travers took one peep at the letter, and was raising his eyebrows, for it had all the melodramatic qualities of the anonymous communication—cheap paper, printed characters, poor spelling and an absence of address, date and name.

> Mr Ammony was burying something in the garden last night right up against his gooseberry bushes in the dark and he hadn't no lantern. Sir I thought this might have to do with the murder as he has been opening his mouth a lot latterly.

The envelope was addressed to no one in particular at the police-station, Edensthorpe, and it had been posted in the town.

"It came by the first post this morning," Feen said. "What do you make of it?"

"On the face of it, it doesn't look the work of the man who talked old Quench into going up to the shed on Saturday night," Travers said. "Perhaps Ammony will throw some light on it."

"What Higgins said about it was this. If the writer was as uneducated as the letter makes out, then he wouldn't have had the sense to write it with gloves on."

"But he had sense enough to print instead of writing," Travers pointed out.

"True enough," Feen said. "Perhaps we'd better have Ammony in. He'll be sitting with his back to that room there, where you'll be, so you can leave the door well ajar."

Wharton came in and Ammony at his heels. That morning the universal provider was wearing a blue serge suit and the tips of his moustache had been specially waxed, but there was a distinct uneasiness about his manner. His greetings had nothing of that breezy deference with which he would have welcomed Feen or Reeper as customers, and he even made something of a bungle of sitting down, for he was casting suspicious looks at Wharton.

"I don't know what you're so nervous about," Feen told him bluntly. "We've only asked you here to lend us a hand."

"I'm not nervous, sir," Ammony said, and threw out his chest. "It's only that this is my first appearance, so to speak."

"Let's hope it will be your last," Feen said, and gave him a look. "But to get to business. You know all about that painting that was done on the wall at Gables. You told Sergeant Reeper here that you didn't sell the paint. Is that right?"

"That's right, sir. We haven't sold any yellow for months, and black we don't stock at all only in enamel."

"So much for that then. And now a quite different matter. I might as well tell you the facts as they'll soon be public—if they aren't now. Every one in Pettistone—except yourself—who is known to have lost money in Brewse's concerns, has been seen by me and has given an account of his movements for two separate times last Saturday. I take it you've also no objection to giving an account of your movements?"

"Me, sir? No, sir. I'll tell you anything you want to know, as far as I can."

"Capital! Then where were you between the hours of three and four in the afternoon?" Ammony repeated the question and wrinkled up his brows in thought. Then he nodded sideways to himself.

"That's easy, sir. I drove one of my vans up to Copmore, because I wanted a word with Haylock, and I thought that'd be the easiest way of getting there—"

"But wasn't Saturday afternoon a busy time for you to be leaving the shop?"

"That's where you're wrong, sir." He looked round at Reeper for confirmation. "Saturday morning's busy, sir, and Saturday evening, but not Saturday afternoon."

"Sounds like jam yesterday and jam to-morrow but no jam to-day," said Wharton, as if to himself.

"Jam, sir?"

"Sorry," said Wharton. "Pay no attention to me. You go on listening to the Colonel."

"Well, what was the particular business you wished to see Haylock about?" Feen went on. Ammony hesitated a moment, then nodded. "I don't see as I shouldn't tell you, sir. I didn't intend to go at all, but I happened to catch sight of Brewster and, thinks I, I'll have no more of it so—"

"Just a minute. Who's Brewster?"

"Haylock's son-in-law, sir, what come round Pettistone twice a week, Tuesdays and Saturdays, with a van, selling oil and household things—brushes and mats and pots and pans." He leaned forward confidentially. "It's like this, sir. I take most of Haylock's butter and eggs, and yet there's his son-in-law taking the bread out of my mouth. I don't sell a pint of oil where I used to sell ten gallons."

"Paraffin oil?" asked Wharton quickly.

"That's right, sir. But as I was saying to you, sir, I happened to see Brewster and my blood sort of flared up, and the van happened to be going that way so I drove it myself."

"Yes. And what satisfaction did you get out of Haylock? I'm only asking that so as to be sure how long you spent with him."

"How long?" He snorted. "Not five minutes, sir. He as good as told me to go to hell, and if I didn't want his butter and eggs he could take 'em into Edensthorpe."

"And then what happened?"

"Well then, sir, something went wrong with the engine." He turned again to Reeper for confirmation. "Right against them two old elms that hang over the road, and there I was stuck for over half an hour. First I thought it was the plugs, and then the mag., and then I worked it down to the petrol feed."

Reeper caught Feen's eye.

"Didn't any one come past while you were there, Charlie?"

"No one didn't come," Ammony said aggrievedly. "Who should be there on a Saturday afternoon? No one ain't at work?"

"Well, we'll take the afternoon as over," Feen said. "Now about the evening, say from a quarter to eight till a quarter past."

Another preliminary frown and Ammony was ready.

"Just before eight, sir, we shut up the shop, and I dare say it was after eight when every one had gone. Then I made up my accounts for the night, and I reckon that'd take me another half-hour."

"Where did you make them up?"

"Where I always do, sir. In my office, behind the shop."

"You were alone, of course?"

"I always am alone, sir."

"Well, we'll take the evening as over," Feen said, and picked up the anonymous letter. "Here's something which I'd like you to read. By the way, you weren't doing any digging in your garden last night after dark?"

"Doing what, sir?" Ammony apparently could hardly believe his ears.

"Digging in your garden."

"What on earth should I be digging in my garden for, sir?"

"Worms, perhaps," put in Wharton jocularly.

Ammony shot him another uneasy look and then began on the letter. In a minute he was looking round indignantly.

"Well, of all the barefaced lies!"

"Exactly," said Feen, and took the letter back. "Doesn't that garden of yours run along that little back lane to those two or three thatched cottages?"

"It does, sir. Why?"

Feen smiled at Ammony's new bellicosity.

"Well, I happened to run an eye over it this morning when I was out that way. It struck both me and Sergeant Reeper that it was a handy spot for anybody else to have done a bit of digging—or burying."

Ammony stared. "What would any one want to go burying things in my garden for?"

"Exactly." He got to his feet. "Why shouldn't we all go and have a look? I happen to be going that way again with a friend of mine, so I'll get hold of him at once. If anybody's been playing monkey tricks with your garden, then we'd better look into it."

Ammony went out with instructions to wait. Feen was warning him about secrecy as he and Wharton went with him.

"Old Charlie's the limit," Reeper said with a chuckle to Travers. "If you were to ask me if he was telling the truth or not, I couldn't tell you, sir. He's got so used to reeling off the lies, I don't believe he knows himself when he's telling the truth." He listened for a moment and his voice lowered. "I don't know if I'm doing right to ask you, sir, but who's this Mr. Higgins?"

"One of those old fogies who fancies himself as a detective," Travers confided.

Reeper nodded knowingly. "Queer looking old gent., sir."

Which was the end of that, for Feen and Wharton came back.

"Well, how'd you find Ammony?" the Colonel asked Travers. "His yarn was pretty convincing, didn't you think?"

"Yes—and no," said Travers. "But what next?"

"You're the friend I was referring to," Feen said. "I don't think there'll be anything suspicious if we all go in my car, and you see what we'll all see. You go on ahead with Ammony, Reeper, and we'll catch you up. Mention Mr. Travers's name, if you like."

Reeper was smiling as he caught Travers's eye.

"That's right," said Travers. "Still with a screw loose somewhere."

Two miles short of the village they began overhauling Ammony's car, and the Colonel let his own car slow down.

"By the way, I saw Gordon Strongman this morning," he said. "He says it was after eight o'clock when he left Bob Quench and Molly Pernaby in the Pernaby garden. I wanted to know how he knew the time, since it was dark, and he said there was a light in the lounge where old man Pernaby was, and he looked at his watch as he went by. Then he said he mooned about a bit and then went to see some one. He said that last very suggestively, as if I'd take it for granted it was some wench or other. I told him point-blank that I'd probably want the name and place and exact time."

"Did that bother him?"

"Not that I noticed."

He shot the car on and passed Ammony just short of the village, then slowed again and went at a crawl into a narrow lane that ran south from Ammony's house. The lane was a cul-de-sac, and he was proposing to back out, for the garden began no more than twenty yards along it. All that back property looked unkempt, and Ammony the kind of owner who puts his money into the shop front and grudges a penny on back repairs.

"There're the bushes," Feen said. "Just under your nose against those broken railings. You sit tight and you'll have a good view. Wonder where the others have got to?"

Ammony had evidently been fetching a garden fork, at Reeper's suggestion, for he came up by the garden path.

"Curious place to have gooseberry bushes, Charlie?" Reeper said. "I don't think I'd have mine right against the road."

"It's them blasted boys broke the railings down," Ammony said, "and I never could catch the young devils."

Reeper held out his hand for the fork.

"Better let me have that. We'll soon see what you've been burying."

"If it was April Fools' Day, there might have been some sense," Ammony said.

"We'll know in a minute whether or not some one's been taking a rise out of you," Reeper told him consolingly. "Better start here, perhaps."

He thrust in the fork and began turning over the soil nearest the garden edge, and, in less than a minute, was standing and gaping. There lay a revolver, and it had been buried not more than six inches in the loose soil.

"Keep back," snapped Feen, as Ammony moved forward. "Don't touch that gun. I want to be sure where it came from."

Where exactly it had been buried was what he meant, for he measured the distance from a railing post, and stuck in a piece of broken railing to mark the spot at ground-level.

"Your gun, is it?" he asked the still staring Ammony.

"Never saw it before in my life, sir."

"But you've got a gun. A revolver if you like."

Ammony shot him a look.

"I say you've got a gun."

"Well, sir, I have."

"Go and get it and bring it here."

Travers's head appeared out of the window as soon as Ammony had gone.

"How long has that gun been buried?"

Wharton had a good look at it. "Not longer than since last night, probably. There's no new rust on it."

"An old Army Colt, isn't it?"

"Looks like it," Feen said. "What I'm wondering is if it could have fired that bullet." He shook his head "I'll get it up to London at once. Better be safe than sorry."

Ammony came back with a blunt little gun of Dutch make.

"Where'd you get this?" Feen asked.

"I really got it through a friend," Ammony said.

"I see; smuggled over. Got a permit for it?"

Ammony opened his mouth, then closed it. A shake of the head and he was saying he didn't know it was necessary, considering all the burglaries.

"Now, now," said Feen. "Don't take me for as big a fool as that."

He read the Riot Act to Ammony. One word made public about the finding of the gun, or about the anonymous letter, and he'd have him up on two charges. It was a remarkably flabby Ammony who was told at last he might go.

"Let your sergeant go after him and warn him on no account to go near this dug soil," Wharton said. "And bring back a pound of flour or rice with you, Sergeant."

"What on earth's the flour for?" Feen wanted to know.

Wharton explained. Whoever it was that had planted the gun, so as to cast suspicion on Ammony, would be anxious to know if the police had taken any action. The gun had been buried in a hole scraped with the fingers less than a foot below the surface of the loose soil, and in an easy place to recognize. If then that marking-stick were removed, and a fairly extensive layer of flour placed at about six inches depth, and then the soil carefully replaced and smoothed over, it would be easy to detect if the soil were subsequently disturbed.

"No matter how craftily he works," the old General said with a nod of satisfaction to himself, "he won't be able to hide the fact that he's been grubbing there to see if we've found the gun."

"And now what?" said Feen when his car was heading for Edensthorpe again.

"Afraid you must count me out," Travers said. "It may sound something of an anti-climax, but I'm playing golf with my missus this afternoon, and it's an engagement I don't feel like putting off."

"Any ideas?" Feen asked Wharton.

Wharton's nod was far from a satisfied one. "I'd like to be getting on a bit quicker. The sooner we get some rubbish cleared out of the way, the better I'll like it. What about a real examination of everybody's alibi." He gave one of his most unctuous looks. "We shan't be able to do that without Mr. Travers."

"Any time after six o'clock, I'm your man," Travers said.

Feen said six o'clock would be first class.

"One little thing before I forget it," Travers said. "I wonder if George here would care to submit that medical evidence to a certain High Authority if Barnes wouldn't mind giving details."

Wharton said he'd arrange that and Feen thought a copy could be got off at once.

"And one other little thing," said Travers. "I'm hoping to jot down a few notes relative to all the alibis, and I'd like one piece of preliminary information about people. Isn't Pettistone a kind of caravanserai? Isn't it rather like a Sussex village, I mean, where not one middle-class resident in twenty is native born?"

"You're dead right," Feen said. "Quench is a Dorsetshire man. Guff-Wimble's the only native product and he doesn't actually belong to this district. Strongman's a Londoner. Pernaby, I should say, is some sort of northerner. The Davidsons are Scots. The people who used to be at Gables were Lancashire."

"I rather thought Pernaby was an East Anglian," Travers said. "I haven't heard him say very much, mind you, but he had the East Anglian clipped way of sounding his consonants. What did you think, George? You heard him talking the other night."

"I'm no authority," Wharton admitted modestly. "But does it matter?"

"I think you'll find you're wrong," Feen told Travers. "I have the distinct impression that they all come from Northumberland."

"So long as he's not local, that's good enough," Travers said, but, being rather proud of his ear for dialect, still had his own opinions.

Then when the car dropped him near the house, he had one final word, and it was by way of revenge on Wharton.

"Nasty one in the eye for you, George, this business about the gun?"

"How do you mean?" said Wharton, and glared.

"Well, didn't you insist that the murder wasn't a local job at all, because none of our suspects had any good motive? Then how do you explain away the planting of that gun. Isn't that a local job?"

But Wharton seemed quite unperturbed. "Other people here, aren't there, besides the local ones? Outside the Guff-Wimble gang, if you like."

"Ammony?"

Wharton snorted prodigiously.

"Ammony! He's a bladder of lard, that's all he is. I'm talking about an outside person who's got no alibi."

"And who's that?" asked Travers, fingers at his glasses.

"Marlin, the man you've all forgotten," Wharton told him.

# CHAPTER X
# TRAVERS ON "ALIBIS"

THE FIRST THING Feen said when Travers arrived that evening was that a big risk had been run in overlooking Marlin. The old butler and his wife had been, with himself, the sole mourners at the Edensthorpe cemetery, the time of which had been kept secret, and after the funeral he had taken advantage of the opportunity to have quite a long talk.

"You found something out?" Travers said.

"I did and I didn't," Feen told him. "You see, it's like this. He has a kind of artless way of talking, as you know; a simple, conversational way I suppose one might call it. He doesn't hesitate and he gives the impression of being genuine and having nothing whatever to conceal. What I'm driving at is this. If he told you he had a perfectly good motive for killing Brewse—told it you without knowing he was saying it—you'd actually take it as a strong proof of innocence. A murderer would be careful what he said, but Marlin answers everything without the slightest hesitation."

"And did he show he had a motive?"

"He did. He told me he and his wife had lost most of their savings in the crash, but that they'd not wished to add to Brewse's worries at any time by letting him know it. Brewse was under the impression that they'd invested less than they had, and that they'd got out in time."

"When you were telling me that, sir," Reeper said, "it struck me as making Marlin a little too good to be true."

"A good many saints and martyrs aren't in the calendar," Wharton told him. "This chap Marlin's either one of them, or else he's one of the most plausible rascals and best actors I've run across yet, and I've met a few in my time."

"When did you see him?" asked Travers.

"Oh, I get about a bit," Wharton said complacently. "I happened to be in the neighbourhood of that funeral too."

"The second thing I found out was about Brewse's will," Feen went on. "Do you realize we ought to have known that the house, for instance, would become Marlin's property in reality, after Brewse's death?"

"I'd thought there'd probably be a deed of gift, transferring back from Marlin to Brewse," Travers said.

"There was never any intention of it," Feen said.

"This is the situation as it was when Brewse came out. Certain old friends and sympathizers collected about two thousand pounds for him, and it was given him in cash. His married daughter and his son together arranged for an annual payment of four hundred pounds, so long as Brewse behaved himself—a condition and a wording which Marlin says helped to embitter him, particularly as he had to take their money."

"I suppose Brewse and the two Marlins could live on four hundred?" Travers was saying reflectively.

"Marlin says they anticipated doing it comfortably," Feen told him. "The house was bought, and there were a few hundreds left over, and Brewse was proposing to use them speculatively. Marlin says he now has the idea that the telephone was kept on so that Brewse could ultimately transact any business with the City. But that doesn't matter. The thing is this, that Marlin bought the house in his own name with Brewse's money, and Brewse was calling himself Mr. Hanley—the name, you'll notice, that Marlin called him by when Brewse's father was alive. Brewse said, 'It's your house and it remains your house. If anything happens to you, then it goes to Clara'—that's Mrs. Marlin—'and she can then make a will, if necessary, leaving the house to me.' In other words, Brewse is dead and the house is Marlin's, and Marlin tells me he'd like to sell it and get away at once."

"Tell me this straight out," Travers said. "How much would you bet that Marlin was telling the truth?"

"A pretty hefty sum."

"I'll venture a fiver," added Wharton hopefully.

"I'm inclined to agree," Travers said. "If Marlin's not genuine, than he's a histrionic marvel. By the way, if you've no objection I'd like to make some excuse to call, just to have a last look."

"And I'm taking the precaution of making inquiries at Brewse's old home," Feen said. "A letter will reach there in the morning and they'll 'phone a reply. And now what about getting on with those alibis? I think it's high time, as somebody else said, that we cleared some rubbish out of the way and saw just where we stood."

Travers produced some rough notes and suggested somebody should start the ball rolling. The others voted him down.

"If you wish it then, I'll lead off," Travers said. "And I've noted down here two things I'd like us to agree on. First of all, the two times are the afternoon hour and the evening hour. The afternoon hour is the more important because it's when Brewse was murdered, and we're after his murderer, and not necessarily after the man who moved the body and—"

"Just a moment, sir," Reeper said. "Are you really making out there were two separate people? One who killed him and another who moved the body to the shed?"

"I'm glad you asked that," Travers said. "We want to know just how we stand, so that when we come to individual alibis, we can go full steam ahead and not have to refer back. But with regard to the question whether one man did the lot, or induced another man to move the body for him, there was a time when I was the least bit undecided. The murderer—X, as usual—killed Brewse. Now you've heard Mr. Higgins's theory, and my own, as to why the body was removed, and if you agree with it, then X did the whole show himself. The entire business was the work of one brain, and the only doubt is the actual removal of the body. Conceivably X induced his friend Y to bring the body to the shed where he had everything prepared. It's an idea I've gone into very closely, and I'm of the opinion at this moment that a man with a brain like X's wouldn't have run the risk of confiding in anybody."

"I certainly agree," Feen said. Wharton nodded.

"We'll take that point as cleared up then," Travers said, "though I may have to make a reference to it later. But to repeat. The 3 p.m. to 4 p.m. hour is the important one, and therefore if a man is clear for that hour, then it ought to include the evening alibi time also. If a man hasn't got an alibi for, say from 7.45

p.m. to 8.15 p.m., then we shall have to pay special attention to an examination of his afternoon alibi, and vice versa.

"Now to the second point—what is meant by a perfect alibi. Am I right in saying it's one that satisfies a judge or jury?"

Wharton smiled dryly. "No Director of Public Prosecutions would advise a charge against a man who had that kind of alibi."

"Right then," said Travers. "So beginning with the afternoon alibis, I say that Old Quench and Pernaby have the most perfect kind. Each is a man of probity who can swear to the other, and each can produce witnesses, like Guff-Wimble who saw him on the course. If we go on ahead to the evening, Quench has an alibi if we believe his tale, which I gather we do. Pernaby has an alibi, because Gordon Strongman unwittingly revealed that he was in the lounge of his house at eight o'clock, and because Pernaby can produce his sister as evidence that he was in her room at somewhere about that time. In other words, I think some rubbish is cleared away already. Don't you think we might, in fact, leave old Quench and Pernaby out of all future consideration?"

All agreed.

"Now to alibis which are highly suspicious and are nevertheless still perfect because they can't be broken. Bob Quench and Gordon Strongman can swear to each other's alibis. And, for what it's worth, my private opinion is that they did spend the afternoon in the vicarage garage, but not at Bob s car."

"Yes," Feen said. "Reeper and I have agreed that he'd have had his car overhauled at the works where there's a pit and everything. And what's the use of being virtually manager of a garage and not making use of the fact?"

"He and young Strongman were repairing that ladder and getting ready for the evening's painting," Reeper said. "I don't deny they didn't take down bits of the car, but that was only a blind."

"Exactly!" said Travers. "Therefore they're ruled out. Their afternoon alibi is suspicious and so is their evening one, but it's good enough. I don't want to go into the question of whether Gordon Strongman did the painting alone, which he could have done, as the lettering is crude enough, because you couldn't even bring that charge against him. He's probably induced some lady friend to give him an alibi for that time. If Bob Quench and Molly Pernaby helped too, and they care to lie steadily about it, we're still helpless. But as I said, the painting's nothing, except in so far as it gives the painter or painters a murder alibi."

"I'm of the opinion we should rule out Bob Quench and Gordon Strongman," Feen said emphatically. Wharton nodded again.

"That's agreed," Travers said. "More rubbish cleared away, and now we begin to see the road. We come to Guff-Wimble, for instance. His afternoon alibi isn't worth a cent. Who's to prove precisely when he was in the secretary's office? Who's to prove precisely when and where he was on the course? He may find occasional witness, but that's no good. If his car was handy somewhere, he could have been away to heavens knows where and back again, and away again and back and so on all the afternoon." He leaned forward, fingers at his glasses. "And remember this about Guff-Wimble. He's the only one who knew Brewse in the flesh. He was the only one who could have rung him up and induced him to come to any rendezvous!"

"My God, sir! You mean he's our man?"

"Not so fast," Travers said. "All I'm saying at the moment is that his afternoon alibi is a dud, and it's up to him or us to prove it otherwise. But let me go back to something. Suppose he did do the murder. Then he certainly didn't do anything else, for his evening alibi is more than perfect."

He was giving Reeper an inquiring look, and Reeper duly obliged.

"But why couldn't some one else have done the rest for him, sir?"

"He's his own answer," Travers said. "Can you imagine any one doing anything for Guff-Wimble?"

"But he's lousy with money, sir. What if he paid them enough? Don't you think any one'd have done it, especially some one like that Gordon Strongman who was going away and wouldn't care what happened after he'd gone?"

"That's a brainy suggestion," Travers said. "But about Gordon Strongman, I still think he was the painter, and I still think Guffy couldn't have sat tight in his house that evening over his dinner while some one was saving his neck."

"I very definitely agree," Feen said. "And as our only hope of breaking his afternoon alibi is to find some one who saw him on the Edensthorpe Road, I think we'd better wash him out, too. If anybody should come along and happen to say they saw him where we want him, then we can act accordingly."

"Good," said Travers. "A little more rubbish cleared away. And now to something more promising—the afternoon alibi of Strongman."

"But isn't he all right for the afternoon?" asked Feen.

Travers smiled. "On the face of it—yes. When you get really down to it—no. In fact, if I were trying to fake an alibi and I could achieve what Strongman's achieved, I should be rather pleased with myself."

Wharton nodded with the approval of a fond parent, whose offspring has just performed successfully.

"You don't think he was telling the truth?" Feen said.

"Yes and no." He was smiling and blinking away as he polished his classes. "I think his alibi might be discovered to be such a delightful fake that it's amusing in an impertinent sort of way."

"You can break it?"

"I can tell you what I might have done myself, if the idea had occurred to me," Travers said, and hooked his glasses on again. "I'd have asked Bob Quench round to see my wife's car—"

"Excuse me, sir," broke in Reeper, "but he did come round to see that car on the Friday night!"

"Exactly," said Travers suavely. "He may also have delivered a spare spare which Strongman had spoken about, on the plea that his spare had something or other wrong with it. Bob Quench was also an excellent witness to the foot-pump which was not replaced. Assume all that, and assume that I'm Strongman, and what do I do? I hide my old spare in the hedge near where I'm proposing to have a puncture, and I make sure the new spare is very flabby. Just before I and my fledgling chauffeur start out, I loosen the valve of a tyre so that it will run flat in about a mile. It does so and I get out to look at it, and jab in a nail. 'Here's the puncture,' I say, and, 'Get out the spare.' The rest you know except that with my quick jacking system I can put on the hidden spare and be away and gone, and back again in the same breakdown position long before my chauffeur is back."

"Yes," said Feen slowly. "That's certainly workable. But it has a flaw or two. Suppose Ammony's man had brought back the chauffeur in another car and found you gone?"

"Oh, I admit the flaws," Travers said. "All the same, I might have said to my chauffeur, 'Take that spare to be blown up and for your sins walk all the way there and back.' "

Feen was still shaking his head. Wharton was looking anxious. Travers resumed cheerfully.

"There's something to get your teeth into, in any case. You can hear the chauffeur's version on the pretence of asking what cars he recognized that afternoon on the road, and you can hear Strongman's version on the same pretext. Also, I've another card up my sleeve. *It was a pump that was hidden*—not a spare, and that would wash out the risk of Bob Quench mentioning the second spare. As soon as the chauffeur had gone, out came the hidden pump and Strongman was away and gone. And remember he could have gone the devil of a way in that powerful car of his. He could have circled round to the Edensthorpe Road and been back in ten minutes, even if his chauffeur had been brought back in an Ammony car. Then he'd have been sitting with the tyre deflated, and he could also exhibit the nail he found."

"Now we're coming to things," Wharton announced triumphantly.

"I like that version better," Feen said. "Tomorrow we'll make a few inquiries."

"As for Strongman's evening alibi," Travers went on, "he hasn't got one. There was early supper and his wife went to the pictures. Gordon was out, as we know, and there Strongman was, entirely by himself. In other words, *we've arrived at last at the first suspect who has no alibi for either time.*" Then he smiled. "There's only one snag. Had Strongman the brains to do all that? I must say he struck me as if brawn and not brain was his strong suit. Well-fed but ill-informed, if you like."

"Any man can pretend to be a fool, sir, but you can't pretend to have brains if you haven't any."

"A very sound remark, Sergeant," Wharton said.

"Yes," said Feen. "Strongman may be the drawling, sluggish kind, but he always strikes me as having more brains than he wishes people to believe. In any case, he's our chief suspect from now on."

"He and Ammony," Travers said. "Don't forget our universal provider. There never need have been a thing the matter with his car in Copmore Lane, and his evening alibi is a long way off being proved yet."

"I don't think somehow you're very keen on Ammony," Feen said. "I still think you're pinning your hopes on Strongman."

"Maybe you're right. Ammony wouldn't have faked all that business with the gun, and I must admit I don't see how he could have lured Brewse anywhere."

"Well, that's all the alibis," Feen said.

"Anything else?"

"Only this," said Travers. "We've got a certain amount of evidence as to the kind of man X must be. Physically he had to be pretty strong to carry the sheer dead weight of even Brewse's body and put it in his car. He had to have a good knowledge of the district, or else he wouldn't have known about that shed. He knew the people or he wouldn't have rung up Quench, pretending to be Brewse, and he wouldn't have rung up Corby. And he has his own car with which he removed the body. He also knew about Ammony's being a likely suspect or he wouldn't have planted a gun and written the anonymous letter."

"Everything fits Strongman," Feen said. "Nobody knows the Pettistone district better. What do you think his hobby was when he first came here?"

Travers shook his head.

"Butterflies! You'd see him wandering all over the place with a butterfly net."

"Hercules among the women," said Travers. "But one thing I forgot. In X's house there's probably an oil-cooker and a drum to keep oil in That's how he got the oil to start the fire."

"I might have a word with Haylock's son-in-law, Brewster, about that," Feen said.

"I can tell you this much," Travers said. "The Strongmans have both oil-cooker and drum, and my informant tells me that most big households in the village have both. Electricity's dear, and having an oil drum means being able to buy in bulk and therefore more cheaply."

Feen made yet another note in his book. "Anything else?"

"As a matter of fact there is," Travers said. "That business of planting the gun in Ammony's garden. Don't you think it was all very crude and theatrical? It wasn't even dug in; it was merely placed in. And dead up against the road, which is the last place Ammony would have buried anything he wanted nobody to see him bury."

"I've been thinking of that," Wharton said. "The whole thing isn't in keeping."

"Exactly. We get a very cunning murderer who carries through a fairly intricate scheme with never a hitch, and yet when he wants to put suspicion on Ammony, he does the things Ammony would never have done! Comic—that's all I can call that gun business. Very well then; what was X's motive? We must credit him with enough brains to know he was being comic. Why did he try to incriminate Ammony in a way he must have known didn't incriminate anybody?"

Feen shrugged his shoulders. "It's beyond me."

"And me, sir," said Reeper. Wharton was shaking his head and saying nothing.

Travers rose to go. Feen said he was most grateful, and next day he—and he hoped Mr. Higgins—would be devoting considerable time to Strongman. "Well, good luck to you both," said Travers.

"Why the dismal Jimmy tone of voice?" asked Wharton.

"Sorry, but I just thought of something. Strongman seems to have every qualification but one."

"And what's that?"

"Motive," said Travers. "Would Strongman have murdered Brewse because Mrs. Strongman lost her money? Would uxoriousness make a man commit murder?"

"Motive or not," Feen said doggedly, "Strongman's got to go through the hoop to-morrow. I've a dozen ways of getting at him."

"You certainly have," said Travers. "So good luck to you again, and this time a bit more cheerfully. By the way, I might be able to see Marlin to-night."

And there the conference ended. A few moments later Reeper was confiding to his friend the station-sergeant that he'd just spent an hour with Mr. Travers and the Chief's pal, Higgins.

"Travers is him with the big specs., isn't he?" the sergeant said. "The one you said had got a screw loose?"

"That was all eye-wash," Reeper said. "If I'd a quarter of his brains, I'd still only have about twice ours. Anything through yet about that gun? It ought to have been there by tea-time."

The station-sergeant passed over a 'phone message.

Bullet not fired from gun. Gun Service Colt not later than 1916. Verify no prints.

Later that night Feen read that message and threw it contemptuously across to Wharton.

"Even more comic than Mr. Travers said. Why bury a gun that didn't have anything to do with the crime?"

"Why shouldn't some one other than X have planted it?" Wharton asked. "Some one who had a private grudge against Ammony and wanted to make trouble?"

"I'm sick of the sight of Ammony," Feen told him testily. "If you ask me, all he's doing is cluttering up the case. And now what about drawing up a chair and working out the best way of tackling Strongman."

"There's just one little thing I still can't make out," Wharton said, "and Mr. Travers didn't refer to it. Brewse didn't know that road very well, if he knew it at all, and there aren't any particular landmarks, especially where he was killed. So when Strongman or whoever it was, got him out there, how'd he know where to go, or where to stop? From what I can see, if Strongman, or whoever it was, had happened to get hung up, Brewse might have kept right on walking till he got to Edensthorpe."

"That strikes me as having been exactly the idea," Feen said. "X told Brewse to come across that path to the Limehurst Road, and then take the back way round the village and keep on walking till he was overtaken by a car. X did overtake him, and stopped, and the two went just inside the wood. Brewse was shot at once and dumped where we found the hat, X reversed his car and that's all there was to it."

Before the two had been at work for five minutes over the next day's plan of campaign, Feen was called to the 'phone. It turned out to be a preliminary report on Brewse's clothes which he had sent for an expert examination to the Yard, and when he came back he was in a much better humour. "Well, something's corroborated at last. Did I tell you there were some small grey stains we noticed on Brewse's coat between the shoulder blades, and which we thought might have been something in the manure? Well, they were lichen. The kind that grows on the trunks of trees."

Wharton's eyes narrowed in thought, as if he was still wondering how it got there. Feen explained.

"Everything works out perfectly. The body was near an oak-tree which was smothered with lichen. On the north side too, as usual, which was farthest from the road. Brewse was leaning his back against it when he was shot."

"That sounds good to me," Wharton said. "Not a single soul in the whole village says he saw Brewse that afternoon, and so he must have come the way you say, and been shot against that tree. So do you know what I'd do if I were you? If I had to put a dozen men on the job I'd get hold of every one who was motoring along the Edensthorpe Road between half-past three and four o'clock that afternoon That might get us farther than tackling Strongman."

Bernice complained of a slight headache that evening, and ascribed it to thunder. As the headache persisted after the belated dinner, Travers suggested a breath of air. He would like to call on the Marlins, he said, and the drive to Pettistone might do Bernice good.

Travers was a kindly and a charitable soul, though only his nearest intimates were aware of the fact, and he had done a considerable deal of worrying about old Marlin. Bernice was equally concerned when she heard what was in his mind, and it was the two of them that Marlin saw that night at the door of Gables.

"Come in, sir," he said, after a quick, peering look. "I didn't recognize you for a moment. You were the gentleman who came that night with Colonel Feen."

"This is an unofficial visit," Travers said. "This is my wife, by the way. We're not going to keep you for more than a minute or so."

Marlin said his wife had gone to bed after that tiring day, and might he make coffee. Travers made him sit down, and then came straight to what was in his mind. Marlin had mentioned the difficulty of obtaining desirable employment during his late master's imprisonment, owing to lack of suitable references.

"Now we have in mind at least a couple of people who might like to have yourself and your wife," Travers said. "A tactful word or two from us, and there'll be no trouble about references."

"That's more than kind of you, sir," Marlin said, "and of you, madam. I only wish I were a younger man and could have accepted the offer—not that I'm not just as grateful, sir."

His plans were to end his days with a widowed niece, thanks to the little nest-egg coming from the sale of the house. His conscience had worried him about that, he said, but now he thought he was entitled to regard it as some compensation for what he had lost.

"Of course you are," Travers said. "You're rightfully entitled in every way." He got to his feet. "Well I'm very glad to hear you're going to take things more easily. I may be seeing you again before you go."

"One moment, sir." The old man suddenly flurried. "There's something I think I'd like you to see, sir, if you'll be so good."

It was a registered envelope, containing twenty-five pound-notes and a short, unsigned letter—

Hope you will regard this as satisfactory compensation for any damage to house, and let the matter drop.

Travers looked at the envelope with its Edensthorpe post-mark, and even more closely at the writing which was a kind of copy-book upright, and the simplest form of disguise.

"You're not worrying whether you ought to take this?"

"Well, sir, I didn't know."

"Hang on to it," Travers told him. "I'll just mention the matter to Colonel Feen, if you've no objections. And might I have the letter and envelope?"

Bernice said she liked Marlin, whose manner reminded her very much of Travers's own man, Palmer.

"Had Zimri peace who slew his master?" asked Travers with an obvious jocularity.

"You surely haven't been suspecting a dear old man like him of the murder?" Bernice said, with a genuine indignation, which, added to his own opinions, was for Travers a good enough reason for removing Marlin once and for all from the suspect list.

He called up at the police-station on his way through the town, and found Reeper there.

"Looks as if some one has got the wind up, sir," the sergeant said. "We ought to find out at the post office who it was that registered the letter."

"I'm betting it was Gordon Strongman," Travers said.

"Gordon Strongman!" Reeper stared. "Why, he's gone, sir!"

"Not back to the Sudan?"

"You can take it he has, sir. The Chief wanted him about a quarter of an hour ago on the 'phone, and his mother said he'd changed his mind and left a day early, first thing this morning."

Travers nodded. "Is the Chief having him back?"

"He can't, sir," Reeper said ruefully. "It looks as if there's a regular conspiracy on. According to the mother he didn't say how he was going, and the Chief reckons that if he caught the midday 'plane, he'd be at Marseilles and on the way to Egypt by now."

# CHAPTER XI
# DEADLOCK

As FEEN WAS AWARE, the Traverses were to be away for a day or so. Bernice was particularly anxious to see the Shakespeare country, which was not too far a run, and it was not till dinner on the Thursday that the two returned to Edensthorpe. The gardener reported that Feen and another gentleman had already been round to make inquiries. Travers rang him at his house, and the Colonel and Wharton turned up at once.

Even the General was extraordinarily pessimistic. Every conceivable thing had gone wrong, and promising roads had become blind alleys. What had happened during Travers's brief absence was this.

Wharton had considered that the best way to approach Strongman was through the very heart, as it were, of his alibi.

"I'm coming to you for help," was what Feen therefore said to him. "Strictly between ourselves we're of the opinion that Brewse was murdered some way along the Edensthorpe Road at somewhere about the time you had your breakdown. What we want to do is to check up by all cars that used the Limehurst to Edensthorpe Road, in case anything unusual was seen, and that's where you might help. Did anybody come by whom you knew, while you were waiting in your car?"

"I don't know that there did," Strongman said, "except old Canticle."

"Major Canticle of Limehurst?"

"That's right," Strongman said. "I was actually out of the car at the time, having a look at the punctured wheel. He spotted me and drew up. As a matter of fact it was he who found that damn' nail that did all the mischief."

"And what time was that?"

"What time? Well, it was after three-thirty, because I remember he looked at his watch and said so. Apparently he ought to have been in Edensthorpe by a quarter to, and he doubted if he'd make it."

That was all the information Strongman could give, and he himself made the suggestion that Feen and Higgins might like a word with Tom Jewry. Tom said it was exactly twenty-past three when he started trundling that spare wheel back to Pettistone, and in the quarter of an hour it took to do the mile, only one car passed him and he met none.

"You didn't see anything of Major Canticle?" Feen asked.

Tom grinned. "Yes, I did, sir. When they was blowing up that spare, he went by in his big Daimler, and I thought if only I'd been a bit later, he'd have given me a lift."

"See anybody on the way back?"

Tom thought for a minute and then said a Mrs. Ware of Limehurst had passed him in her baby car when he was half-way back.

"Which Mrs. Ware? Not the rector's wife?"

Tom said she was the one, and he thought her daughter was with her.

"By the way, why didn't the garage people run you back in one of their cars?" Feen asked him.

Tom said they would have done, only there wasn't a car or van available, and also they were shorthanded.

Off went Feen and Wharton to Limehurst and saw Major Canticle, who confirmed Strongman's times but had no information of his own to give The really curious thing was that he had passed no man wearing a green hat.

"I'm a bit bat-eyed," he said, "but I think I should have noticed him. As a matter of fact I don't remember seeing any pedestrians along that woody stretch."

"Did you happen to meet Molly Pernaby?"

"Molly Pernaby?" He shook his head. "Don't know her."

Feen described her and her car. Canticle still had no recollection of having met her. As he pointed out, one's chief concern on the local roads was to pass safely. It was the road and the on-coming car one saw, and not its occupants. And, as he admitted, he was rather in a hurry.

The two went to the rectory next and saw Mrs. Ware. She remembered a car drawn up on the verge and her daughter even remembered that a man in the car had been reading a book.

"I suppose you didn't overtake or see Molly Pernaby?" Feen asked.

They had seen nothing, and, as the daughter happened to mention, Molly Pernaby's little sports saloon was so closed in that you never knew who was driving it.

"And did you by any chance happen to see a man walking to Edensthorpe?" Feen asked. "He'd be somewhere near the second milestone out, and he was wearing a green hat and had a short dark beard."

But they also had seen nothing, and Feen could only conclude that Brewse had been warned not to let himself be seen, and he had therefore dodged through a handy gap when he saw or heard a car.

"Not a very satisfactory solution, do you think?" he said to Travers.

"Most unsatisfactory," Travers said. "The very way to call attention to himself was to be seen dodging through a hedge. But what about times? Have you checked up with Molly Pernaby?"

"I'll tell you about her later," Feen said. "Here are the times, just as we wrote them down."

BREWSE. Must have been walking along the Edensthorpe Road from 3.20 p.m. till 3.50 p.m. approx.

MOLLY PERNABY. If she reached home at just on 4 p.m., then she met Brewse at 3.50 approx.

CANTICLE. Went through Pettistone at 3.35 approx. and therefore should have passed Brewse just over a mile along the road. The fact that he did not meet Molly Pernaby may be accounted for. Even if he had known her car, the two passed each other in the suburbs of the town.

MRS. WARE. Drove at what she called medium pace. Arrived Pettistone 3.40 and was therefore ahead of Molly

Pernaby. Should have met Brewse between first and second milestones.

"Molly Pernaby's story fits in," Feen said, "but Brewse doesn't. Men in green hats with dark beards are still uncommon enough, and the Ware girl must have noticed him. Since she didn't, where was he?"

"There is a solution," Travers said, "even if it is a little too obvious. He may have slipped into the wood for private reasons, or he may have spotted the car coming and have gone in till it had passed."

"It's beginning to beat me," Wharton said despondently, "and I don't mind telling you I take some beating. When we'd worked for a whole morning and done nothing but establish Strongman's alibi, instead of breaking it, I don't mind saying we both felt the whole bottom had gone out of things. Then we had a look at Ammony's garden where the gun was planted, but nobody's disturbed the soil."

"And that's not all," Feen said. "On top of all that, was a smack in the eye from Bob Quench and Molly Pernaby."

What had happened there was this. Just after midday Feen and Wharton ran Bob Quench to earth at the course where he was playing a round with Molly, and went across to them on the sixteenth green.

"Can you spare me a minute, Bob?" Feen said, and introduced Higgins.

Bob smiled at Higgins and grinned at Feen. "If so it'll be the last minute I can spare anybody, I'm going back into harness this afternoon."

"As a matter of fact," Feen said, "I'd like a word with both of you. About Gordon Strongman, for instance. Know why he changed his mind and went back early?"

Bob shrugged his shoulders. "Ask me another."

"Did he say anything to you about sending Marlin compensation money for painting all that vulgar rubbish on his house?"

"Just a minute," Bob said. "Are you hinting that Gordon did the painting?"

"Well, didn't he?"

Bob grinned again. "Even if I knew, do you think I'd tell? What sort of game is this you're trying to get me to play?"

"Merely a straight one," Feen told him. "You and he may both look fools if I bring him all the way back again."

"I'm not worrying," he said. "And if that's all you want to know, we'll be pushing on. We're a bit late as it is."

"There's nobody behind you and you'll stay here," Feen told him grimly. "All the same, you can move on when you've both looked me in the eye and answered one question. Will you swear that you weren't out of your garage that afternoon?"

"I'll swear it on anything you like and before whom you like."

"Thank you," Feen said. "And about you Molly—"

"Sorry, I don't know a thing."

"You don't know what I'm going to ask you," Feen said dryly. "Are you still sure it was not till four o'clock when you got home?"

"I think so," she said.

"Did you give your aunt a powder?"

"Oh, at once," she said. "She was feeling frightfully ill, poor darling, but she knew it was four o'clock."

"Where'd you go then? To the garage?"

She gave him a long level look. "Why the garage?"

It was Feen's turn to shrug his shoulders. "Well, why not? Where did you go?"

"I went straight across to the golf course through the gate opposite the eleventh, and I saw Uncle and the vicar finishing their round. I went to see who'd won and then we had tea there."

"And after that," Feen said to Travers, "I could only sort of wave them through. But I was furious, though I hope I didn't show it. All the time, whenever I've been dealing with those three younger people, I've felt I've been up against a wall of silence and—well, I'll say it point-blank—pre-arranged lies and Wharton agrees with me. As for that Pernaby girl, I never knew anybody who could be so infuriating and not say a word." He got to his feet.

"Still, we won't keep you from your dinner. See you later, perhaps."

Travers went with them to the gate. "My sister-in-law's due down on Saturday and I've got to be away from here early on Tuesday morning." He shook his head despondently. "It's a bad hat and everything keeps letting us down."

"The really annoying thing is this," Feen said. "Both Wharton and I are now dead sure the job must have been done by a local man. He's here, right under our noses, and we just can't put our hands on him."

"I know," Travers said consolingly. "I'd lay a thousand to one on it at this moment." Then his fingers were fumbling with his glasses. "Feel like trying a hopeless chance?"

"You've got an idea?" Wharton said quickly.

"Well, there is something that did occur to me," Travers said. "Have a go at Mrs. Strongman. She hasn't an alibi for the afternoon and her husband hasn't one for the night. She might have done Brewse in during the afternoon and then confided in her husband who did the rest. It's fantastic, but she's an obstinate, headstrong, scatter-brain kind of woman."

"I'm as good as my word," Feen said. "I'll try what I can do, and if that comes to nothing, then we shall all have to put our heads together and do something or other. Public opinion here won't stand for any more shilly-shallying."

That night Travers lay for a long while awake. He had always been something of a night bird and his brain never functioned more clearly than in the late hours, but as he lay in the dark and reviewed that case, he arrived like Feen at a blank wall, and it was not till just before he at last fell asleep that he came to what seemed to him the inner core of the mystery, and a question whose answer would be like the sun in a fog.

The time of the murder was sure. Brewse was dead before four o'clock that afternoon, and X had at once got to work about proving his own innocence and buttressing the already perfect alibi.

What he had known from the beginning was that if the body were left in that wood and not found for days, then the medical evidence could not determine the time of death to within less than twenty-four hours. That was the last thing he wanted. Death must be determined as at the time for which his alibi held good.

At once then, he got to work. Probably the shed was drenched with paraffin during the afternoon, and he then rang old Quench and arranged for him to be at the right spot at the right time. After dusk he fetched the body but lost the hat owing to its green colour in the bad light. Then the body was put in the heap so that its legs could be seen and the fire was lighted. Off went X, with a choice of roads for his route, and he wondered if Quench had smelt a rat after all and had not turned up. If so, the fire might not be seen, so he rang Corby.

A local man beyond all question, thought Travers, nodding to himself in the dark. He knew the 'phone calls could never be traced, and he knew enough about Quench—as everybody in the district did for that matter—to get him to consent to come in the dark to that comparatively lonely spot. And it was then that Travers asked himself the vital question, and at once he knew in his very bones that if he knew the answer, then the case might be as good as over.

*Why had X gone to all that risky trouble of removing the body three miles away to that shed?* If he wanted the body to be found, then there was the easiest way in the world. That road, as everybody knew, was used by traffic on a market day till a late hour, and eight o'clock was comparatively early.

*Why then had not X done the obvious thing, and merely put the body in the middle of the road where some car must see it?*

That was indeed the vital question, and it was one to which Travers could find no answer. Compared with the safety of one line of action, the other seemed risky to the point of madness, and incredibly unnecessary. Put the body in the road, and there would have been no need to 'phone either Quench or Corby, or stage that melodramatic fire. Indeed it almost seemed as if two men had after all been concerned in the drama of that Saturday: one a man of cold-blooded purpose and sanity, who had done the killing: the other a lunatic who had gone out of his way to run unnecessary risks and bungle all that the other had done!

There were times when Travers would wake and find that the subconscious mind was waiting with an answer to some problem, but that next morning he woke as far from a solution as ever to that vital question that had lingered in his mind on the borderlands of sleep. It still seemed to him that two men—the sane and the mad—had been concerned in that tragedy, and the only additional idea that had come was that a further manifestation of the madness of the one had been that preposterous placing of the gun to incriminate Ammony.

But if the success of the police inquiry seemed as far off as ever, yet it was not for himself or Wharton that Travers was worried. Failure for them was all part of the game, and the last thing he wanted in the event of success was applause or publicity. But Feen was different. Personally and professionally Travers had acquired for him an enormous regard, and the Colonel's triumph would have been the most fitting end to an unforgettable fortnight.

Bernice was thinking something of the kind, and she mentioned it during breakfast.

"Ludo, I do think we ought to do something in return for how kind every one has been to us here."

"Certainly we ought," he said. "If it's the Feens you're thinking of, what about a present of some sort?"

"Well, yes," she said. "We might do that. What about an autographed set of your books?"

"Heavens, no!" said Travers hastily. "Something from one of the antique shops would be far nicer."

"Well, we'll see," she said. "But I'm thinking of other people as well. People at the golf club have been awfully good to me. You know how bad I really am, and yet Mrs. Strongman's simply making me play in that foursome this morning. Molly Pernaby's been perfectly charming too."

"Well, what's your worry?" he said. "Just how to thank them, or what?"

"I know," she suddenly said. "I might give a really nice tea-party here and then take everybody on to the cinema. Let me see. Laura Feen, Mrs. Strongman, Molly Pernaby, and her aunt. I feel I ought to ask the aunt."

Then she was giving an oh! of dismay.

"But I can't. Joy will be here to-morrow."

"All the better," he said. "Have your show tomorrow, which will leave Monday for packing and so on. Joy will help entertain and she'll make the party six—a nice round number."

"But my dear, don't you see? I have to introduce her as my sister, Miss Haire, and every one will hear us calling her Joy. Joy Haire—well, now do you see?" Travers shrugged his shoulders amusedly. "As far as I'm concerned, I don't care a button what people discover. We're an old married couple by now. Also by Saturday we shall virtually be gone from here. And we've got to keep Joy amused somehow."

"I do wish you'd be serious," she said, and Travers promptly agreed. Objections, he rather gathered, had been expected of him, and once they were made, the party would again be recognized as the ideal way out. And so it proved. Before the meal was over, Bernice was in a minor fluster. This and that must be done at once, and Laura Feen, with whom she was going to golf, must be asked to allow time to call at the Pernabys.

Travers, who had left the morning free in case Feen and Wharton might need him, found himself at a loose end. But Pettistone drew him like a magnet, and at half-past ten he was amusing himself on the small practice course.

"You wanting a game by any chance?"

It was Pernaby, and Travers hailed him with delight.

"I'd like one very much," he said. "If you'll put up with me, that is."

Pernaby smiled in his usual grim-lipped fashion. "I noticed you playing some pretty good stuff against Quench the other day."

"That was a flash in the pan," Travers said. "Still, we'll see what happens on handicaps."

It was a dullish morning and excellent for golf, and Travers enjoyed it if only for the reason that Pernaby was a deceptively fast mover, which should have suited his own game. Yet he played abominably that morning, for his thoughts were always wandering to the case and were busying themselves with trying to find a way out of the *impasse* at which things had suddenly and unexpectedly arrived. Pernaby, poker-faced and laconic, was four up at the fourteenth, and he should have been more but for bad luck with a lie or two.

"Well, I call that positively ill-mannered!" Travers said, when Pernaby's drive crashed straight as a line over the menacing trees at that dog-legged fifteenth.

"Go thou and do likewise," said Pernaby dryly. "Try playing with a slice, if you like. It'll come to the same thing. I always do it that way when I want to be safe."

"The game's as good as over," Travers said, "so you show me."

Pernaby put down a ball, stood for a slice and played with a low tee. Out went the ball to the left, then it took the slice and disappeared along the fairway dip.

"Damn' good," said Travers. "But not as far as the first, do you think?"

"Does it matter? You can get on the green with either of them in two."

"Of course," said Travers, and tried the safety shot with the slice. It was badly foozled, and away went the hole and the match.

"I wonder if you'd mind if we went straight back?" Pernaby said. "I'm just a bit late."

They walked across the tenth fairway to the clubhouse, and all the time Travers was thinking how he had misjudged Pernaby. He had always rather liked the manner of him, but now he knew that that exterior aloofness was nothing but a veneer. Pernaby was probably the kindest-hearted of men behind that protective colouring, and he had a dry humour that was like a November sun.

"You know I'd have sworn you came from East Anglia," Travers happened to remark. "There's occasionally something in those consonants of yours."

"Well, I'll tell you something," Pernaby said. "I was brought up by an aunt and lived in Suffolk till it was time for me to go to school. Then she died and the family trustees brought me back north." He broke off. "Isn't that Strongman going into the club-house?"

"Looks like him," Travers said. "Doesn't he drive a colossal ball, that chap!"

"Smites it, I think, is the word," Pernaby said. "And yet, you know, he's got the daintiest touch of any man I've ever seen. He's the loveliest billiards' player. A marvellous shot with a revolver, too—so they tell me."

"Really?" said the interested Travers.

"Only what I've heard," went on Pernaby. "I know he's got a collection of cups and things he's won." He held out his hand. "I'm taking my clubs with me. Playing with a man at Edensthorpe this afternoon. Some other time, perhaps, you'll give me another game."

Travers treated himself to a short drink, then sat on the loggia to watch the approach of Bernice's four. They had reached the sixteenth, and Bernice's side had evidently won the last hole, for Bernice, or some one in a red jumper remarkably like hers, was driving off first.

"Here you are then."

Travers gave a little startled jump, for Feen and Wharton had come unheard round the corner and were at his elbow.

"Damn you both and your pussy-footing!" Travers said. "You nearly scared the life out of me. What about a drink?"

"Can't stay a minute," Feen said. "I thought you were here somewhere, so we came round just in case."

"I've just had a game with Pernaby," Travers said. "Picked up a bit of information, by the way. I don't know what good it's going to be to you, but Strongman's a crack revolver shot. He's won cups and things."

To his amazement Feen received the information with even more of a casual indifference than Pernaby had given it.

"What we thought you ought to know was this," he said. "Reeper got hold of it this morning purely by chance. His uncle's the local Registrar, and he happened to look in on him at the Register Office this morning. What do you think he discovered? Just nosing round instinctively, and there were a couple of names he knew. Bob Quench and Molly Pernaby!"

"Married?"

"Not yet," Feen said with a shake of the head.

"That wouldn't suit our ideas nearly as well. What it is, is a notice of the intended marriage which has to be more or less publicly displayed. And handed in and the fees paid—when do you think?" Travers shook his head.

"Last *Monday morning!* You get the idea?"

"The first available moment after the discovery of the murder," said Travers reflectively.

"Exactly!" chimed in Wharton. "And you see the point? As a wife, she can't he forced to give evidence against her husband."

# CHAPTER XII
# NEARING THE END

AT SIX O'CLOCK that evening Bernice was giving the usual sigh of relief.

"That's all settled," she said, and hung up the receiver.

"Good," said her husband, who had thought it just as well to dissociate himself entirely from the proceedings.

"I told you Grace Pernaby couldn't come, didn't I?" Bernice said. "I'm rather relieved in a way, because I don't know her so well as the others, but everybody else is all right. It's a very good picture, so they tell me, and they've none of them seen it. You heard me just asking the manager if the seats were good, and he said they were the best in the house. Awfully lucky, wasn't it, getting the whole six together?"

"Six?" said Travers, with a sudden apprehension.

"But of course, darling. Can't you count? Mrs. Strongman and Molly, and Laura Feen, and we three."

"Oh, my hat!" said Travers. "I didn't know you were counting me in."

Bernice laughed at an idea so deliciously preposterous as leaving him out. Travers, presented with the *fait accompli*, had merely the consolation of possessing yet a little more knowledge of what marriage was likely to involve.

Feen and Wharton turned up after dinner, and they were looking rather less despondent,

"Enjoying your holiday?" Bernice asked Wharton. Wharton was gloomy at once "Holiday! I oughtn't to be here at all. I come down here for a day or two's rest and before I know where I am, I'm kidnapped."

"But when are you really going, George?" Travers said.

"Monday's my latest," Wharton announced belligerently.

"Make it Tuesday," Travers said. "We're leaving on Tuesday morning."

Wharton shook a dour head. "Of course he'll stay till Tuesday," Bernice said, guessing that Ludo had something important in mind.

"Well?" said Travers when the men were left to themselves.

"Not too well," Feen said. "I told you that we didn't get any change out of Mrs. Strongman, didn't I?"

"You did, but you didn't give me any details."

Feen told him just what had happened. As he and Wharton drove up, Strongman was crossing the road to that private entry of his to the course, which was lucky. The two waited down the road for a minute or two till he was well on the way, and then called on Mrs. Strongman, who also was just off to golf. Feen spun the old yarn about seeing Brewse when she was out on the Saturday afternoon.

"Out?" she said. "But I wasn't out!"

Wharton looked suitably staggered and said that surely their witness hadn't been deceived.

"We'll soon settle that," she said indignantly and rang the bell for the parlour-maid. Wharton and Feen were all apologies when it was confirmed that Mrs. Strongman had been in full view as it were from soon after three till well after four o'clock.

"We mightn't have looked a couple of fools," Feen said, "but we felt a couple when we left the lady. George tried to placate her by admiring the garden but she nearly bit his head off. After that we made inquiries at Ammony's garage, and got the names of three people who'd been identified as using the road between Pettistone and Edensthorpe during the three to four hour on the Saturday afternoon. We saw the lot and not one had seen anything of a pedestrian in a black beard and wearing a green felt hat. The last chap we interviewed was at Limehurst. When we got back to Pettistone we saw Reeper who'd just brought old Quench's ladder back. By the way, our expert found traces of paint on it, but more about that in a minute. That was when Reeper told me about his discovery at the Register Office."

"And when you two left me, where did you go?"

"We went after Bob Quench," Feen said. "Called at his garage here on our way to lunch and found him out and so left a message for him to come round to my place and give me the exchange value of my car. Perfectly genuine, that, by the way. What time was it when he turned up, George?"

"Just after five," Wharton said, and nodded so grimly that Travers had an idea he was egg-bound with ideas.

"That's right," Feen said. "We did the car business and then I mentioned people who'd been using the road on the Saturday afternoon. I said I knew he'd been overhauling his own car in his father's garage but had he by any chance tried her out on the road afterwards, because, if he had, then he might have seen somebody, too. He said he and Gordon started her up in the garage but didn't take her out. The first time they took her out was on the Sunday morning. You remember, when they drove down ostensibly to see the scene of the fire."

Travers nodded.

"Then I added, as an afterthought, that if he'd excuse my butting into his business, I'd like to congratulate him. He looked surprised at first and then I told him what I'd found out by accident and how I was proposing to keep it a secret, if he wished. His face simply flared, didn't it, George?"

"Red as a tomato," Wharton said. "And I could see his mind working. Racing over, it was, like the engine of a baby car."

"He had plenty of good reasons for getting married though," Feen went on. "Apparently things are always in a state of muddle at the vicarage and the maids play old Quench up. Molly will keep things in order."

"They're going to live there?"

"That's apparently the idea. Old Quench doesn't know it yet but I gather he'll be amenable. Still, that was that, and then I suddenly told Bob that traces of yellow and black paints had been discovered on his father's ladder. Do you know he didn't turn a hair? Merely looked politely surprised. All he said was that he wasn't responsible for Gordon's actions and that Gordon knew where the ladder was and would have been quite capable of helping himself to it. Not that he'd admit any knowledge of Gordon's having done so."

"That Gordon Strongman is a young fellow I'd like to clap eyes on," Wharton said. "I'm not so sure he did the painting. I'm beginning to think he was in the other matter a damn' sight more deeply than we've thought. People don't go bolting back to Africa because they've disfigured some one's property. And he paid twenty-five quid damages before he went, didn't he?"

"But we've got to prove that," Feen reminded him.

"Well, you get on with the proving and I'll get on with my idea," Wharton said. "I'm open to bet that those three young people—young Strongman, Bob Quench and Molly Pernaby—will stand a damn' sight more investigation than they've had up to the present."

"Let's hope you're right," Feen said. "And talking of Molly, she'll have to be at Monday's inquest. I made no definite promise to let her off, and if you two fellows are going away, it won't concern you."

"Why do you want her there?" asked Travers.

"Merely to make her statement about seeing Brewse It'll be reported at length in all the Press—I'll see to that—and then some one may come forward and corroborate and help to fit in the times. Some one may even have seen Brewse."

"It should start the ball rolling again," Travers said hopefully. "The soil in Ammony's garden disturbed, by the way?"

"Devil a bit," Feen said. "Nothing's happening at Pettistone at all. Never a soul who saw Brewse that Saturday afternoon, and no clue to anything. But we're still not down and out ourselves, are we, George."

"Not by a damn' sight," Wharton said grimly. His look shifted to Travers. "What's gone wrong with you the last day or two? Brain gone back on you?"

Travers smiled. "When I theorize, as you call it, you simply cackle with laughter, and when I bust people's alibis, all you and Feen do is stick them together again with cement."

"No stamina, that's what's the matter with you," Wharton told him. "You do a little thinking about those three young fly-by-nights I was talking about."

"Thanks," said Travers. "Perhaps I will."

That night, in his last waking minutes, Travers did let his thoughts dwell on Bob Quench and Molly Pernaby, and particularly on Molly Pernaby. There was one essential fact, as he soon was knowing, that had somewhat escaped his notice. Gordon Strongman, the last in that triumvirate of the Pettistone Bright Young People, had bolted—and there seemed no other word for it. Had he bolted to avoid trouble over the painting, or was it—as Wharton had said—because he was avoiding all questioning over the major affair? Was there, in fact, something he knew? Did a strong sense of loyalty to Bob Quench make him take that way out?

Travers's thoughts ran on. That car overhauling in the garage might have been a fake. Bob Quench and Gordon Strongman might have arranged it deliberately, so that Bob, with impunity, could meet Brewse, whom he had inveigled down the Edensthorpe Road. There had been a scheme, perhaps, of frightening him with a revolver, and making him promise to repay. The man could afford to buy a house, the two would have argued and therefore he could afford to hand back something of what he stole. Then Bob came back to the garage to say there had been an accident and Brewse had been shot.

Then late on the Monday afternoon Molly told Bob that she had just given information that she had seen Brewse. Bob was in a panic at once. There was danger in every possible word she might say, and then he saw the way out. Perhaps a Register Office marriage had been talked of before, but at any rate, that same evening, just before the office closed, Bob was there to give the notice of marriage.

Other confirmatory facts began to crowd in on his thoughts. As Bob had said, marriage at Pettistone was surely the last thing Molly Pernaby would want, and she would have been easy enough to persuade. There had been that Sunday morning visit by Bob Quench and Gordon to the scene of the fire, and there had been that afternoon on the practice course when Bob had definitely sent Molly over to make various subtle inquiries. There had been that curtly annoying manner of hers to Feen when he had questioned her and Bob that recent morning during their round.

Travers, in fact, was fairly sure at last that though Wharton and Feen might at the moment be no more than hopeful, yet Bob Quench was probably their man. Then suddenly the pleasure of the thought of Feen's success brought him nearer to sleep. The thoughts shifted drowsily and, with anticipation of the morrow, he remembered Joy and how he would be meeting her at midday at the station.

When Travers next stirred in his bed and opened his eyes, the sun was shining through the window, and almost at once the maid was bringing in the early cup of tea. Then Travers, hastily putting on his spectacles, was hooking them off again, and blinking away in the morning light. The last thoughts of the night had returned to his mind, and with their remembering had come an idea. A mad idea, but full of promise. Bernice must never know a thing about it, but it was something that Joy would surely revel in, and if there was one person in the world who could carry it through, it was she.

In view of Joy's arrival, the Traverses were to spend a domestic morning. Bernice announced that she had a hundred things to do, if she were to be ready for the station by noon. Travers, to come round in half an hour. Which gave him leisure to write a few notes.

"You're looking a bit more intelligent this morning," Wharton said, himself in more cheerful vein. "Got any ideas about what I told you?"

"I may have a few to fit in with you own," Travers told him.

Wharton grunted. "Well, we've got some news for you. You-know-who agreed with the medical evidence. Brewse was dead before four o'clock, and that's that."

Travers had to smile at yet another of Wharton's changes of front, and his little tricks of concealment. Even Feen must be aware that You-know-who was a camouflage for Sir Barnabas Craig.

"Did he set any limits?"

"No," said Wharton contemplatively. "He hinted that if he was most certainly dead before four o'clock, then he was most likely killed at a quarter to. That's how both Feen and I read it."

Travers's fingers were at his glasses. "Doesn't that kybosh all Molly Pernaby's times?"

Wharton shrugged his shoulders and his air was one of much injured innocence. "Well, since you mention the fact, it does rather look as if the old hand wasn't so far out after all. Facts are facts, and Molly didn't see Brewse at all. She saw some one else: some man wearing a green felt hat—Brewse's own hat—and a false beard."

Travers couldn't forbear a dig. "But you said that theory was fantastic!"

Wharton peered at him over the tops of the antiquated spectacles, then peered at Feen.

"Fantastic? Suppose it is. What's that got to do with it?" He grunted, then his voice took on a dove-like coo. "Still, perhaps it doesn't sound the kind of thing you'd expect from me, but when I'm up against miracles, I'm liable to run a bit off the rails. Not that there's any miracle about it when you come to work it out. What I say is that X, who killed Brewse, had come prepared with a false beard. He killed Brewse where he was found, then put on the beard and Brewse's hat. Now do you begin to see it? As *Brewse,* he was off to let Brewse be seen somewhere else. In other words, he was going to fake an alibi. Then something went wrong, and it was this."

Wharton paused to bring his chair forward, and his finger wagged impressively.

"Shall I tell you what went wrong?" Travers cut suddenly in.

The wagging finger dropped. Wharton's smile had something startling in its politeness.

"I should think this is what went wrong," Travers said, "and I'll mention names. Bob Quench killed Brewse while Gordon Strongman faked the alibi in the vicarage garage. He didn't know Bob had killed Brewse. All he knew was that a disguised Bob was to meet Brewse and hold him up with the gun and get some promise of restitution out of him, and Gordon was tinkering with the car, ready, if necessary, to swear Bob was there too. But something went wrong and Bob shot Brewse. After the first panic had gone he had some idea of creating for himself a new and perfect alibi—just how, can be worked out by you two people—and so he put on Brewse's hat and stepped warily out to the road. He was Brewse's precise build, if you remember, and his height. The road was clear and he decided to walk back to Pettistone to fake the alibi there.

"Then what went wrong is that suddenly Molly Pernaby's car was heard and as he turned it came snarling round the corner from Edensthorpe. Somehow the idea came to disguise his original intention, so he turned *towards* Edensthorpe and began walking that way. As Molly passed he caught her eye and he was sure she had recognized him through his disguise. No sooner had she disappeared round the next, bend than he was darting back into the wood again, and he was once more in a panic.

"A few moments and he saw a way out. He had re-entered the wood some short distance away from Brewse's body and he didn't feel like going back to it, so he dropped the hat where he was, which was where you found it, Colonel. I should say he had a bicycle hidden somewhere handy, too, and as himself—no false beard that is—he cycled off like blazes to the vicarage garage and Gordon Strongman."

"My God! it fits in," Wharton said triumphantly. "What we've got to do, Feen, is to see all those road-users again and ask if they met or overtook a cyclist." He shook his head. "Bob Quench would have disguised himself in some way, even as a cyclist. He wouldn't dare to be seen. Still, that can all be worked out later. What do you think happened next, Mr. Travers?"

"Probably this," said Travers promptly. "Gordon told Bob that Molly had looked in and had been surprised at not finding him there, but Gordon had told her Bob had gone to the house for something or other. Then Bob told Gordon what had happened."

And then Travers whipped off his glasses and began polishing them, but it was not because he was at a loss, and as he blinked away in the sunny garden, he was trying to arrange in some logical order, the sudden swirl of thoughts.

"Jot these ideas down in your note-book, George," he said, "in case any of them escape me. Number them as you go:

"1. Bob knew his garage alibi was broken if Molly divulged that he was not there when she looked in.

"2. That was the real reason for the quickly arranged marriage.

"3. Bob and Gordon talked the situation over. Bob paraffined the shed and spoke, as Brewse, to his father over the 'phone, and Gordon removed the body and did the rest.

"4. Bob and Molly did the painting at Gables.

"5. In order to avoid the consequences of that painting, Molly had to lie like blazes. She was forced to lie about Gordon being in the Pernaby garden till eight o'clock.

"6. Molly told Bob nothing about seeing Brewse till after the murder news got out. Sunday afternoon, shall we say. Since Gordon was backing his garage alibi he didn't mind at all when she came to you, Colonel, with her news about seeing Brewse. It suited his alibi perfectly.

"7. And finally, Gordon Strongman bolted back to the Sudan to avoid all questioning by the police."

Wharton wrote the last word, gave a final peer, then closed the book with a triumphant snap.

"Well, not a bad bit of work, even if I was the one that put it in your mind. But you're not going?"

Travers reminded him of Joy's arrival.

"Well, if I don't put in an appearance for a day or so, you'll know what I'm up to," Wharton said, and rapped that note-book significantly with his knuckles. Then he gave Feen a dig in the ribs. "You and I are going to be busy for a bit."

Feen smiled hopefully.

"Mind you, it's all theory," Travers felt bound to point out. "It's up to you people to find the flaws."

"Don't you worry about us," Wharton told him. "You get away home and forget about everything. Feen and I'll have this case ended long before Tuesday, or my name's Higgins."

Joy Haire resembled Molly Pernaby to the extent that she was of the type turned out in hundreds since the War by the most expensive of our schools, but whereas Molly was blunt and off-hand, Joy was embarrassingly alert, and always something of the *gamine*.

"There you are, darlings!" she called from quite two carriages away from where Bernice and her husband were standing, and no sooner did she spring out of the compartment than Ludovic was being publicly embraced.

"Lovely to see you both," she said. "And you're looking so well."

"Why the surprise?" asked Travers dryly. "Bernice, I think we're going to find that young sister of yours rather an embarrassment."

Travers had to laugh, the imitation of himself had been so perfect. Bernice, not nearly so amused, was all at once fussing over luggage.

"Have you got any particular nickname?" Travers asked Joy when the car was on the move.

"Not nowadays," she said. "At school they used to call me 'Tish'." She explained. "My auburn hair, which is the Titian colour, I believe. Hence Titian, and so to Tish."

"That's what you'll be called here," Travers told her, and mentioned Bernice's apprehensions about the discovery of her name, and thus to the newly married status.

"I don't mind," she said. "I think it will be rather jolly to be called Tish again."

Bernice mentioned the afternoon's party.

"I do hope you'll be discreet, darling. Everybody here has been so kind and charming that I'd like them to think the best of us."

Joy nudged Ludo.

"If you mean I'm not to give impressions of any of them, I haven't the faintest intention. Or do you mean that you'd like me to give some very charming impressions, and that's why you've asked me down here?"

"Since you asked yourself, the latter question hardly arises," Travers told her.

But he was very fond of his young sister-in-law, and he was more than ever sure she would fall in with his plan. So it was he who mentioned at lunch the local excitement there had been about the murder. Joy said she had seen it in the papers and was excited to hear that two of the afternoon's visitors came from Pettistone. Travers said the murder had better not be mentioned, and then proceeded to give a quick and none too serious résumé of what the public knew.

It was not till almost the last minute that he managed a word with Joy alone, when Bernice was still upstairs dressing.

"I'd like to explain about that Tish business," he said. "It was my idea really, though Bernice thinks it's hers. The point is that nobody must guess you're Joy Haire."

She smiled. "Didn't you tell me all that?"

"Not quite all," he said. "I've got a job of work for you to do, and even Bernice mustn't know about it. Nobody must ever know a word about it. Remember how I told you quite a lot about a girl called Molly Pernaby, who's coming to tea? I rather think you and she will get on well together, and I'm most earnestly hoping so. I'm contriving, by the way, to let you sit together at the cinema. In fact, I want you to make a study of her, to get clean under her skin."

"Why?"

"I'll tell you later. Her mannerisms don't really matter. It's her voice I want, and it's got to deceive the very elect. Later on this evening I'll make an opportunity to try you out, and Bernice will be our judge, though she won't know it. But we've got to have Molly Pernaby better than anybody you've ever done in your life."

He had spoken with such a quiet earnestness that she was looking genuinely alarmed.

"Is it something to do with that murder?"

"Yes," he said slowly, "it is. It may make all the difference to somebody's life."

"But you're frightening me."

He smiled. "Nothing to be frightened about. You do your stuff, as they say. And you will, won't you?"

"All right," she said. "I'll try."

Laura Feen arrived first, and within a minute Mrs. Strongman's car appeared. Molly Pernaby had come with her. Joy was introduced as Bernice's sister.

"Usually known as Tish," said Travers flippantly.

"Haven't I seen you somewhere?" Molly Pernaby said.

They compared schools, but Molly said it was fairly recently that she knew she had seen Joy or some one like her. Travers cut in by asking about Aunt Grace. Molly said she was feeling heaps better, and in a week's time was going for a holiday. Which, thought Travers, would be after the wedding.

Small talk ended with the announcement of tea. Then to kill the hour that remained, came a putting competition on the lawn—Travers's contribution to the festivities.

"But what a lot of prizes!" Mrs. Strongman said, beaming at the boxes of chocolate that Travers had provided.

"I think the only sort of competition that ought to be allowed is where everybody gets a prize," he said, and lent Molly his putter to be shared with Joy.

Then to the cinema where Joy and Molly sat at the end, with Travers next, then Mrs. Strongman, and Bernice and Mrs. Feen. Everybody voted the picture delightful, and then came another surprise. In a private room at a smart local restaurant was a light supper for the whole party.

"That was a perfectly lovely evening, Ludo," Joy said. "Everybody was simply thrilled."

"Sure?"

"Of course. Everything was just wonderful and I think Bernice has married a wonder."

Bernice laughed and said Joy said the queerest things.

"Not queer, but apt," said Travers. "You and Molly Pernaby seemed to get along well together, Joy?"

"Didn't we," she said, waiting for the lead.

"What was the idea? Studying her for an impression?"

"Maybe."

"Bet you a new hat you couldn't do her. Close your eyes, Bernice, and see if you're listening to Molly Pernaby."

A little cough and Joy was off.

"I simply love shocking people, not that I intend to—don't you? The other day I walked into the women's club-house and there were two of the frightfullest old hags and a girl called Davidson who was down on holiday, so I called right across the room: 'Hallo, Jean'—that was her name—'Hallo, Jean. Bob says you're a bloody marvel.' My God! you ought to have seen their faces."

Travers laughed like blazes. Bernice pretended to be the least bit shocked.

"But wasn't it Molly Pernaby?" Travers asked her.

"It was very good," Bernice said. "Very good indeed. I'd almost have thought she was in the room."

"Try a more serious vein," Travers said. "Take her when she was talking to me."

"That's going to be harder," Joy said, but had a shot at it.

"Of course I don't get much time for reading, Mr. Travers, but I used to simply love it. I think books are so marvellous, how people think of things, and write them all down; don't you think it is? You really think I could write a book about golf? Oh, but you're pulling my leg. I simply write the foulest of stuff, and the most poisonous handwriting."

"Good," said Travers. "Very excellent, good. What did you think, Bernice?"

"I didn't think it was quite so good as the other. It didn't seem so much like Molly." Just before bedtime Joy managed to whisper. "Was it really all right?"

Travers shook his head. "Magnificent, but not just quite good enough. There was still just a little bit of yourself."

"You mean I've let you down?"

""Not a bit of it," he told her. "By this time to-morrow you'll really be Molly Pernaby, or, as George Wharton says, my name's Higgins."

# CHAPTER XIII
# THE GREAT EXPERIMENT

Bernice had told her Pettistone guests that she might be seeing them again, which was why her husband took it for granted that the family would be going to church. Bernice said that what she had been thinking of was a final round of golf in the afternoon, but she would certainly like church as well.

Quench had exchanged pulpits with a local man, and the congregation was larger than that of the week before. On that last Sunday morning, too, Travers had no need of any subterfuges, for the Strongmans hastened to overtake the Travers party as soon as service was over, and the Pernabys caught up with them at the wicket gate.

Travers said they would all walk a short way towards the golf course for exercise. Then the good-byes were said, though Bernice did mention that final round for the afternoon.

"Everybody will be sound asleep by then," Molly said. "Pettistone simply gorges at Sunday lunch, and it's always on roast beef."

"Well, there are worse crimes," said Travers. "And talking of crimes, I hope by the time we're down here again, all that Brewse business will be over and done with."

There was a little silence, as if he had dropped some sort of a brick. Then Grace Pernaby remarked that she hoped it was true that the Traverses *were* coming down again.

Joy's golf was far too bad for public exhibition, but she said there was nothing she would like better than walking round. The three arrived early to avoid the after-lunch rush, and it was about half-past three when they came up the rise at the thirteenth and were in sight of the club-house again. Travers had bet himself a new hat that Molly Pernaby would put in an appearance sometime that afternoon, and, sure enough, he caught sight of her coming through that opening in the woody fringe that led from her house to the course. The Strongmans had a similar private entrance, he remembered, and a remarkably handy entrance it was if a man wanted to practise with a club or two for a spare half-hour.

Molly waved a cheery hand as she came across the twelfth fairway, and she paired off with Joy at once.

"Well, had your gorge and your nap?" asked Travers.

Molly said nothing, but she had become sufficiently friendly to make a face.

"You're not to watch while I make a stroke," Bernice said. "I'm feeling frightfully nervous already."

So Joy and Molly prattled at a discreet distance, and it was only when the club-house was reached that Molly announced why she had turned up at all. Aunt Grace insisted, and Molly identified herself with the insistence, that the Travers party should come in to tea on their way back, instead of having it at the club-house.

"I waited till I could see you all from my bedroom window," she said, "and then I came across."

Bernice and Travers looked at each other and Travers gave a quick frown.

"We're most frightfully sorry," Bernice said, "but we weren't going to have tea anywhere, except a quick cup at home. We're due out again almost at once."

"I told Aunt Grace you wouldn't be able to come," Molly said. "But you'll call up and say good-bye. I might as well have a lift, too."

So the Traverses said good-bye once more to all the Pernabys, and just as they were going, Mrs. Strongman and her husband strolled along. They had caught sight of the party and had come to say another good-bye, too.

Bernice sighed when the car turned right from the little village into the Edensthorpe Road.

"I almost wish we weren't going away after all. It's been so lovely here."

Bernice had promised to see Laura Feen that early evening on some matter or other, which gave Joy an opportunity for a private talk with her brother-in-law.

"Ludo, can't you tell me what's behind whatever it is you want me to do?"

"I don't know that I can—altogether," he said.

"Is it going to do Molly Pernaby any harm?"

He smiled. "Why do you ask that?"

"Well, just because I like her. I think she's a real good sort, and as genuine as can be."

"Perhaps I do, too."

She looked surprised. "Oh, but I thought you were thinking she had something to do with the murder."

He shook his head. "You'll have to trust me. But may I put it this way, in the very strictest confidence. Suppose—and it's no more than suppose —she was likely to marry a man who had committed the murder. Wouldn't you like to do something to stop it?"

"Yes," she said. "I would."

"Then I'll tell you no more. I oughtn't to have told you even that—though it's only suppose. And now about what I'd like you to do, so that you can try it out by yourself. It's going to be rather like playing chess, in the sense that your answers will have to be in accordance with what you hear over the 'phone. But here's what I've written down to begin with, and you'll see I've left out names till the morning. We shall go along to a local telephone box and you'll go in and do everything by yourself, in case I embarrass you."

*Question.* "Is that you,—?"
*Probable Answer.* "Yes, it's me."
*Continuo.* "Listen,—. The most terrible thing has happened. Everything's been found out."
"What do you mean?"
"What I say. The police have found out everything."

Joy read it through twice, and was still frowning. "You must take it that what it means is this," Travers said. "Out of a sense of loyalty, she may be shielding somebody who isn't worth shielding. If she isn't, then no harm's done, and she and the man will share a mystery till the end of their days. Neither can by any conceivable chance ever know who it was that rang him up and spoke like her,"

Joy nodded. "And what do I say next?"

"Nothing at all," he told her. "You'll be able to judge by his answer whether or not he's guilty, and that's all I want to know. If he gives any other information, listen but don't say a word beyond yes and no, and then hang up quietly so as to make him think the 'phone's out of order."

"And if he's guilty, will it mean staying on here?"

He shook his head. "It won't make any difference whatever. This is an experiment that hasn't anything to do with the law. Something for my private satisfaction if you like to think of it that way."

"And on behalf of Molly Pernaby?"

He smiled, perfectly content to leave that much understood. "Like to hear a try-out?"

He shook his head again. "No need for it. Last night you were as near right as made no difference. To-morrow morning you'll really be Molly Pernaby."

Breakfast was at eight that Monday morning, but Travers was in no hurry to move till half an hour later, for he had ascertained that Bob was never at the Edensthorpe garage till just about that time.

Bernice had just begun the preliminary packing up when he and Joy slipped away to the garage and the car.

"It's only a minute from here to the kiosk," Travers said, "and I'll get the tank filled and so on while you're doing your act."

"I'm terribly nervous," she said. "Just look at my hand. It's shaking like a leaf."

He laughed. "Tell that to the Marines. You, nervous! What about facing an audience of thousands and never batting an eyelid?"

"But this is different," she said. "It's like broadcasting and speaking into the microphone. When I broadcast in America for the first time, I thought that every minute I'd flop on the floor."

His face fell, then all at once he was chuckling.

"The very best thing in the world. Don't you see? You've got to sound nervous. You've got to sound scared to death! When you get inside that kiosk, you won't have any need to act."

Just short of the kiosk he drew the car up.

"The system's automatic, just like town. The number you want is 212, which you can't forget, or if you like I'll jot it down for you. The man you're speaking to—and keep this as secret as the grave for the rest of your life—is Bob. That's all you need to know. When the garage answers you, you ask if Bob is there. If he says, 'Speaking,' then you'll give a nervous titter and show surprise. After that, straight on."

A quick rehearsal, and she was ready.

"Good luck," he said, "and don't forget that old adage—when in doubt, ring off. Wait for me afterwards over there, at the corner."

As a matter of fact it was he who was the bundle of nerves, and while the car was being serviced, his fingers were most of the time hovering near his glasses. When at last he came round the bend and saw Joy waiting, his heart began to thump violently beneath his ribs. But he did manage a smile

"Well, how'd things go?"

"Something went badly wrong," she said.

He drew the car in at the kerb again, and halted. "How do you mean?"

"Well"—she frowned—"I couldn't understand what was happening, so I rang off."

He nodded. "I see. But tell me just what did happen. Give me the exact words if you can."

"Well, a voice said, 'Hallo,' and I said, 'May I speak to Bob, please?' and the voice said, 'Right-o, miss, I'll fetch him.' "

"Good," said Travers. "That showed they knew you were Molly Pernaby. I guessed she'd refer to him as Bob. And what happened then?"

"Well, another voice said, 'Hallo,' very quickly, and I said, 'Is that you, Bob?' and Bob said, 'Of course it's me. What on earth are you doing?' I said, 'Listen, Bob, I've got to speak to you. The most ghastly thing has happened.' He said, just like this, 'What d'you mean?' I said, 'Just what I say. The police have found out everything!' His answer was as quick as lightning. 'What do you mean? About your mother?'"

*"About your mother?"* Travers stared. "The police have found out about your mother? That doesn't make sense."

"My dear, it didn't make sense to me," she said. "But that wasn't what scared me and made me ring off. All at once he was saying this and I'll try to give you his exact tone. 'But I say, what is all this? How could you have found anything out since I saw you?'"

"Oh, my hat, yes!" Travers smiled feebly and his fingers went to his glasses. "He must have seen her this morning, just before he left for the garage."

"Then it's all been for nothing?"

Travers was still smiling feebly as he moved the car on.

"Yes. I think the mountain's been in labour and has produced a remarkably miscroscopic mouse." He gave a Whartonian grunt. "Perhaps I ought to have said, a dead cat."

"But what was that about her mother?"

"Don't know exactly," he said. "She's an orphan, so I've understood, and presumably the mother's dead. Wait a moment, though." Then he was shaking his head again. "Still, even if that's right, I'd rather not think it."

"Think what?"

He smiled. "Well, I suppose you're entitled to your pound of flesh. I was thinking this. Suppose Molly were an illegitimate child. She's thinking of getting married. Well, wouldn't that make complications in the statement of parentage which has to be made?" Another Whartonian grunt. "As a matter of fact, the statement has been made, and that's why the Bob man is very alarmed. He thinks the police have discovered that she's committed perjury."

But he was thinking something else, too. The 'phone might have been indistinct, and Joy might have heard some other word than *mother*. She had had no chance of asking Bob to repeat, and the word might have been anything—bother, for instance, or even *murder!* But when he contrived another quick talk to Joy she was insistent. Mother, had been the word. What Bob had said had virtually been: "So the police have discovered all about your mother."

A minute or two later Travers was ringing Feen to hear the latest news. Feen said Wharton was already at Pettistone ferreting out heaven knew what in his own way.

"Any progress along the lines we discussed?" Travers said.

"The Three Young People?" Feen said guardedly. "If so, we haven't got very far. Wharton and I saw Strongman and practically got him to admit that his boy had been mixed up in the painting affair. If so, it doesn't look as if he was doing you know what."

"Surely a question of re-arrangements," Travers said. "Three people, so to speak, and there's no telling who did what."

"Talking of that," Feen said. "I've just had a bit of a facer. Miss Pernaby has just rung up to say Molly can't be at the inquest this morning. A bad bilious attack, and a doctor's certificate is coming along at once."

"Sounds rather—well, very apposite, don't you think?"

"That's what Wharton said," Feen told him. Travers replaced the receiver feeling very much of a fool. That experiment with Joy had been carried out too precipitately, and no wonder Bob Quench had been surprised. Probably he had seen Molly that morning before leaving for Edensthorpe, and yet apparently within a few minutes of that she was ringing him and saying the police had discovered everything.

And then Travers was all at once beginning to think. Bob *had* seen Molly. That much was evident from the brief 'phone conversation. Had Bob arranged for Molly not to appear at the inquest, and was that what they had been talking over? A bilious attack, thought Travers. Maybe, and maybe not. Molly Pernaby would make no bones at all about swallowing an emetic, and if she set her mind to it she could hoodwink any doctor in the district. A fake bilious attack, that was it, and designed so that she should not answer under oath at the inquest any question that might incriminate Bob Quench.

No wonder Wharton was at Pettistone, thought Travers, and no wonder Feen had sounded quite hopeful over the 'phone. At any moment some vital connecting link might be discovered and that intricate net of lies that had been fabricated by those three young fools would collapse like the flimsy thing it really was.

Joy came down and was told about Molly.

"I've just heard she's down with a bilious attack," he said. "Probably the result of that Sunday gorge. The devil of it is that

Bob almost certainly saw her a few minutes before a certain party 'phoned him."

"Well, it's your funeral," Joy said. "I only carried out orders."

"I know," he said. "And all you and I are going to do now is forget all about everything. It never happened at all. Isn't that so?"

Joy's nod and her smile were as grave as his own, and then, as
soon as she had gone again, Travers began thinking once more
about Molly Pernaby. That she had had a hand in the murder
was something he altogether refused to credit, and yet, now he
came to think back, Molly Pernaby had kept bobbing up like a
cork throughout the whole of that murder inquiry. In some ways
she had been the most prominent person in it, and the more the
fact struck him, the more he became intrigued by the Pernabys
generally. Had Grace Pernaby been aware of what Molly knew,
and was that why she had been overcome by faintness at that
first public mention of the murder? Bernice had said much the
same things about Grace as Feen had said about Arthur, that
there was something somewhere at which you never seemed to
arrive, and a feeling of concealment that went beyond ordinary
reticence.

Travers, in fact, was almost inclined to credit his own scan-
dalous solution of those words that Bob Quench had uttered
over the 'phone—that there was some mystery about Molly's
parentage which constituted the secret the Pernabys were holding so close. Then there was that question of Arthur Pernaby's
native county.

If there was one thing that could nag at him like an aching
tooth, it was an unsolved mystery, whether that mystery were
the simple forgetting of some name he ought to have remembered, or some major mystery or problem in detection. Now, as
he began to think over that question of Pernaby's accent, and
those mysterious words of Bob Quench's over the 'phone, he
was prowling restlessly about the garden. Then all at once he
halted, fingers at his glasses.

But it was not some sudden revelation that had given him
pause. What he all at once knew was the nearness of his own
departure from Edensthorpe, and how little he had really done

and how vitally much remained to do. At that moment he knew he would have given some incalculable all, if only Feen could succeed in getting his man.

And within the wider scope of that urge, was the smaller nagging one, insisting, as it were, that he should follow up that heaven-sent information that Bob Quench had given over the 'phone and begin some lightning inquiry into the Pernabys, and Molly in particular. His fingers went to his glasses at that, and then all at once he was making for the house and fairly sprinting up the stairs to Bernice.

"My dear, I'm going to surprise you," he said. "I've got a job of work to do and I simply have to be away all day."

"But, darling, why not?" she said. "You know if it's important."

"It is," he said. "At least, I'm beginning to think it is. I may be home frightfully late, by the way, but I'll certainly be home to-night."

Within ten minutes the Rolls was heading east, for what he had thought was this. The Pernabys had never divulged the exact place from which they had come, but had described it vaguely as up north, and Feen had thought it to be Northumberland. Pernaby's own accent and intonation, Travers was sure, had definitely possessed an East Anglian quality, and when more or less cornered by the embarrassing questions of Travers himself, Pernaby had accounted for the fact by mentioning a Suffolk aunt. But, as Travers was well aware, a few years in very early boyhood affect speech little compared with the extent to which it is influenced from the age of puberty onwards. If, therefore, Pernaby had had something to conceal and had been more or less forced to mention Suffolk, he had done so with the deliberate intention of concealing the fact that his real county was not Suffolk but Norfolk.

Which was Travers's own opinion. Pernaby's speech had nothing of that singing intonation which is the Suffolk mark. His had the curt and clipped and more blurting features that betrayed the neighbouring county. In any case, Travers proposed to try Norfolk, and to consult such old telephone directories as were available at the District Headquarters of the Telephone Service.

But since he had asked no help or credentials from Feen, but was making the matter a purely personal one, he was anticipating difficulty. Yet none arose. When at last he arrived at Norwich and said he was most anxious to obtain copies of old directories for the years 1930 to 1933, he was provided with them at once, and had nothing to do but pay.

It was long after lunch time and he took his purchases to the hotel where he had left his car, and over his meal he went most carefully through all the P's, and for every district covered. Never a Pernaby appeared. Then he went through the names again, and felt like a crossword solver who knows a word must be right but cannot find that word in any dictionary.

Then he made inquiries of the waiter, and the inquiries must have been audible to a man who was sitting at a nearby table, for he came over with apologies and asked if he could be of any help. But he knew nobody of the name of Pernaby.

"What sort of a man is he?" he said.

"Tall, raw-boned and in the early fifties," Travers said. "He may be even fifty-five or six. He's still a very fine golfer."

"Sure he used to live in Norfolk?"

"Reasonably."

"Then if he was a good golfer, why not call at the *Eastern Daily Press* and see one of their men on the sports' side?"

Travers called himself several kinds of a fool, and went off to the newspaper office, where he was put on to a man who might help.

"Pernaby?" he said, and shook his head. "There's no golfer of that name that I know." Then his expression changed. "Wait a minute, though. Was Pernaby part of his name, or his whole name?"

"Might have been either," said Travers hopefully.

"Why I mentioned it was because there was a man called Pernaby Grant who was a very fine golfer. He won our county championship some years ago. What sort of man was he?"

Travers described Arthur Pernaby again, and he certainly seemed likely to be the man. But where he had lived, the informant couldn't remember.

He suggested a visit to the local courses, but Travers had a quicker way, and it worked. Those telephone directories of his gave A. Pernaby-Grant, Peatwold Hall, and a study of the map showed that Peatwold was not too far off the homeward road if one went by Newmarket.

In less than an hour he was down in the southwest corner of the county, with curiosity even more aroused. If Pernaby had dropped that latter half of his name, he had done it for some good reason—the reason perhaps that had led him to leave his county and come to a secluded corner of England a hundred and fifty miles and more away.

In that flat country the church had been visible long before he reached it, and it was from the vicar that he was hopeful of hearing the Pernaby history. Then something made him change his mind. The children were just coming out of the little school, and an elderly man, who could be no one but the schoolmaster, was standing just outside the porch. Travers drew the car up.

"I wonder if you would be so good as to spare me a minute or two of your time," he said. "I was looking for a Mr. Pernaby-Grant who used to be at the Hall here, but they tell me he's gone away."

"He's been gone for some years now," the schoolmaster said. "I don't know where he went to. It was a bit of a mystery, to tell the truth." He nodded reflectively. "I expect it wasn't a mystery really. You couldn't wonder at it, if you think things out."

He seemed the quiet, philosophical type, and Travers thought it best not to hurry him.

"You've been to the Hall?" the schoolmaster was going on.

"Not actually to the Hall," Travers said. "That was his home, wasn't it?"

The other nodded reminiscently. "About three generations I suppose, the Grants had it. Nobody about here used to call them anything but Grant, even when they did take on that name of Pernaby."

He rambled quietly on about the connection that had meant the Pernaby addition, till Travers at last brought him gently back.

"You've known them all for a good many years?"

"Yes," he said. "I was educated in this very school as a boy and I came back to it as headmaster over twenty-five years ago. Another year and I'll be retiring."

"Grants?" He smiled to himself. "There was only Mr. Grant and a regular bachelor type he was, if I may say so. And I don't know that it was much of a surprise after all. Every one was sorry at the time, but I don't see how he could have done anything else."

"You'll pardon me," Travers said. "But just so that you and I shouldn't be talking at cross purposes, what exactly was it that made him leave?"

"I'm talking about that Brewse affair," he said. "Perhaps you don't remember anything about that."

Travers's heart had missed a beat. For a moment he could only shake his head.

"Hanky Brewse," the other was saying. "The one responsible for all those swindles. At least, that's what we always reckoned round here."

Then he was breaking exasperatedly off. A child was telling him that Miss Somebody-or-other wanted to see him. In a couple of minutes he was out again, and he was smiling.

"That assistant of mine was wondering if you were an inspector. I told her even inspectors didn't ride about in Rolls-Royces. And where were we when I left off?"

"You were telling me just why Grant left the village," prompted Travers.

"That's right. He sold up everything and went clean away, and where to nobody knows. That Hanley Brewse came down here once, by the way. I saw him myself, and little did I think how he was going to end up, nor Mr. Clarke, either."

"Clarke!" gaped the astonished Travers.

"He was Mr. Grant's brother-in-law. Didn't you know?"

Travers shook his head.

"I knew the whole family, every one of them," the school-master said. "I remember Miss Grace being born, though I was only a little chap at the time. She married Merrick Clarke, son of the Rev. John Clarke, who was rector of Fenwold."

"I seem to remember things now," frowned Travers. "Wasn't he mixed up in the Brewse affair?"

"Mixed up, if you like," the other said. "We didn't put it that way about here. We always reckoned that he was no more to do with it really than you and me. The judge said as much at the trial—and then sent him to jail."

"Culpable negligence, I expect," Travers said. "And so Grant left here to avoid all the scandal. Well, one can't blame him. By the way, I think I knew the sister Grace. She bore a very strong resemblance to her brother."

"That's right; she did. Those two were always very much alike. I suppose you knew, by the way, that her husband died in jail?"

"I think I do remember it," Travers said. "Any children, were there?"

"Only one—a daughter, and she was born down here, as a matter of fact. Margaret, her name was, but every one knew her as Miss Molly." He smiled. "Very well liked, she was too. Every one said she ought to have been born a boy."

Travers nodded again as Pettistone came vividly back. And he had one last question to ask. "Let me see, Grant was a clean-shaven man, wasn't he?"

The schoolmaster said he was, and that was all that Travers learned, and all indeed that he needed to know. The school-master pointed out the lie of the land, and in ten minutes Travers was out at the turnpike again, and making for New-market, and home.

In the outskirts of Cambridge he stopped for something of a meal, and then drove slowly and deliberately across those long stretches of open road. There was no triumph for the success of what seemed to him no more than the most obvious of deductions. All that had come at first was a kind of bewilderment and now he was feeling the overwhelming need to think.

So Grant had become Pernaby, and Travers could somehow only admire the man for his sacrifice, and how he had given up what must have become dear, and made a new home among strangers. But for his sister's sake, and not his own, though she had been something of a problem. So closely did she resemble himself, that she still had to be his sister, and therefore she must carry his own new name and be childless. Her own daughter had to become her niece; daughter of some dead, fictitious brother.

But when Molly became engaged, Bob Quench had to be told the truth, though doubtless her mother and uncle were unaware. That must have shown Molly was sure of Bob Quench and trusted him implicitly. And a false statement of parentage must have been made before the Registrar, hence Bob's alarm that morning when the pseudo Molly told him the police had discovered all.

As Travers drove on, one main fact seemed to stand more and more out. Molly Pernaby was the daughter of that Merrick Clarke who had been convicted of fraud and had died in jail. What would it have meant for her if the news came out? The Pernabys on the move again, trying to find some other secluded corner of England where they could be unknown? It would certainly have meant Bob Quench's going too. Life in Pettistone, with Molly as his wife, would have been impossible once the facts were known.

Soon Travers was driving even more slowly. The case had narrowed itself down to three suspects only. Not the three Pernabys, for Arthur Pernaby had an unquestioned alibi. Grace Pernaby and Molly were two, and Bob Quench was inevitably the third. Which brought things back once more to something of Wharton's theory.

And yet Travers hardly knew. Now there was a reason for that perturbation shown by Grace Pernaby when she heard of the murder, he was inclined to make her very much of a suspect. There had never been any question of inquiring into any alibi of hers, for it had been assumed that she was in no way connected, and that her afternoon had been spent in her room, owing to that bad headache. But now it seemed that she had no alibi at all! With her daughter off to buy the powders, and her brother playing golf, she had the house to herself. And was she not the one person in the world who could have lured Brewse anywhere? And what about mother love, and the defence of her daughter? Motives everywhere, thought Travers, and no lack of opportunity.

Or was the Bob Quench idea right after all? Had he done the killing for Molly's sake, and had she discovered the fact, and was that why she was marrying him at once? Was that an additional reason for her avoidance of the inquest?

On went the questions till darkness came and he was forced to thrust the case from his mind, and push the car along. The miles went by till Edensthorpe was a bare twenty minutes away, and then the thoughts began circling again. Molly Pernaby, Grace Pernaby, Bob Quench, each alone and each in combination. Did Molly herself kill Brewse, and was the information she so gratuitously gave Feen, merely an attempt to make her above all suspicion? If either woman killed Brewse, then did Bob Quench remove the body and do all the rest? Did Gordon Strongman discover the fact, since Bob had been unable to join him till later than arranged for the painting, and was that why he had bolted back to the Sudan? Was Brewse killed in the Pernaby garden, where Grace had lured him, and was Molly's whole story therefore nothing better than a pack of lies?

The lights of Edensthorpe were in sight and once more Travers forced the case from his mind. The Town Hall clock was striking eleven as he drove by, and in another five minutes he was in the house. It was a chilly night and Bernice and Joy were sitting over the electric-fire.

"We didn't expect you for ever so long," smiled Bernice. "Dreadfully tired, are you?"

"Just a bit," he said. "And hungry. Anybody inquire for me?"

"George Wharton came round," she said. "He didn't know you were away, but he stayed with us for quite an hour."

Travers went up for a quick wash while supper was being laid, and he also changed into an older and more comfortable jacket. Then as he transferred things from the pockets of one to the pockets of the other, he came across a folded sheet of paper and wondered for a moment what it was. It was the original map of Pettistone, from which he had made a better specimen for the use of George Wharton.

Then, as he looked at it, something caught his eye. He stared, frowned in thought, then his fingers were all at once at his glasses. Another moment and he was making his way downstairs.

"What about breakfast in the morning?" he asked Bernice. "Earlier, shall we have it?"

"I think we might," she said. "No end of things always turn up at the very last moment."

"Seven-thirty then," he said. "And we leave here at nine. Now if you'll excuse me just a moment I'll try to get hold of Feen."

Wharton was not a late bird. Feen reported he had been in bed for over half an hour.

"Don't disturb him," Travers said, "but I want you two to be round here at eight o'clock sharp in the morning."

"Discovered anything?" Feen asked quickly.

"Quite a lot," Travers said. "If everything goes right I might even be able to tell you who killed Brewse."

## CHAPTER XIV
## TRAVERS KNOWS

BREAKFAST WAS OVER that morning by a quarter to eight. Travers had been up since six and everything was ready for his own departure. Now, with Bernice and Joy busy about final odds and ends, he had leisure to collect his thoughts again before the arrival of Feen and George Wharton. But of the facts he was now sure, and what was soon passing through his mind was something rather like judgment and comment, coloured as they were by the vague sadnesses of departure and the beauty of that last autumnal morning.

He had woke with nothing new in his mind except a queer depression that was hard to trace to its source. But the cause had been a shaft of autumn sunlight through the window and a quick, unconscious recalling of those sunny days on the Pettistone links. Happy, untroubled days they had been, with Pettistone going about its work and its leisure, and yet beneath the placid surface of things there had been a strange and terrible stirring.

A grim tragedy had been played in the silence and the dark, and that same tragedy was hidden and yet still living in those intenser silences which were the thoughts of those who knew, or had played their part. Those thoughts, imagined Travers, would be an endless fear and a torture. Grace Pernaby, go where she might, would never forget. Those new lives planned by Bob Quench and Molly were being built on worse than sand. And as Travers sat on in the quiet garden, listening for Feen's car, he knew something else. Even his own life would be coloured by that tragedy, and golf would never be the same again.

With that he was thinking of Arthur Pernaby, the tragedy of the man himself and his sacrifices and the queer twist of fate that had brought Brewse into his life once more, and with him all the past from which he himself had run. Pernaby, said Travers gently to himself, and, as he closed his eyes, he could see him that morning on the fifteenth tee, and that master shot of his that had skimmed the trees and swerved in. to circle them, and then had come to rest not ten yards from that first crashing drive that had whizzed its way across the menacing angle of the woods.

The sound of a horn and Travers was opening his eyes. A moment, and there was Feen's car at the gate.

"What's all this?" began Wharton. "I'm told you've finished up the case for us."

Travers shook his head. "I wouldn't go as far as that. What I'd like to do is tell you a few things I've happened to discover and ask you to tell me if I'm right."

"We'll talk here if you don't mind," he said, halting at the summer-house. "Light your pipes and let's take it easy. Half an hour ought to see us through."

Wharton began filling his pipe.

"Tell me one thing. Was that Bob Quench theory right?" He gave a none too hearty chuckle. "Not that I'm afraid it was wrong."

"Just a minute before you commit yourself" Travers said. "I'll give you this much of a clue. When I come back to this case in future, I shall think of it as The Case of the Green Felt Hat."

Wharton frowned, pursed his lips, then snorted

"That's easy."

"Maybe," Travers told him with another shake of the head.

Wharton smiled suggestively at Feen. Travers wondered what lay behind the quick complaisance, and was ready for some craft or guile, and, sure enough, Wharton was leaning forward with a kind of conversational unconcern.

"How'd you find the flaw in that alibi of his?"

"Whose?" countered Travers.

"Well, Bob Quench's."

"Bob Quench," said Travers slowly. "I don't know that we're concerned with him very much. But Molly Pernaby's different. She was in it up to the neck."

"I knew it," said Wharton triumphantly. "Collusion, that's what there was."

Feen smiled dryly. "What about letting Travers tell the story in his own way?"

"Well, first of all there's something I've discovered," Travers said. "I'm not at liberty to tell you just how I discovered it, but it took me all yesterday. It's this. Pernaby's sister isn't Miss Pernaby. She's Mrs. Merrick Clarke. Her daughter is Molly Clarke."

Feen gave a gasp of astonishment. Wharton's pipe stopped an inch from his mouth, and his eyes were goggling. Then he smiled, and the smile was the one which Travers always described as that of a lion which has spotted a particularly plump Christian.

"So Molly Pernaby is Merrick Clarke's daughter. I'm taking your word for that. Brewse was responsible for everything that happened to her father. Everything's getting better and better."

"But not necessarily clearer and clearer," Travers told him gently. "I admit that on the face of it, it appears to give the three Pernabys a motive."

"And Bob Quench. What concerned his future wife, concerned him, too."

"Admitted. All the same I'm wondering what the motive precisely was. Was it hate of Brewse because he really killed Merrick Clarke?"

"Of course it was!" Wharton said with a snort. Feen said nothing, but his eyes never left Travers's face.

"I'm still not sure," Travers said. "Arthur Pernaby sold up his old home and left his friends and—don't mock at this, George—the very graves of his people, and went into a far county, where his sister and her daughter could have a new home. He grew a moustache to disguise himself and he hoped he would never be recognised, and he hoped also that he and his people would forget. He was lucky. They all settled down well in Pettistone. But that amazing arrival of Brewse wasn't only the arrival of some one the Pernabys had cause to hate. It was even more than that. It was a threat to a new security. It might mean selling up again and trying to find a place to plant new roots." He shook his head. "When people are of the age of Arthur Pernaby and his sister, there comes a time when they refuse to begin life all over again. Remove the threat, and the change would be unnecessary. Isn't that a stronger motive than hate? And wouldn't both the elder Pernabys have the interests of the daughter at heart?"

"So Grace Pernaby was in it, too?" Wharton gave an exasperated click of the tongue and looked round at Feen for confirmation. "Most of this is new to me. How can any one be expected to handle a case when half the information isn't available?"

"True enough," Travers said. "All the same, George, I still hold that before I had that latest information; before the middle of last week, in fact, I should have known for a certainty who killed Brewse."

"You mean that?" asked Feen.

"I do," Travers told him. "And I'm not hinting that you and George should have known too, even if I did mention to you both that curious fainting feeling that Grace Pernaby had when I mentioned the word murder on the Sunday morning. That should very definitely have told me that Grace Pernaby knew something about the murder. She wasn't the kind of person to be suspected herself, but I ought to have known she was somehow implicated. Later on I tried to fit her in, but it was in the wrong hole."

Wharton shook his head. "I think that's rather far-fetched."

"Not a bit of it. I'd already been intrigued by Pernaby—his accent-intonation, if you like—and I couldn't quite reconcile it, as you'll both remember with his claim to have originated somewhere up north. I've known the time when those two clues would have been enough to set me off with my nose to the Pernaby trail."

"And where to?" asked Wharton ironically.

"To a simple study of the map of Pettistone," Travers said calmly. "To the study of a map I drew for you and of which I have a copy in my pocket. Take that map out and look at it, George. The answer to who killed Brewse is written there as plainly as if the murderer had painted his name on the side of Gables, instead of painting that cheap advertisement."

Wharton was bringing out his own copy and Feen was on his feet and looking at it over Wharton's shoulder.

"How should I have known the murderer from this map?" glared Wharton.

"Just one moment," Travers told him. "I still don't want you to have a grievance. Listen to this first. Molly Pernaby saw Brewse at the second milestone along the Edensthorpe Road at as near to four o'clock as makes no matter. Isn't that so?"

"Not at all," said Wharton, at once looking at Feen for confirmation. "She saw some one wearing the green felt hat, and a beard."

"I'll concede the point," Travers said. "She saw a man wearing a green felt hat. But very shortly after Molly Pernaby had volunteered that evidence, she herself came under suspicion. You'll admit that?"

"Why not?"

"Exactly. But if she was under suspicion, why was not her volunteered evidence under suspicion, too? And again other motorists were known to have been between Pettistone and that second milestone at the time the man in the green felt hat must have been there, and yet none of them saw him, And—incredible as it now seems—Molly Pernaby's evidence was still believed."

Wharton gave a grudging kind of grunt. Feen looked the least bit uneasy.

"But wait a minute," Travers said. "There's something even more incredible to come. Molly Pernaby had a bilious attack yesterday morning which arrived at the precise moment to stop her giving that volunteered evidence of hers before a coroner on oath. And yet she was still believed!"

"Don't blame us," said Wharton virtuously.

"I'm blaming nobody but myself," Travers said. "I'll even mention the matter of a gun that was put clumsily in the soil of Ammony's garden and was claimed to have been dug in there by him. Who'd have made a mistake like that but a woman? And there was I, absolutely obsessed at one period by the idea that two people had been at work—"

Yet once more Wharton turned triumphantly to Feen. "Two—Bob Quench and Molly Pernaby."

"George, I do wish you wouldn't commit yourself," Travers told him reprovingly. "What I sometimes suspected was that two people had been concerned, one of them cool and sane, and the other perfectly mad; and that the two were working at cross purposes."

Wharton paused in the act of lighting his pipe.

"Why not come straight to the point? Tell us just how our young friends did it."

"All in good time," said Travers imperturbably "I say I ought to have guessed that Molly Pernaby planted that gun in Ammony's garden, and in order to shield some one. To divert suspicion to Ammony it you like. Therefore, as the next logical step,

I should have known she also planted the green felt hat in the wood."

"But Brewse was killed in the wood!"

"I know he was."

"Then he was killed where his hat was."

"Granted."

Wharton glared. "What is all this? Brewse was killed in the wood, and there was lichen on his coat where he had been leaning against a tree. When his body was removed at night, his hat was left behind, and yet you say that Molly Pernaby planted the hat in the wood!"

"So she did."

Wharton stared, then let out a breath. "Here, what in God's name are you talking about? Are you mad or am I? You agree the hat was left there, and then you say she planted it there. How the devil could she plant a hat in the wood when it was there already!"

"Now we're coming to things," Travers said. "The answer's this, and it's a simple one. *It wasn't the same wood.*"

Neither Wharton nor Feen had never stared harder in their lives.

"It was the simplicity of it that beat us," Travers was going on. "Remember my old reference? *If the prophet had bid thee do some great thing, would'st thou not have done it?* We've been looking for complex things when the simple ones were under our noses. We're Naaman the Syrian all over again."

"Damn Naaman the Syrian!" said Wharton exasperatedly. "What was that about not being the same wood?"

"This," said Travers, and took out his own map of Pettistone. "Here's what was under my nose." Wharton had another good look at his own map, then polished his antiquated spectacles, spread the map for Feen, and looked again.

"Damned if I can see anything under my nose." Then an idea. "Unless it is that the map's too small to show the Edensthorpe Road and the second milestone."

"Then I'll ask the question I should have put to myself," Travers said, "for that second milestone matters even less than a damn. Here's the question. *Where did Brewse go for his walk on that Saturday afternoon?*"

"Where?" Wharton had another look at the map, then shrugged his shoulders. "Well, where did he go?"

"The answer's on the map," Travers said. "We had the alibis of various people and we didn't use them in the right way. We should have used them to tell us where Brewse was killed, instead of trying to break them. Let's start off at about three o'clock that afternoon, when Brewse went out of his front gate. Let's see where he must have gone by where he couldn't have gone. And let's remember that every house in Pettistone has been canvassed and every person questioned, and nobody ever saw Brewse that afternoon.

"If he'd gone through the village—which was the last thing he'd want to do—he'd have been seen. If he took the lane by-pass, he still might have been seen, and he certainly would have been seen by those motorists when he was walking along the Edensthorpe Road. Secondly, if he went south by the wood path to the Limehurst Road but didn't then turn right but went left, in the direction of Limehurst, then Strongman must have seen him for Strongman spent half an hour there in his car. Now take a third possible direction.

"If Brewse went left towards the golf course, he still must have been seen. If lastly he went right, towards Copmore Farm, then Ammony must have seen him, for Ammony spent over half an hour in the lane. And therefore there's only one possible remaining way. Brewse went fifty yards or so to the left, then took the path through the wood that comes out at the track that goes round the golf course to the west, and then up to Copmore Farm. And he had an enormous stroke of luck. Ammony's breakdown was on the wrong side of another fringe of wood, or else our grocer friend must have seen Brewse walking along that unused track."

"My God, you're right!" burst out Feen. Wharton was peering over his spectacle tops. "But why was he going to Copmore Farm that way round?"

"He wasn't going to Copmore Farm," Travers said. "He was going to a certain spot long before that track turns uphill to Copmore. See that little path I've marked that leads into the wood? It's a kind of grassy ride, and there's a small deserted hut there, probably once used by woodmen. That was what Brewse was making for."

"But why?" asked Feen.

"Because that's where Pernaby told him to come. That's *where Pernaby killed him.*"

"Pernaby!" said the staring Wharton. "But Pernaby had a cast-iron alibi. He and that old parson never lost sight of each other all the afternoon!"

"I agree," said Travers calmly. "I agree on principle. Or what I'm prepared to admit is that old Quench would swear in any court of law—if the facts weren't pointed out to him—that he had Pernaby under his eye the whole time. Sorry if I'm being unduly exasperating, but let me explain. You know the rudiments of golf. You know some courses are up and down with hills and valleys and deep bunkers and heaven knows what. You disappear into a bunker, or I take one valley parallel to the one you're in, and we'd still swear we were in sight of each other. So we arc, in the sense that the continuity of the game hasn't been broken. I know you'll reappear from your bunker and you know I'll reappear from my valley. You follow that, don't you."

Wharton nodded.

"Then let's take the probable course of events," Travers said. "Pernaby told his people the frightening news that Brewse, of all people, was living in Pettistone, and that he would be bound in course of time to recognize one of them, and so their own secret would be out. He had heard the unsuccessful attempt of Guff-Wimble to buy Brewse out, and I think that he was at once making up his mind to a certain course of action. He knew, by the way, that it was no use keeping the matter a secret from his people, because Bob Quench would be bound to tell it to Molly, so what he probably said to Molly and Grace was, 'Keep your heads, both of you, and don't worry at all. A movement's on foot to get Brewse out of the village, and I have an idea it's going to succeed. I'm not at liberty to say what it is, but whatever happens, we still know nothing.'

"Then Pernaby fixed his game of golf with old Quench for the Saturday afternoon when the course was always very clear. He got in touch over the 'phone with Brewse, who would of course remember him, and suggested the rendezvous. He said, 'I may not be there exactly on time, but wait for me, whatever happens.' Brewse did wait, with his back against a tree.

"Only a golfing master can slice or pull or use a spared shot at his pleasure, and make the stroke effective. Pernaby was such a golfer. He and his partner arrived at the fifteenth tee at a time that was near enough to Pernaby's schedule, and he deliberately sliced and spared his shot so as just to leave it in doubt whether or not he had cleared the trees with his drive.

"'Believe I've cut things too fine,' he would say. 'I may be in the wood after all.'

"Old Quench, who had played for safety well to the left, would go off hoping to heaven Pernaby had gone into the wood, whatever pious hopes he had uttered to the contrary. Such is human nature, and golfers are the biggest hypocrites in existence. Quench is a slow walker and he went well out to the left. Pernaby went more quickly and to the right, and probably cut through the wood. Out of his bag came the gun. There may have been a silencer, and there may not. Old Quench is quite deaf and he'd never have heard a thing. In any case, Pernaby, without his golf-bag, came panting up to Brewse, apologizing for the lateness. Another second and Brewse was dead and his body was behind the hut or in the undergrowth. In less than no time Pernaby was back at his bag, and reappearing on the fairway in time for Quench who had played his second shot.

"'Afraid my ball's lost, Quench. No use looking for it in there.'

"Quench would be sympathetic, but inwardly elated. Our point is this. He knew just where Pernaby was all the time. Pernaby, in fact was, from his point of view, never out of sight.

"Later that night, Pernaby removed the body. A man of his raw-boned strength could have carried it across the meadows to the shed. But we needn't go into all that. All we need look at is

Pernaby's eight o'clock alibi. When Gordon Strongman said he knew it was eight o'clock because he saw the time on his watch by the light from the lounge where Pernaby was, he didn't mean he saw Pernaby. He saw the lighted room—the light through the drawn blinds of the room—where Pernaby presumably was, but actually wasn't. And when Pernaby said that at eight o'clock he went to his sister's room and asked how she was, all that means is that he went to a room, where she would be lying in the dark, and asked how she was. Then he either volunteered the statement that it was eight o'clock, or said so in answer to her question."

"You're right. You're dead right," said Feen.

"I don't know that he isn't," said Wharton, pursing his lips and nodding away to himself.

"I'm only too glad you think I am," Travers told them. "But now to go back. Remember how you asked Mrs. Feen when she saw Molly Pernaby? She said it was before three o'clock, and she was right for once. Molly Pernaby's accounts of her Saturday afternoon movements were made up afterwards to suit the circumstances. I should say she was back in the house at half-past three to a quarter to four. She took the powders to her mother, then had a peep out of the window, and she was in time to see her uncle either slice into the wood or going into the wood to look for a presumably lost ball.

"So she went through that short cut and to the woods to have a look for the ball herself, and there came across the body. She had seen Brewse in his beard, and she knew him, and I imagined she had a good idea that her uncle had killed him. In any case she knew he had been in the wood and was likely to be suspected. A later visit found the hat that had been missed when Pernaby removed the body, and she planted that hat in a place, and told a yarn, that would give her uncle a perfect alibi.

"And that's the gist of everything. We could go on elaborating for hours and talking about details, but I doubt if we'd get nearer the truth."

"It's near enough to satisfy me," Wharton said with a sideways nod.

"It satisfies me too," Feen said. "All we've got to do is get ready to call on Pernaby."

"Wait a minute," said Wharton. "What about that Molly Pernaby, or Molly Clarke or whatever she is? Is she to be allowed to get away with it?"

"That's what I'm worried about," Travers said. "And about Bob Quench. He must have guessed something when she got an old gun from him to plant on Ammony."

Wharton knocked out his pipe and got to his feet. Travers reached across and gently pushed him down.

"Don't be indignant, George. Just think instead. And you be patient for a minute too, Colonel. You've got a daughter of much about Molly's age, George. What would you have thought of her if she hadn't tried to pull you out of something like the same mess? Wouldn't your daughter have lied and schemed for you? My God, she would!—or she wouldn't be George Wharton's daughter."

Wharton was replacing his old-fashioned spectacles in their case, and shaking a dismal head. Then he got to his feet again.

"Well, it's nothing to do with me. That's the Colonel's affair."

"It's going to be difficult," Feen said, and was frowning away to himself. "It might be done, but I don't know. Two young people's lives oughtn't to be ruined if we can help it."

"Lu-*do!* Lu-*do!* Where are you?"

Travers grimaced. "That's my young sister-in- law. Afraid our time's up."

"We must go to the house and say good-bye to every one," Feen said.

"Just one minute," Travers said quickly. "Another quarter of an hour and we shall be on our way. You won't be doing anything about—at Pettistone, before then?"

Feen shook his head.

"I'm glad of that," said Travers, and smiled with a queer kind of gravity. "You and George are the tough kind. I'm not. What I mean is . . . well, I rather liked Pernaby."

"Do stop the car for a moment," Bernice said. At the top of the hill Travers drew the Rolls in to the verge and the three looked back. Edensthorpe lay in the valley beneath them, its smoke a faint mist in the morning haze. Away to the right was Pettistone, church steeple visible above the trees, and shimmering and greyly blue against the clear autumnal light were the golf-course woods, and a glint of red which was the roof of a house.

Joy sank back in her corner seat.

"I wonder if they'll ever find out who did that murder?" Then she was answering her own question. "If they do we shall see it in the papers."

"No papers where we're going," Travers told her.

Bernice was still looking back, and at last she sighed, and smiled.

"I shall always love Edensthorpe, and Pettistone. I almost feel I want to cry."

Travers was hardly listening. His eyes had been fixed on the roof that he thought was Pernaby's. A mad way out old Pernaby had taken, but who was he to cast a stone? It was the good in Pernaby that would be remembered, and as he closed his eyes he was standing once more on that fifteenth tee and hearing that friendly, laconic voice and watching a club that crashed against a ball.

Then a queer thought came to him, about Pernaby already dead, and dead souls released from Limbo to wander till cockcrow across their human, accustomed fields. Then Travers shook his head, and as Bernice finished speaking, he was moving the car on again.

"Fields," he thought to himself. "Elysian fields, perhaps."

Then as the car gathered speed, he was smiling gently and once more shaking his head.

"Golf in the Elysian fields," said Travers to himself. "Who knows? Who knows?"

THE END

Ingram Content Group UK Ltd.
Milton Keynes UK
UKHW021317250723
425753UK00021B/349

9 781912 574056